Assassin's Arrow

Journey From The Wilderness
Michael J Spanhanks

Bible References

Dedication—Numbers 24:9

Target/Part 1 - Ephesians 6:12

Ch. 34 - Rom. 10:9-10

Ch. 37 - Proverbs 18:10

Ch. 2 - Psalm 121:1-3

Guardian/Part 2 - Psalm 23:4

Ch. 21 - Hebrews 13:2

Ch. 26 - Matt. 6:26

Ch. 34 - John 15:13, Rom. 10:17

Ch. 35 - John 15:13

Encounter/Part 3 - Romans 8:31

Ch. 55 - Psalm 23:4

2 Corinthians 13:11 ESV

Dedication

The Journey From The Wilderness Post-Apocalyptic Series is dedicated to a free America. Today, it appears our nation is under attack, not from other countries, but from oppressors within. This series presents a prospective vision should matters continue to disintegrate around us. I pray Old Glory stands resolute, warding off threats from both abroad and within, safeguarding our cherished freedom. May the Church worship without oppression until the glorious return of Jesus, and may Israel remain free.

Michael J Spanhanks

—

'He bows down, he lies down as a lion;
And as a lion, who shall rouse him?'
"Blessed is he who blesses you,
And cursed is he who curses you."
Numbers 24:9

Prologue

The sharp crack of high-powered rifles echoed through the streets, drowning out the screams of terrified crowds fleeing for cover. Bullets riddled cars and pickup trucks, splintering glass and metal. Overhead, Apache helicopters thundered, their rotors slicing the air as they unleashed a barrage of fire into the dense woods below, where survivors huddled with their loved ones. By the end, soldiers were the only ones left standing in the streets.

In the wake of a presidential executive order declaring martial law—enforced by the full might of the military—the scent of fear hung heavy in the air. Christians everywhere struggled to escape a tragic fate. A boundary was drawn along the thirty-sixth parallel, selected because so many Christians already resided south of it. Those who engaged in the conflict or defied the North, if not slain on the spot, were captured by the military to serve as examples.

A thirty-year-old man gripped the blanket covering his five-month-old son. His wife ran alongside him, her mouth clenched tight and her eyes fierce with determination. They slipped quietly through the dense trees where others huddled, hearts pounding, desperate to evade detection. Spotting the safe zone markers, they knew they were close—the boundary at the thirty-sixth parallel. The man, with his wife and son, sprinted across the boundary. Many sobbed in terror, yet everyone felt a profound relief to be alive.

A burly man who had crossed with them wheeled around, shouting at the soldiers, "This injustice won't stand! We're citizens, and you're violating the Constitution. You've turned communist and have ruined everything!"

Just beyond the forest, seven military jeeps braked as their crews watched from the northern side. Though barred from crossing the parallel, they hurled accusations and threats at the escaping Christians.

The man, unwilling to tolerate the lies, shot back, "We'll build our army and return to reclaim our freedom."

The First Lieutenant burst into laughter and barked an order for his men to open fire on the crowd. He knew he would receive no accommodations for his actions and might face reprimand by his superiors, but today he was the one giving orders. Two soldiers hesitated, drawing the captain's fury. "Do what I said, or face the consequences!" Reluctantly, the pair complied, their rounds mowing down men, women, and children, killing seventeen outright and wounding others.

A wave of anger swept through the survivors. "Murderers! You sick murderers, all of you!"

"Quiet," someone pleaded, voice trembling, "they'll wipe us all out."

The platoon leader, prompted by their defiance, signaled a second volley. Bullets tore through the group again, wounding more and claiming six additional lives.

The survivors plunged to the ground, wailing over the bodies of their loved ones.

The First Lieutenant strode from his jeep to the boundary, a smug expression etched on his face. "You're lucky I've been ordered to spare some of you. But don't forget—you're here because of your obsession with some invisible God. You can ask him to provide for you. Maybe he'll send his sparrows with food or make it magically appear. You might just survive." With a final mocking laugh, he climbed back into the jeep and ordered his men to pull out.

The young man lay on the ground, cradling his wife's lifeless body, his infant son still bundled against his chest. Fury narrowed his eyes as he glared at the burly instigator. "She's dead because of you!" he accused, pointing a trembling finger. "They would have left us alone if you hadn't incited them."

With a chilling stare, the burly man locked his gaze with him, eyes flicking briefly to the slain wife and the other bodies lying on the ground. "Not my fault—you saw what they did. I'll raise an army and make them pay for this." He then rose, the weight of the fallen on his shoulders. Turning southward, he strode away, four others trailing behind, leaving the rest to bury their grief.

Target

For we wrestle not against flesh and blood, but against principalities, against powers, against the rulers of the darkness of this world, against spiritual wickedness in high places. Ephesians 6:12

Chapter 1

Twenty Years Later

Travis Weston crouched at the edge of the dense pine woods on the east side of the narrow creek. The air carried the cool, mineral scent of moving water and the faint resin of crushed needles underfoot. The undergrowth—wild viburnum, holly, and blackberry briars—rustled once, then settled. The day before, he had seen fresh whitetail tracks pressed into the clay beside the stream. He needed meat for himself and for his father, Logan, whose illness had stolen the strength from his legs. They had once hunted these creeks together—now the task fell to Travis alone.

In the southern states, hunting had become the only reliable source of meat after the supplies were exhausted. Many families had never drawn a bow until hunger forced their hands. The Westons were more fortunate than most: Logan had spent years teaching his son to read sign and move quietly through the forest searching for game.

The brush stirred again as Travis heard the soft crunch of leaves—too deliberate for deer. *Human.* He eased a compact pair of binoculars from his pack—a gift from his father before the sickness worsened—and focused on the far bank. A figure in a dark hooded jacket kneeled beside a freshly killed doe, the knife flashing as they worked.

Black Arrow!

The name tightened his throat. Whispers in the Faith camps spoke of them and their refusal to walk in the ways of God. They often hunted in pairs or groups, yet this one was alone.

Hey, that's my deer! No, you don't!

He leaped to his feet and dashed across the shallow water, cold against his boots, with his bow in his hand. The figure spun, arrow nocked in a heartbeat, the yew stave firmly gripped.

When he reached the other side of the creek, bow drawn, heart pounding, Travis's eyes locked on the shrouded face beneath the hoodie, standing ten paces apart as the creek rushed quietly behind them. One wrong move, and arrows would fly from both sides.

Gazing into his adversary's face, he saw something surprising. This isn't the enemy his father told him about. Brownish blonde hair spilled from beneath the hood and cascaded down the sides of the face. Travis had never heard Logan mention women among the Black Arrow archers. Yet here she stood, bow gripped tight, poised to strike.

She stood unflinching, her eyes the color of river hazel, studying him through the shadow of her hood. Travis saw no immediate danger in them—only caution.

A nervous knot coiled in Travis's gut. He forced words out before the silence concluded. "That's my deer you're cutting up."

She stared, eyes narrowing. "Today, it's not."

"I've been watching this creek for a week," he barked.

The huntress stood firm, prepared to defend her kill. "That changes nothing."

An eerie silence thickened—even the jays seemed to hold their breath. Travis searched for a path to peace. "What's your name?" When she remained silent, he said, "I'm Travis Weston."

She tilted her head, her piercing gaze probing for a hidden agenda. "Wren Daniels," she said softly, catching herself staring at the attractive young man even as her father's warning echoed in her mind: *Be careful if you meet one.* Finding him at the creek felt wrong after her father had said they hunted to the east. *I should see if Father was right.*

A faint smile appeared on her face, and she sensed no animosity. "As long as you don't shoot, I won't either."

The unexpected lightness in her tone unsettled him more than hostility would have. Was she truly Black Arrow, or had she simply taken the jacket from someone else? His father's warnings echoed, yet something urged him to answer in kind.

"I won't," Travis answered.

Wren eased the tension from her string, set her bow and arrow on the ground, and turned back to the carcass. Travis kept a grip on his bow a moment longer, then relaxed the string.

"Hungry?" she asked without looking up.

He nodded.

"Help me cut and finish the butchering, and we'll cook some."

He hesitated, scanning her movements for any sign of threat. None came. Slowly, he set his bow aside, drew his skinning knife, and kneeled opposite her. The rich, warm scent of fresh blood mingled with campfire smoke as she coaxed a small flame to life among the river rocks.

"You're Black Arrow," he said quietly. "Why didn't you shoot me?"

She laughed once, surprised at herself. "Day's not over yet." Then, more seriously: "I was a child when the Separation happened. I don't carry the same hate some do."

He sliced off a piece of meat and slipped it into her pack. "Then why wear the colors?"

"My father commands our fighters, so the jacket is practical, and we all wear them," she said, meeting his eyes across the low flames. "Tell me, Travis Weston—what do you think caused division among our people? I was born after the Separation and still don't understand why it happened."

He shrugged, turning a strip of meat on the wire rack she had rigged. "Faith, maybe. My people hold to it. Yours don't."

"Perhaps." She tucked a strand of hair behind her ear. "I was never taught about faith. Asked my father several times, and his answers were vague and confusing. After a while, I stopped asking. I don't believe he knows."

Smoke curled between them, carrying the sweet scent of roasted venison. Somewhere deeper in the woods, a squirrel chattered.

"Some of my people call faith in an unseen God foolish," she continued. "Others see it as madness. I honestly don't know where I stand."

Travis glanced at her. "But you want to know?"

Her eyebrows lifted, and she smiled, lightly this time. "It's important to consider all points of view? Perhaps one day I'll understand."

"I hope so."

"Why are *you* hoping?" she asked.

"Hope is good—a story for another time," he said.

She looked into his face once more. "I'll bet you've heard some brutish stories about us?"

"You might say that," Travis replied, wondering about her questions while hearing his father's warning that they could be manipulative. He needed to be cautious with her.

She tossed a few pieces of meat onto the wire rack over the fire and turned to him. "Ever wondered what our lives would be like if all our groups united?"

"United?"

"Yes, all the groups as one. Once, we were a strong people."

"That'd be something," he said.

"If we banded together," she continued, "maybe we could go back North someday—to our first homes."

Travis recalled that his father said the North had very powerful weapons—a losing cause, he claimed. "Have you ever been to the thirty-sixth parallel?"

"My father called it the periphery. He and my mother came through together, and he told stories about their army and the hummers. Have you heard of them?"

"No, what's that?"

"Father said, mechanical flying contraptions carrying something called missiles," she replied.

Travis turned and looked at her. "Yeah, the drones. Some of our people have seen them."

She nodded. "Father warned us they can track you."

"Mine too," he replied. "I've often wondered if my father would have fought against the North, except our weapons aren't equal. The government took them from the people. He shared some stories with me. Must've been terrifying reaching the periphery while being shot at."

"For sure," she said. "Do you think we'll ever go back?"

"I don't know. We make out okay now."

The meat had cooked, and they sat by the fire to eat, sharing stories of their people—hunting triumphs, failures, and hardships. They concluded that the division among the people stemmed from their differing ideologies.

"My father was an officer prior to this," Wren said, wiping her hands on some moss. "Before the groups separated, Brody Myles—our leader—got pinned down near the periphery, and my father drew the gunfire away so he could escape. That's how he earned his position as commander."

Travis watched her bend down to pack the remaining meat. A sudden ache surprised him at the thought that this might be the last time he saw her.

"I'd like to meet again," he said. "If that's possible."

She sighed and nodded. "It is. But no one from our camps can know. In my camp, there are serious consequences for associating with someone from another faction."

"Understandable. Here tomorrow?"

"I'll be here." Her grin returned. "I'll even give you time to get that doe."

Distant voices rose through the trees—male, urgent, calling a name that sounded like hers.

Wren's face tightened. "Our hunters. They'll be looking for me."

"Won't they stay the night if they find this fire burned out?" Travis asked.

"They've likely been hunting and have fresh meat," she replied. "I believe they'll return to camp tonight."

"You don't want to be found?"

"Not with you here," Wren whispered, her voice low and urgent, hazel eyes flicking toward the western pines where the voices echoed. She swung the heavy pack onto her shoulders and shifted the weight for comfort.

"I'll take a different trail back to my hideout—quickly, before they get closer." She tugged the straps tighter, leather creaking softly. "They won't like finding me with someone from the POF."

Her gaze returned to Travis. "There's no telling what they'd do to you. I've seen them strip a man bare—clothes, knife, bow, everything—then lash him to a tree and leave him for the night, vulnerable for whatever comes sniffing around." Her words were flat, as if she forced herself to recall that moment without sympathy. "You need to go now, Travis. Take the east trail. Don't wait.

The distant shouts grew louder, boots cracking through the forest and dense briars. Travis felt the grip of the bow under his palm and nodded once, his throat tight.

"Tomorrow?" he asked.

Wren's expression softened for an instant. "I'll be here." She reached out, fingers brushing his forearm—warm and brief—I like your name, Travis. You must have been born for something special."

He walked away through the creek, the scent of smoke and venison still lingering on his clothes. Glancing back again, he watched her vanish into the green shadows on the other side.

Strange girl, he thought—but the words carried wonder more than warning.

Chapter 2

Pastor Greyson Parker finished praying and rose, prepared to share the message the Lord had given him. Knowing that few in the congregation owned Bibles, he would deliver it in plain language that everyone could grasp.

The morning crowd exceeded expectations, with everyone finding a seat. Two young men with acoustic guitars and a middle-aged woman with a mandolin stepped forward and struck up a lively melody. Then an elderly woman from the congregation led another song. With the music concluded, Pastor Parker walked to the front.

"My prayer this week has been that you all found sustenance," Pastor Parker said. "I know times are tough, but even if it's meager, let's not forget to thank God for supplying our needs."

Parker flipped through the pages of his timeworn leather Bible. "Today, I'm reading from the one hundred and twenty-first book of Psalm, beginning with verse one, through verse three." *I will lift up mine eyes unto the hills, from whence cometh my help. My help cometh from the Lord, which made heaven and earth. He will not suffer thy foot to be moved: he that keepeth thee will not slumber.*

"That passage should be familiar to you, who are older among us. However, the younger folks might appreciate some guidance.

It comes from the time David fled from Saul. Though the young warrior was afraid Saul would execute him, he had faith in the Lord's protection. Scripture calls him a man after God's own heart. In another place, it says his help came from the Lord. Like David, God has watched over and sustained us through the dark times.

"Our God never sleeps, people, and is always there for us, even when we struggle. He walks with us, as he did with David, even when we feel lonely and helpless."

Travis listened to Parker's sermon. Like many others, it offered encouragement. Life in the wilderness had grown harder year by year. Without machinery, planting and cultivating crops was a monumental task for all, even the experienced. Hunting in the forests had turned perilous as rival factions encroached on their territory, sometimes sparking skirmishes. Pastor Parker saw it as his duty to remind the people of God's faithfulness and urge them to keep believing.

The pastor concluded the sermon and offered a brief prayer, bringing the service to a close. The people shook hands with friends and neighbors as they filed slowly out of the building.

Frantic cries suddenly erupted as the crowd reached the outside, disrupting the peaceful moment. Onlookers gathered, others stood outside the nearest homes observing Edmond Lester, a respected town council member and longtime friend to most, writhing in agony on the ground.

Several men noticed the council member collapse and ran toward the crowd on the crumbling paved street.

Travis felt a sharp twinge in his gut at the sight of his father's old friend, sprawled lifeless on the ground. He remembered how

Edmond and his wife, Lila, had joined them in tending a garden for several seasons. Edmond was also a trusted friend his father relied on when drafting the town's regulations. If the councilman died, it would spark a fierce reaction from the others—and from his father, whose grief might undo the fragile peace.

Dr. Sedric Duggan pushed through the crowd. "Everyone, please stand back. Allow me to tend to this man." Duggan was a reformed alcoholic, thanks to Pastor Parker's continued urging. Parker kept him busy hunting for food, which took precedence over everything else. Though he was an excellent doctor, the medical supplies had run out long ago, causing him considerable difficulty when operations were required. When he wasn't helping folks with minor cuts, bruises, and other medical emergencies, he took time to hunt—sharing the meat with the widows in town.

"Oh, this is bad, Edmond," Duggan stated, gazing into his eyes.

Edmond struggled for breath, finally rasping, "It's okay…Duggan." His eyes fluttered shut as he lay there bleeding, an arrow buried deep in his chest.

Duggan leaned in to check for breath. "He's passed out. We need to get him to the office so I can remove the arrow and close the wound.

As some men stepped forward to help, Antoine Fisher, the local magistrate, arrived to assess the scene. Travis had been only five-years-old when Antoine, his wife, and their son had wandered into town from North Missouri—starving, thin as rails.

When the townspeople learned of Antoine's law enforcement background, they naturally leaned on him for law and order.

With a grave expression, Antoine kneeled beside Edmond, who lay barely breathing. "Did anyone see what happened?"

Nevan Buckley raised his hand. "I couldn't spot the culprit, but the arrow came from the top of the old city hall. Out of the corner of my eye, I caught movement as it flew in and struck him—but by the time I turned back, he was gone."

Antoine gazed at the arrow embedded in Edmond, spotting the insignia, a small A carved near the notch. "Well, it's obvious who's behind this."

"Yeah, Black Arrow!" someone shouted from the crowd.

"It's time to stop this nonsense," another added. "We haven't caused them any trouble."

"We ought to track him down," a bold voice called from the back.

Antoine rose from one knee with his hands raised. "Don't be foolish! You wouldn't get within fifty yards before more of you are hurt—or killed. You don't know how many of those archers are waiting for you to make that mistake."

The murmuring crowd fell silent as the men lifted Edmond from the dirt. A shrill scream pierced the air. Everyone turned to see Lila Lester, Edmond's wife, sobbing as they carried her husband away. "Why? Why? Doctor, please help him!"

Duggan took her hand. "I'll do everything I can for him."

A few women rushed to comfort Lila as he hurried off to tend her husband.

Travis spotted his father standing nearby, taking in the scene and shaking his head. Logan looked up at him intently. He often railed about Black Arrow's atrocities and urged the men around town to stand their ground—though none took him seriously. Travis knew that his father would hunt them down alone if he were able.

Turning to his friend, Jacoby Myers, Travis said, "Let's get out of here."

"I heard someone say they should track him down," Jacoby whispered.

"You know they won't. No grit," Travis muttered, heading toward the trading post—the town's sole store, little more than a large garage covered with metal where folks bartered scavenged goods.

They reached the post and stepped to the counter, ordering honey nectar using Travis' prior trade credit. Travis paid him with credit from a trade he'd made days earlier. After pouring drinks, they claimed one of the three tables.

"I'm furious, Travis," Jacoby said. "That assassin struck in broad daylight. I have a friend from Blossom who said the same thing happened there not long ago—they killed the mayor. I can't understand why they're doing this—or why we're letting them."

Travis recalled his new huntress friend's words: "What if we could unite all the factions?"

"What's more sensible than making peace with Black Arrow?" he said.

"Black Arrow is no friend, Travis," Jacoby replied. "They'll never make peace with us—and what happened today will only make our people more determined to fight them. And maybe they should."

"But why are we even divided in the first place?" Travis inquired. "Hasn't it only led to conflicts with our own kind?"

"Travis, each faction has carved out its own path," Jacoby said.

"So, is it too late for change?" Travis asked.

"Buddy, what's got you so fired up today?" Jacoby eyed him with curiosity. "You're awfully passionate about this."

"Seeing Edmond lying there in the street has convinced me we have a problem, Jacoby—one that'll take more than just wishing for change."

"You sound certain that joining them is the solution."

"It might be—but how to go about it, is the real question," Travis said.

"If you ever unravel the Black Arrow mystery, let me know," Jacoby said with a shrug. "Now, I've got to get home."

"Me too. I'll see you later."

As Travis turned to head toward home, his thoughts drifted to Wren. She seemed enthusiastic about uniting the groups, despite their deep differences. But what would they do if they learned of her intention? Would Black Arrow ever consider friendship with them, anyway? And what about his father? He would have a strong opinion if he learned Travis was talking to a member of the rogue group.

None of this mattered now; he needed to find meat. Tomorrow, he'd hunt where he'd spotted the huntress—and hope for the best.

Chapter 3

As twilight deepened into night, the rider and his weary horse trudged into the camp, aware of the two lookouts at the tower stepping from the shadows. The hour was late, and the rest of the camp had long since retreated to their bunks, leaving the cool air thick with silence broken only by the distant hoot of an owl.

After guiding the mare through the gate, he turned her toward an empty stall in a weather-worn barn, the musty aroma of hay mingling with the sharp tang of seasoned wood. He tended to her needs first, scattering a scant handful of oats—collected from a mill shut down since the separation—into a worn oak trough and drawing water from a nearby barrel. The brutal two-day journey had ravaged the poor creature—her coat matted with sweat and caked in dirt, her sides rising and falling in ragged gasps, her eyes dulled by bone-deep fatigue. As she dipped her muzzle into the sparse meal, the rider whispered soft reassurances, swatting at the persistent flies tangled in her mane.

Reilly Brewin, a former decorated Army Ranger who served in Afghanistan, felt a sigh of relief wash over him. Even a warrior with a spotless record knew that the unforgiving wilderness could break the strongest will in mere days.

The crunch of gravel underfoot outside the barn tugged him from his task, halting the strokes of the brush against the mare's flank. *Someone's stirring.* He edged toward the doorway, peering into the moonlit premises where a shadowy figure approached with purposeful strides. *What does he want now?*

Seconds later, their leader, Brody Myles, stepped from the darkness inside where a lantern burned bright. "I had a hunch you'd make it back tonight, so I stayed up. How did the mission go?"

"Boss, the target was still breathing when I rode out, but it was a clean hit. By now, he's surely dead."

"That's what we want—striking terror into those rival factions. Black Arrow will become a shadow that haunts their every move. Once we gain leverage over them, all the food supplies and resources will be ours to manage."

Reilly sank onto a wooden crate, exhaustion pressing down like a burden. "That mare can't take much more riding, sir. She's slowing down and getting harder to handle."

"No need for concern," Brody said. "We've got some prime horse stock lined up from a goods trader west of here. He said that in some places there aren't any horses because folks have eaten them."

"I'm not surprised," Reilly replied.

"The old man demands a full wagonload of cured meat," Brody said. "A steep price to pay, but we need those horses to survive. He'll deliver soon—or we'll take them by force."

"You don't have to give him our meat, sir—it's so hard to come by. Say the word, and I'll handle it."

"I appreciate your enthusiasm, soldier, but we might require horses in the future. It's best to keep that bridge open, my friend."

Reilly had never considered Brody Myles as a friend. He endured his commands only because of their mutual disregard for the outsider clans. They agreed to propel Black Arrow's ambitions forward, yet Reilly harbored no illusions: this allegiance would vanish like smoke if Brody ever wavered from the cause. The moral tightrope they walked—the search for provisions, the elimination of enemy threats for the sake of existence—tortured him in quiet moments, a reminder that survival often demanded choices that weakened the soul.

"Are you hungry?" Brody asked.

"I'm good."

"Very well, rest up. I expect everyone assembled right after breakfast tomorrow."

"Understood, boss. I'll be there."

As Brody turned to leave, Reilly's mind drifted back to the dusty heat of Afghanistan and his fallen Ranger buddies. Even now, when exhausted and depressed, the one constant he counted on was memories of the Steel Patrol—his team. Now most lie buried somewhere. He and Drake had dreamed of starting a cattle ranch together, but one day at Drake's grave, noticing how the grass had reclaimed the dirt, Reilly realized how shallow their plans had been—mere wishful fantasies. They'd all boasted of grand ambitions, knowing deep down that few might ever materialize. Some returned home in flag-draped boxes, and the survivors to a nation unraveling at the seams. Reilly knew little of the northern states, his roots firmly planted in Alabama soil, so staying south of the designated periphery line had always felt like the safest choice.

Pulling back the frayed blanket on his bunk, he sank onto the thin mattress. As sleep crept in, he wondered how life might have unfolded if he'd ventured north like so many others.

***

The rich scent of freshly brewed coffee invaded Reilly's senses, dragging him from the depths of slumber. He swung his legs over the edge of the narrow bunk in the cramped sleeping quarters, stretching his taut muscles and scrubbing the grit of weariness from his eyes. Emerging into the brisk morning air, he made his way to the campfire crackling between the old wooden barn and the makeshift barracks. The savory aroma of frying meat, intertwined with the men's lighthearted chatter, painted a deceptive picture of camaraderie amid their precarious existence.

A vacant chair caught his eye.

Before he could claim it, Cohen Daniels stepped forward. "Sorry, Reilly—that's my spot."

"No problem, sir," he said. "I'll just fetch some coffee."

He veered toward the modest table bearing the coffee pot, poured a mug, grabbed a pair of warm biscuits and a small piece of deer meat from the serving tray, and settled in a secluded nook beside a rusted old tractor, away from the others.

Coco, the fiery Spanish woman who managed the meals with tireless energy, approached with another pot of coffee. "Reilly, why are you sitting all the way over here, away from everyone?"

He shrugged, blowing on his coffee. "I overslept, and by the time I got here, there were no other spots."

"Alright, just wanted to see if you needed a refill," she said with a warm smile, before turning to serve the others.

Standing back from the fire, Brody Myles waved at the smoke drifting toward him as he flipped through the pages of an old notebook, filled with exercise routines for the men and his strategy to seize control of the rival groups in the coming days.

Pleased with a particular notation, he looked up at the men as they laughed at a young man's amusing remark. "All right, everyone, I see you've all eaten, so we'll get down to business," he said, allowing their giggling to subside. "We've had a solid week—plenty of meat brought in, which will help us get through. The daily drills are sharpening our edge and sustaining readiness. So let's keep that momentum going.

"I've updated the duty roster—check it after breakfast. Reilly, Grady, and Solomon, meet with me afterwards about your assignments.

"On another note: we're expecting a delivery of horses any day. I traded for six saddle horses on my journey west, which will cost us a hefty chunk of our meat reserves. While you're out hunting, look for more places that might still have grain. We'll also need to restock and smoke meat. If you're not on an essential task, you're pulling hunting duty." He scanned the group until his eyes landed on Cohen. "Any sign of your daughter since we spoke earlier?"

"No, sir," Cohen Daniels replied, his voice laced with dread. "She'd be a huge help hunting for meat."

"Where do you figure she's gone?" Brody probed.

"Sometimes she hunts the Newman Lake area. That's about a two-day trek from here. I was certain she'd have returned by now."

Brody met his friend's anxious gaze once more. Black Arrow's protocol mandated a seven-day wait before dispatching a rescue team for a missing trooper, and he'd already bent the rules for Cohen's sake. The possibility of her being captured by hostile factions hung unspoken between them—how far must he bend the rules before they become meaningless? "Maybe she'll bring home some meat. Keep me updated, alright?"

"Will do," Cohen replied.

"That's all for now," Brody said, dismissing the fighters.

As the group dispersed, Cohen Daniels lingered by the fire, his mind consumed by thoughts of Wren. Since her mother's death, he'd watched her blossom into a formidable archer and hunter, which made her a valuable asset to Black Arrow. Two days ago, he and his new wife, Mallory, had grown increasingly concerned when Wren left so shortly after overhearing Brody's daring plan to assassinate the leaders of the other groups using the archers.

Mallory had urged him to search for her, and they'd argued about Brody's rigid seven-day rule. Initially, Cohen had hesitated, mindful of the consequences—banishment or worse. However, upon realizing that Brody had come to regard Wren as the daughter he never had, he decided the risk was worth taking. Surprisingly, his boss agreed to the search. But Cohen promised himself that if she didn't return soon, he would gather another search team—rules or no rules. The ache of her absence gnawed at him, sharper than the morning chill, a stark reminder that in this chaotic world, loyalty and love could propel one into dangers that threatened everything they'd built.

Chapter 4

A thin layer of ice encircled the edges of the creek the following morning, creating ideal conditions for hunting. Travis scanned for whitetail through the trees, his thoughts drifting to Wren Daniels. Why did she have to be part of Black Arrow? They shared a passion for hunting and the outdoors, and he felt an unexpected connection. Still, could he trust her? His father had warned him about the rogue group, insisting they were different from the others—more dangerous.

What about his father? Logan had seemed eager, almost hungry for confrontation, mainly where Black Arrow was concerned. For a man known for his calm, steady ways, the sudden edge in his voice for them puzzled Travis. There had to be more to it—something Logan had not yet told him.

Two does wandered into the clearing and paused as they tested the air, glancing left, then right, before drifting from the cover of the trees toward the water. Travis caught his breath at the size of the larger one. She carried her head proudly, nostrils flaring as she sampled the breeze. For a moment, he thought she would wheel and run, but she lowered her muzzle to drink.

Seizing the moment, he released his arrow, piercing the doe's side. She bolted into the woods, hooves thundering through leaves and underbrush. With each step, her legs weakened until she collapsed. The other deer sensed the danger and vanished over an embankment, rustling the leaves as it leaped away.

Travis reached the fallen animal, looped a rope around her hind legs, and hoisted her onto a sturdy limb. He skinned, quartered, and portioned the meat into loads he could carry. As he added the meat to his backpack, he realized the sheer volume would require two trips back to town.

An hour into the task, Travis heard footsteps splashing in the creek. Glancing up, he spotted Wren Daniels wading through the shallow water.

"I knew she was a big one," she said, a quiet smile touching her lips as she kneeled beside him.

"You called it." He nodded toward the meat. "Care to lend a hand?"

"I'd like that, and I can help you get it home. You can't manage it in one trip."

"Thanks," he said. Her offer surprised him, knowing she couldn't venture beyond the wood line near town.

"She's a nice one, Travis."

"Yes, she is." He dropped a piece of meat into the pack. "There's something I need to ask you."

Their eyes met. Wren felt the pull of his rugged features and the gentleness in his voice—qualities rare among the young men she knew at camp, who often pressed too hard. Travis seemed different, genuinely attentive and caring, yet the divide between their worlds remained wide. He was one of the People of the Faith, sworn enemies of hers. Shared passions were a beginning, but a lasting friendship would require cautious trust.

"So, go on and ask," she said, curiosity resonating in her tone.

"Where is your home? Some of my people think the Black Arrow camp lies west—maybe near Paris."

She suppressed a smile, weighing her response. "Um, we have people in other places," she replied, mindful of her father's warnings about the People of the Faith. She'd only known Travis for a day, but his involvement with the POF made sharing unwise. Cohen had often described them as a zealous religious sect whose extremism may have sparked the separation. Yet, the more time she spent with Travis, the less he fit that description.

Travis noticed how she'd dodged the question, but the omission didn't bother him—they were just getting to know each other. He hoped to glean some insight about them by recounting the assassination.

"There was an attack on our town last night," he explained.

Her expression shifted, a flicker of unease crossing her features. She knew it could only mean one of their own had struck Travis' people. "How did it happen?"

"We exited the church service when an arrow flew in from the woods, striking him in the chest." He paused, studying her face.

Wren lowered her gaze, picturing the scene. Days earlier, she'd overheard her father and Brody Myles discussing a new strategy: Brody's plan was to attack towns and provoke conflict among the groups. The exact strategy she was unaware of, though she knew they had dispatched Reilly Brewin and two other archers. Wren sensed her father opposed the idea but went along with it. "It's what the boss wants," he always said. She slipped out later that night, after everyone had gone to bed.

"Travis, I'm sorry to hear about your friend. Did he... survive?" she asked.

"He died an hour later. The doctor did everything he could, but the blood loss was too much."

Wren drew a slow breath. "I need you to know I don't support these kinds of attacks—from either side."

Her face revealed more than any explanation could. "Did you know this was coming when we met yesterday?" he asked.

"No, I only heard bits about the plan when Brody told my father," she explained. "I never heard the name of any towns."

"So you didn't know they were going to assassinate someone?" he pushed.

"I didn't," she said softly, regret evident in her voice. "And I'm really sorry this happened. What I overheard was about spreading fear among the other groups. I told my father he should leave it alone, but he had his orders. That was the evening I left, and I'm sure he thinks I'm hunting at Newman Lake like I often do."

Travis let out a heavy sigh, sensing no deception—though a subtle redirection in her words. "How long have you been gone?" he asked.

"Four days," she replied. "He'll be worried by now."

"Maybe you should head back."

"He knows I can look after myself. I'll return home in a day or two. Besides—" she glanced at the thickening clouds "—bad weather's coming our way. We should find shelter."

Travis followed her gaze. The sky had darkened considerably. "I noticed."

"You won't get that meat home before the storm hits," she said, nodding toward his backpack.

"I have to try," he insisted. "There's nowhere to keep it safe out here. Besides that, my father could use the fresh meat."

"Go on home if you prefer, but I know of an old shack a few miles through the woods," Wren declared. "I stayed there the past few nights while I hunted. The old place isn't much, but it's dry. Maybe you can smoke your meat while we hold up there and take it home the next day."

The suggestion was reasonable. Logan could find food, and it made sense to hunker down inside somewhere as the storm bore down. "All right. We'll head to your shelter."

She tilted her head. "Unless you want to get soaked," she teased.

Travis smiled. "Not today."

"All right, then," she replied, satisfied.

"But what about your people?" Travis asked.

"My people?"

"Won't they come looking for you again?"

"Not likely with our protocols and surely not into a storm. I'm surprised Brody allowed them to come yesterday. They must have been out hunting, and my father directed them to look around for me as well."

The wind intensified as they shouldered the heavy packs and headed east. Dark clouds loomed closer, lightning flashing more frequently by the minute.

"We'd better hurry," Wren warned. "I've been caught in storms like this before. It starts with rain, followed by ice, and snow—and it all comes fast."

Travis nodded as he gazed into the clouds. "Yes, we'd better. We also need to gather dry firewood when we get there. I expect it'll get cold tonight."

She smiled at him. "Don't worry about that—we could always share our body heat if it gets too cold." A blush colored her cheeks. "I was only joking."

He watched her as she walked ahead of him along the trail, cutting through vines and underbrush. *I still believe she's peculiar.*

They pushed onward as rain began to patter down, hoping to reach the shelter before the storm worsened.

Chapter 5

Logan Weston paced the dim interior of the old café on Main Street, his breath fogging in the cool air. Once a lively establishment before the separation sent them northward, it now languished as a neglected remnant—crumbling walls etched with graffiti, a leaking roof pooling rainwater on the cracked concrete floor, and shattered windows that let in drafts of cold air.

Footsteps echoed inside, pulling him from his thoughts. He turned to see Randall Sweeney, bundled in a winter coat, staring at him. "Randall—finally. I was thinking everyone bailed."

Shaking his head, Randall walked closer, his boots scraping across the concrete. "I've been gathering firewood to get ahead of this storm. Have you heard from Derrick or Kincaid?"

"I haven't," Logan replied, "but I'm sure they'll be along soon."

"Logan, is this meeting really necessary? I have a lot to do."

The small group of men would sometimes call a meeting when they heard about new resources—food or other essentials—that the people desperately needed.

"Maybe we can meet right after the storm," Randall suggested, putting his hands into his pockets.

Logan fixed him with a stern look. "This is something you'll want to hear—and be glad I told you."

A door slammed behind them as Derrick and Kincaid entered the building, bringing in a gust of cold wind.

"Good, we're all here," Logan said, nodding.

Derrick Griffin shrugged. "Sorry that I'm late, Logan. This storm looks to be a devil."

Logan motioned for them to gather around the counter, where weathered crates served as makeshift seats. "Look, I know everyone needs to get things done before the storm arrives, but I want to share something with you—and it'll take only a few moments."

Derrick and Randall nodded, pulling up crates to sit.

Kincaid Mackill gave a curt hand gesture, a quiet habit he'd acquired after the devastating loss of his wife and two sons during the separation.

"What do you have, Logan?" Derrick asked, leaning forward on the counter.

"I've talked about my friend from Oklahoma before, Roy Wayne Sam," Logan said. "Roy Wayne and a few friends came through this way a few days ago.

"Roy Wayne was granted permission to hunt on a piece of land near an old reservation now called the Wichita Mountains Wildlife Refuge. One day, while walking through the woods, he heard some curious sounds and went to check it out."

Derrick gave him a curious glance. "What are you getting at, Logan?"

Logan scanned the room, his eyes meeting those of his friends, convinced his news would brighten their spirits. "Did I mention that my friend, Roy Wayne, lives near one of the places the government stashed the arms and ammunition they confiscated from us? He thinks they meant to hide it deep in the woods. One day, he spotted the military unloading a fresh batch—maybe transferring from elsewhere—but the best part is, they left and never returned. He slipped inside and found loads of guns and ammunition hidden in a bunker. It's been over thirteen years, and the weapons are still there."

"What! All this time?" Derrick questioned, his voice rising in frustration. "We could have used those guns for hunting."

"Yes, and to take back what was taken from us!" Logan shot back. "Don't you guys get it. These weapons are a great start for building our own army, so one day we can fight our way home."

Randall shook his head, a bitter scoff escaping his lips. "Oh, yeah, back to a government that took away our right to defend ourselves? Not much worth returning to, if you ask me."

"I respect your opinion, Randall," Logan replied, undeterred. "But I just hope none of you have forgotten how they forced us here—basically left us to die. These weapons... they could give us a new life."

Derrick shook his head. "We already know how to survive in this godless wilderness, Logan, and we have families to think about. I can't drag them back through that periphery zone again. I know you believe we stand a chance against the North, but I'm not sure I do."

"Do you want to keep scavenging for green plants and berries for food, along with whatever supplies we can scrape together?" Logan said, his voice getting louder. "Those trucks that once brought food to our stores haven't run in twenty years—and they won't again unless we strengthen our clans and push back against the northern tyranny."

"I agree it's not easy to find everything we need," Derrick replied. "But to go back north and face them again—I don't know. I worry I can't keep my family safe now."

Logan reached out and laid a hand on Derrick's shoulder. "You guys are all like brothers to me. I would never knowingly put you in harm's way. If we head north someday, it won't be without the capabilities to make a real difference. We'll invest serious strategic effort in our preparations, so we come out of this fight on top. Hang with me, Derrick." He turned to address the entire group. "Guys, we're only going after weapons, which we could use to guard against more assassination attempts. And besides, how bad can it be in Oklahoma?"

"We're with you, Logan. No matter how long it takes." Kincaid said firmly. "My family died because of them—they didn't even get a chance to leave with me. So, I'm ready when you are to reclaim our liberty and make them pay for what they've done. But let's make sure going after those weapons isn't a trap."

"You're right, Kincaid—we have to prepare for any possibility," Logan agreed. "Maybe we can get them out before the military returns."

Derrick peeled off a small piece of wood from the counter and whacked it against the surface. "Alright, I agree if there are guns and ammo in that building, we have to get them."

"And you see why this meeting was important," Logan said as he met their gazes.

"But why has your friend hidden this information for so long?" Randall asked.

"Roy Wayne figured we'd go after them to start a war with the North," Logan explained. "He believed that by holding us back, he was saving our lives."

"Well, we do plan to start a war," Randall replied, a grim smile tugging at his lips.

Derrick shrugged. "So, what caused Roy Wayne's sudden change of heart?"

Logan shifted uneasily on the wooden box, his fingers drumming lightly against its surface. "Well, he said rumors are coming down from the north side of the periphery that the military is engaged in a fight near Minneapolis. Roy Wayne worries it might spread south. We'll need those weapons if it does."

Randall looked down at Kincaid's foot, tapping restlessly on the concrete floor. "Easy, Kin—we're not at war yet. Just take a deep breath."

"No, not yet," Kincaid shot back, his voice edged with unsettled anger, "but I told you guys we'd fight them someday. I'll never forget what they did."

Derrick's right eyebrow shot up sharply as he fixed his intense gaze on Logan. "Do you think your Indian friend is truthful about weapons being in that bunker?"

"Roy Wayne's a man of God, and he's never lied to me," Logan replied with a firm voice.

Kincaid turned to Logan with an earnest nod. "I'm ready. So, when do we leave for those weapons?"

"As soon as we put a plan together. First, we'll need horses and a good wagon."

"Are you gonna disclose this to Travis?" Randall asked. "He'll know when you leave for Oklahoma."

Logan knew Travis was opposed to fighting the other groups and was more than certain he would refuse to go to war against an enemy like the North, known for its military might. He grimaced, the weight of secrecy pulling at his features. "Yeah, I'll have to at some point, but let's keep it between us for now. If he learns of it, Travis will be furious."

"Our people won't talk," Derrick said with confidence, "and we aren't close friends with any of the other groups. But if they catch wind of these weapons, they'll all want to be friends."

"Then we'll deal with it, however we need to," Logan replied, his jaw set in resolve.

"I just wish we had a working truck for this adventure," Kincaid remarked, glancing at Logan. "It'll be a long trip to Oklahoma and back in a wagon. We're talking two-hundred fifty miles or more. Might take a couple of weeks, and we have no idea what the roads are like."

"Yeah, it'd be great—except there's no gasoline," Derrick responded, shrugging.

A wide smile spread across Kincaid's face.

"What are you smiling about, Kincaid?" Logan asked, tilting his head in curiosity.

"It's just that there might be," Kincaid replied, his grin widening."

Logan looked at him, a confused expression on his face. "Might be what?"

"Oh, only gasoline," Kincaid replied.

The other men fixed their eyes on him. Gasoline hadn't been available for more than fifteen years.

Kincaid nodded and continued, "I know of an old fuel tank with gasoline—if others haven't drained it. Haven't been there in years."

Randall gave Kincaid a hearty slap on the back. "Why didn't you mention this before? Might've been some other uses for it around town."

"We manage just fine with firewood," Kincaid replied, shrugging. "Didn't tell you because I thought there might come a day when we'd need that gasoline for something just like this. Besides, gasoline isn't safe for much else."

"All right, save your energy," Logan responded. "We don't need the gas at the moment. What we need is permission to borrow the town's wagon and horses for a few weeks."

Derrick raised his hand. "Um, have you all forgotten that my old truck is sitting in the barn?"

"That old Ford dually?" Logan questioned, eyes widening.

Derrick chuckled. "Yep, the supercab. It'll need a lot of work. Hasn't run since the day we ran out of gas."

"Hmm," Logan mumbled. "That might alter our plans. Randall and Kincaid, you two get together when the weather clears. Borrow the town's wagon and horses. See if you can locate that fuel tank again and bring some gas back to Derrick's place so we can get his truck running. He and I will stay behind and work on it while you two are gone after the fuel."

Kincaid nodded. "We'll get it done." He gave Randall a quick affirmative nod.

"You can count on us, Logan," Randall replied. "We'll head out as soon as the storm passes and will take along an empty fifty-gallon drum. Not worth the trip if we only bring back a small amount."

Logan's crate creaked as he stood, a huge grin spreading across his face. "Okay, men, let's do this. Our town needs those weapons for protection, and someday we may need them to take our country back."

The main door suddenly flew open. "We'd better get home," Randall said. "That storm ain't waiting."

"Right," Logan said, slapping Randall on the shoulder. "I'll see you, guys, soon."

Chapter 6

As the storm intensified outside, the shack walls groaning against the wind, it proved to be an ideal place for Travis and Wren to wait it out.

Travis dreaded sharing the night with her. He had slept alone since childhood, and Wren had given no cause to doubt her intentions.

They kindled a fire atop the uneven rock floor in the dim space, while a ragged hole in the roof funneled the smoke upward. Outside the door, another low flame burned beneath a makeshift rack, where strips of meat had smoked all day, saturating them with flavor.

Wren slung her backpack over one shoulder. "How about we pull my meat off the smoker and swap it for yours? It can cure overnight."

Travis hesitated, glancing toward the door. "What about the storm? The meat will get wet and won't cook."

"I've packed the smoker with clay," Wren replied. "Hardly any rain will get through. We'll need to scrounge up wood and keep the fire going through the night."

Watching her manage these tasks filled Travis with confidence in her resilience—she seemed more than capable of facing any environment.

After swapping out the meat, they retreated to the small shack, settling on the floor to rest and ride out the storm. Wren pulled a towel from her backpack and dried her hair. "Your meat will be easier to haul home after smoking."

"I've never cured meat while hunting," he admitted.

She flashed a smile. "You never expected to learn something from a woman, did you?"

He shook his head. "It's not that. I just always stick to what I know. Relying on other methods doesn't come naturally to me."

She suddenly wondered whether this might be the ideal moment to raise their earlier discussion. "So, what's your opinion on finding peace between our groups? Or does that even matter to you?"

Travis looked into her eyes, the firelight dancing in them, stirring memories of their former conversation. She'd mused about what their groups might become if they united. "If you mean about joining up, yes, if it's crucial—though it makes me uneasy. Speaking to people about something this important has never come easy to me."

"Yeah, me either," she admitted, her voice soft against the wind's wail. "I keep imagining the fallout when my people discover we've been discussing a merger. There'll be serious consequences. They might even banish me from our group—and I'd find myself living alone in this old shack. Still, I believe it's worth the risk."

"Then we're in agreement," Travis said, "but we need help."

"Perhaps we can find someone who shares our vision and has an ability with words," Wren suggested.

A sudden memory of his gift for her flashed through his mind. "Yes, maybe," he answered, reaching into his pack. "I have something for you."

Surprise flitted across her face, and her eyes widened against the fire's glow. "What do you mean?"

"During our last meeting, you mentioned that your father never answered your questions about God," he said in a gentle voice.

"I remember," she replied, curiosity slipping into her expression.

"You don't have to wonder anymore." He reached for her hand and handed her a small black leather Bible, its cover worn from years of study.

"What is it?" she asked.

He placed it gently in her hands. "A Bible. It contains the beliefs of my people—words from God Himself. Read it, and you'll understand who we are."

Wren's expression shifted, a shadow of sadness crossing her features as she averted her eyes.

"I'm… sorry," he stammered, concern marking his brow. "Did I say something wrong?"

She leaned against the coarse wooden wall, her gaze finally meeting his. "It's not that I don't appreciate the gift—but I can't read. My father said Mom would've taught me, but she died when I was just a child. Then he married Mallory, who refused, saying her own reading was too poor to teach anyone else."

"Your speaking skills, though, are remarkable," he said, with a note of admiration.

She tilted her head, a faint smile forming on the right side of her lips. "If you knew my father, you'd understand. He has no tolerance for what he calls *improper grammar*. We practice speaking all the time."

Travis chuckled softly. "Then I'm curious—why didn't he teach you to read?"

Her jaw tightened, a hint of anger whetting her words. "Father is more devoted to teaching the men and keeping Brody Myles happy than worrying about me."

Travis realized it was a sore topic. "Well, if we keep meeting, I'll teach you how to read."

"You would do that?" she asked.

"Sure," he replied with a grin. "Teaching someone to read can't be too complicated."

Wren's face lit up as she lay down, resting her head against the backpack, her eyes gleaming with gratitude. "Travis, thank you," she said softly. "You're not so bad, you know?"

***

The night brought fierce winds and relentless rain, morphing into a wintry mix of sleet and snow that pelted the shack's tin roof. Inside, the aroma of burning wood filled the air as they took turns stoking the fire.

Come morning, a light coating of mixed snow and sleet lay on the ground. They ate some smoked meat, packed the rest into their backpacks, and set out toward Pattonville under a gray sky.

Fallen trees lay scattered across the cracked pavement, the road's edges bordered by overgrown bushes. Despite an overnight deluge of pounding rain that gave way to sleet and snow, the temperatures remained modest, warding off any treacherous accumulation on the road. After trudging several miles, they reached a collapsed bridge where a creek churned in violent fury, its thunderous roar drowning out all else. The ruined span left no choice but to detour onto a path through the woods.

Travis shouted, his voice straining against the deafening tumult. "This isn't my usual route! I normally follow the creek bed, but with last night's weather and these heavy meat packs, I thought sticking to the road might be easier!"

"You were right, except for this broken-down bridge," Wren replied.

Travis gestured with his hand. "We should shorten our path here anyway. Follow me. We'll take to the woods."

They bounded over a fallen tree and picked their way alongside the washed-out culvert.

Glancing back to check their trail, Travis caught a flicker of movement in his peripheral vision. On the other side of the road, a few hundred yards into the forest, a lone figure sat astride a black horse. "Look," he said.

They ducked behind the gnarled trunk of a fallen tree and watched as the rider urged his mount forward at a steady pace.

"I know him," Wren murmured. "He's not a good man."

"I bet he's good with that bow," Travis replied, eyeing the weapon slung across the rider's back.

"Deadly accurate," Wren confirmed, her expression somber.

Travis squinted into the distance. "I wonder where he's headed."

Wren's eyes narrowed with determination as she emerged from behind the oak toward the rider. "Who knows where he's going or what my father has planned for him, but it can't be good," she muttered in defiance.

"What are you doing?" Travis hissed with concern, grabbing her arm.

She shook him off. "I'm going to tell Reilly exactly what I think of him—and that he shouldn't take orders from my father."

"Wren, if he's not a good person, as you said, he might not like your berating him—and he could turn that bow on us."

She seemed to have ignored his words and pressed on, branches crunching under her determined steps.

"Wren, please stop!" Travis pleaded. "What if something happened? How would anyone find us here?"

She halted mid-step as the weight of his words sank in, recalling Reilly Brewin's reputation—one of the most ruthless fighters in her camp. If he spotted Travis, he'd demand answers: who he was, which faction he was from—no mercy for outsiders. "You're right," she conceded, turning back and closing the distance. "But you should know he's from my camp."

Travis frowned. "You sure know a lot about this man. Anything else I need to know?"

His tone carried a probing edge, and she bristled inwardly, reluctant to provoke an argument. "Maybe later, when we have more time," she responded. "For now, just know he's dangerous—and it's best to keep your distance."

"I'll keep that in mind," he said, his gaze lingering on the rider.

Once the archer and his horse vanished from sight, they hastened onward, reaching the outskirts of Pattonville as darkness settled in.

"You know, it's almost dark," Travis said, scanning the area toward town. "It might be better if you stayed the night. Otherwise, you'll be trekking back in the dark. I can head to the shack with you tomorrow and then to your home."

His concern for her well-being was refreshing, but how dangerous could it be for her to linger in the enemy's town? If the roles were reversed, Travis couldn't even approach her camp without Brady killing him on sight.

"If your people catch me here, they might execute me—being Black Arrow and all. They're probably patrolling right now."

"We have no patrols," he assured her. "Wait here, and I'll hurry back for you. There's an old storage building behind our house. I'll set up a spot for you there. We'll slip out before sunrise, and no one will ever know."

"Well, I am exhausted after that long walk with the meat," she declared with a weary sigh. "Are you certain it's all right, though? What about your father?"

Travis shook his head. "My father hasn't set foot in that old storage building in forever—I can't even remember the last time. You won't see him; he sends me to get whatever he needs from the shed, anyway."

She studied his face and nodded slowly. "Okay, I'm going to trust you."

"I'll be back for you soon," he promised, flashing a quick smile before turning and disappearing into the shadows toward his house.

Chapter 7

Early the next morning, Travis rolled out from under his warm blanket and made his way to the storage building, where he'd set up a sleeping area for his new friend. As he approached, he heard voices—one high-pitched and the other his father's, who was leaning against the doorframe. Travis crept up behind him to eavesdrop on their conversation.

"I hunt a lot, sir," Wren explained. "Thanks to my father, I have the skills for hunting and fishing, which, as you know, are essential for survival."

Logan tilted his head curiously. "Did your father also teach you how to speak so clearly?"

"He did," she replied. "Travis asked about it, too."

"Perhaps in the future I'll have the opportunity to meet him."

"Maybe so."

"How did you come to meet Travis?" Logan asked.

"A few days ago, we were hunting in the same place. Travis helped me with a deer I killed, and I wanted to return the favor, so we brought the meat here from a doe he took."

"I see. So, you're why Travis didn't come home the night before?"

Logan's assumptions aside, the question was partially accurate. Travis had heard enough. "Father, are you implying we did something wrong? I assure you, we didn't. A storm came in while we were hunting, so we waited it out together. There was no time to start back home until the next morning."

Logan turned to meet Travis's stare.

"We smoked our deer meat while we waited in an old shack," Travis added.

"Uh-huh," Logan murmured, his voice laced with intrigue as he turned back to the young woman. His eyes narrowed on her bow propped against the wall, the arrows' shafts bearing the distinctive mark—a letter A carved into the wood. He recognized it instantly: the insignia of the Black Arrow group, those elusive rivals from the outskirts of the wilderness. A chill of unease settled in his gut. *Does Travis know?* He wondered silently. *Has my boy entangled himself with our enemy?* He kept his expression neutral, but the discovery gnawed at him. His urge to confront Black Arrow was genuine, but they weren't prepared—not at the risk of them discovering Travis wasn't one of theirs, but aligned with the POF. He couldn't bear to imagine what brutal reprisals they might unleash on his son.

Wren rolled off the mat and slipped her feet back into her socks. "Travis was a proper fellow, if that's your concern."

"Father, why are you here at the storage building?" Travis inquired, hoping to steer his father's thoughts in another direction. "You never come out here."

"Maybe it's a good thing I did come," He let those words settle in the air for a moment. "If you must know, I was about to grab my toolbox when I noticed this beautiful young lady occupying this space."

"Tools? You haven't needed tools in a while. What are you working on?"

Logan wasn't ready to reveal the nature of the project he and his friends had planned, but a tease wouldn't hurt. "Oh, we're going to try to start Derrick's old truck, and I needed to find some tools for working on the motor."

"So, you're feeling better?" Travis asked, a note of relief in his voice.

"Today's starting off great, son," Logan replied.

Travis's curiosity surged again at the casual mention. "Did I hear right? You're working on a truck? Why?"

"Well, you know us old timers—we get bored," Logan answered with a chuckle, winking at his son. The gesture carried a silent message: *Not in front of her.*

Wren caught the wink and smiled politely. "But where'd you get the fuel?"

Surprise flickered across Logan's face as he turned back to her. "You know about combustion engines?"

"Well, I've heard they need fuel to run," she said matter-of-factly.

"Yes, they do," Logan answered, a nervous hitch in his voice. "Um, before the separation, I was a mechanic—worked on vehicles for a living." *If she does have Black Arrow ties, I dare not share anything that might disrupt our plan,* he thought. "Recently, my friends and I scraped together just enough to maybe get it turning over. It's a long shot, but it'll give us something to do besides hauling firewood or scavenging wild plants and game."

Sensing their lingering confusion, he continued to steer the conversation. "Older men like me love to tinker; boredom's a killer. Back in the day—"

"Father, we're not in the mood for history lessons today," Travis cut in with an exaggerated eye roll. "Wren and I are heading back to the woods."

"You're going hunting again?" Logan's voice rose, sharper than he intended. "I was hoping you'd help with our engine. There's plenty you could learn from it."

Travis sighed, frustration churning. "No one uses those things anymore. Why are you really doing this? You already said fuel's scarce."

"For the enjoyment," Logan said, not missing a beat, locking eyes with his son. "Thought it'd be a chance for you to join the guys and me—spend some quality time together. But I understand if you've got other plans."

"The thing is, I promised to help Wren carry her meat back to her camp," Travis explained, carefully avoiding details about her family and the name of her group, unsure what she'd revealed before his arrival. "She helped me out, so it's only fair I return the favor. By the way, Wren has an impressive meat-curing setup you should check out. I'm sure you could build one."

"Oh? Where's this contraption?" Logan responded, pivoting toward the young huntress with feigned casual interest. He avoided mentioning the Black Arrow mark he'd spotted on her arrows, his mind racing with concern for his son. *I hope Travis knows better than to waltz into that viper's nest*, he thought. The weight of old rivalries pressed on him like the chill of an approaching storm. For now, he'd play it discreetly.

"I don't know the creek's name, sir," Wren replied smoothly, her voice steady as a hunter's aim. "It's a place I frequently hunt for game, about a day's walk that way." She pointed toward the hazy horizon, where the forest thickened into a tangle of trees.

Logan shifted his gaze to Travis. "Am I familiar with that creek, son?"

"We've hunted there before, a long time ago," Travis said, keeping his tone casual despite the knot of unease twisting in his gut.

Logan scratched his head, brow furrowing in thought as memories stirred—old hunts, rival territories, and now this girl's evasive charm. *If it's Black Arrow territory, you're walking into trouble, boy,* he mused silently. "Hmm, maybe I have. I'll try to swing by sometime."

"You're welcome anytime, Mr. Weston," Wren said, her voice softening. "Though I might not always be around—hunting keeps me on the move, and the game doesn't wait for anyone."

Logan offered a half-grin, his expression masking his keen awareness of the subtle evasion in her answer. He turned to Travis, his eyes narrowing slightly as he pondered how their cryptic remarks mirrored his own guarded secrets about the truck. *They're hiding something.* "Well, how long will you be gone this time, son?"

Travis shrugged, meeting his father's scrutiny. "Shouldn't take more than a day or two. I'll leave some fresh smoked venison in the smokehouse for you."

"Thanks," Logan said with a wry smile. "Beats the poke salad I've been choking down—had enough to last a lifetime." He spun toward Wren once more. "It was nice meeting you." Then, with his toolbox in hand, he turned to Travis before walking outside. "Be careful, son. You never know where the danger will come from."

Travis nodded and watched his father disappear around the corner. "That was close. I wonder if he saw your bow?" he murmured, exhaling a breath he hadn't realized he'd been holding.

Wren gazed at him, shaking her head with a mix of amusement and concern. "So, *you're* the one who usually fetches things from the shed, huh?"

"I promise, that's how it always is," Travis replied, his voice sharp and defensive. *But today feels off.* "Who knows why he came in here today of all days?"

Concern engraved deeper lines across Wren's brow as her eyes locked with his. *If Logan finds out, it could unravel everything we are planning.* "I don't think your father would approve of me if he knew I was from the Black Arrow group."

"Honestly, I don't know—he's fooled me before," Travis admitted, rubbing the back of his neck as a familiar mix of exasperation and worry settled over him. "I wish I knew why he's messing with an old truck—it's got no chance of running, and there are plenty of those mechanical hulls rusting away everywhere. But I'm just glad he's feeling better."

"I'm sure he gets bored, as he says—another man itching to get his hands dirty," Wren said thoughtfully, her fingers absently tracing the edge of her bow. *If only they knew how alike our worlds are,* she thought. "We have plenty like that back home, my father included."

"Maybe so," Travis conceded, his voice trailing off as he glanced toward the forest's edge. *Boredom doesn't explain Father's wink or the mention of fuel,* he mused. "I've got a feeling something else is up, and he's keeping it from me."

She laughed lightly, the sound cutting through the tension like the morning mist. "But what about you? You insisted I stay here because you thought it was unsafe for me to head home in the dark—and you never mentioned I'm from Black Arrow. You're keeping that from him."

"I really did think traveling at night was too risky, and I didn't tell him the group you're from for good reason," he said.

"You don't have to protect me, Travis," she replied. "I can take care of myself from your father, too."

"I have no doubt you can," he said with a warm smile. "So, how about we grab that meat and hit the trail? The weather's holding clear—perfect for our journey."

"Ready when you are," she responded, slinging her pack over her shoulder as they stepped into the crisp dawn.

Chapter 8

The barn door creaked open, revealing the dual-wheel Ford truck—its red paint faded to dull crimson, blanketed in dust and cobwebs that caught the morning sunlight.

"There she is," Logan said. "Besides tires, gas, and a wash, what else is wrong?"

"Isn't that enough?" Derrick shot back, circling the truck with a critical eye. He kicked a flat tire, stirring up dust. "Converter's plugged solid, motor needs spark plugs—good luck finding those here. Battery's dead, but I can scrounge a charger and generator."

Logan looked at the hulking relic. "Plenty to fix before it will get us to Oklahoma. What about that Ford by the old sawmill near Morris's farm? Let's check it for parts."

Derrick nodded. "Yeah, I thought of that one too. Motor the same?"

"Won't matter with plugs and batteries," Logan said confidently. "We'll pull what we can and test 'em. Henderson's junkyard might have some parts."

"I forgot about that one."

The morning turned into a grueling hunt as they scoured wrecks for parts, salvaging spark plugs, a battery that might hold a charge, and scraps of tail pipe.

Back at the barn, they tackled the clogged catalytic converter. Lacking a torch, they hack-sawed the tailpipe to length and fitted it after removing the converter.

With repairs done, they hauled a generator from Derrick's parents' home to charge the truck's battery. By lunchtime, they rested in the shade, waiting for their friends to return with the fuel.

"Logan, we've got to find a place to store those weapons, don't you think?" Derrick asked, taking a swig of water from his glass.

An idea popped into Logan's mind—*Raines Road*, far enough from Black Arrow for concealment. Then he felt a sharp ache, recalling that Travis was heading toward them with the young huntress. He prayed he discovers who she is before something happens.

"How long's it been since you walked along Raines Road?" Logan asked.

"Not long," Derrick replied. "I hunt for meat like everyone else."

"There used to be a few farms left along that road," Logan said, squinting into the sun. "Travis and I found one years back—a big hay barn in the field behind the farmhouse. Old Salisbury place, I think. A couple of rolls of hay sat inside, nothing else. Driveway's overgrown and rutted, but your truck'll manage."

"We could drag it with the truck," Derrick suggested.

"Right, provided we find that fuel."

"How far away do you say it is?"

"About three miles," Logan replied, wiping sweat from his brow.

"Hmm, that won't be too far," Derrick mused. "Should be a great spot to store the weapons—not many farms have buildings still standing these days. But Logan, how do you know we can use it?"

"I don't—we'll have to ask," Logan answered.

The distant squeak of a wagon and the rhythmic crunch of wheels on the road caught their attention. "I'm sure that's Kincaid and Randall," Derrick said, shading his eyes against the sun.

The men guided the Murgese workhorses to a halt near the barn, the animals snorting and stamping in the dust, while Logan and Derrick hurried to assist.

"Okay, how much fuel was there?" Logan asked, peering at the barrel strapped to the wagon.

Kincaid shrugged, unhitching a rope from the load. "There's no way to measure that old tank. We took a rope, tied a chunk of steel to it, and dropped it in. It came up wet for about ten feet—maybe more."

"That's a lot," Derrick uttered, a grin forming on his face. "I suppose you siphoned a barrel full?"

"Sure did," Kincaid replied, patting the barrel with a satisfied grin. "Wish we'd had another—felt like we had struck liquid gold."

Logan gestured to reposition the wagon. "We'll lift it out with Derrick's hand hoist. If we can siphon a small amount, we'll test the generator."

They backed the wagon into the barn, lowered the barrel to the dirt floor, and drew out fuel for the generator. The four men coaxed it to life.

Plugging in the 12-volt charger, they watched the meter's needle climb to full charge in minutes. With the truck's tank fueled, they prepared to start the ancient beast.

Derrick slid into the driver's seat and turned the key, only for the motor to grunt. "It's been sitting forever," he muttered. "Hope the rings aren't stuck."

Logan nodded with a faint smile, worry gnawing at him. If this heap runs, he thought, it could shift the balance against the factions. "Don't be so optimistic—it's only thirty years old."

"Thirty-five, but who's counting—if it runs?" Derrick quipped, wiping his hands and trying again. He turned it, and the motor sputtered and died.

"Try again, Derrick!" Randall urged.

On the third attempt, it roared to life, rattling the fenders.

"Pump the accelerator!" Logan barked, heart pounding with hope. The engine coughed and stalled, but the next try brought it sputtering back, spewing dark exhaust before settling into a steady rumble.

"Yeah!" Derrick shouted, pumping his fist. "Knew this old thing would start—it was always dependable."

Logan rolled his eyes. "You knew it, huh?"

After several more starts, they shut the truck off, the silence highlighting the need to conserve every drop of fuel.

"Okay, guys, we've got a truck," Logan said, as he wiped oil from his hands on a ragged shirt. The shop fell pin-drop silent, the lingering echo of the engine's roar fading into the air with the faint metallic tang of fuel. He perceived a wave of uncertainty rippling through the group, their faces shadowed in the dim light filtering through the open door. "Now's the time to push forward with our project. Roy Wayne won't believe we're really gonna do it." Pausing, he scanned their expressions. "Are you guys still with me on this? I'm sensing something's changed."

"Logan, you know we want to go after those weapons," Derrick said, gazing down at the grimy shop floor. "Randall and I talked it over when we took the wagon and horses back to the town. We have families to consider—and so do *you*. If something happens to us on that trip, what would *they* do?"

"We're just going for guns and ammunition," Logan countered. "For our protection, nothing more—no one's starting a war. Black Arrow's our problem, and they won't be in Oklahoma. Just prep the truck properly, carry along tools and spare parts, and we'll be fine."

"But Logan, *with* those guns, we could easily start a war," Derrick pressed, his voice low. "You don't know what we'll run into along the way—scavengers, more faction groups, or worse."

Logan stood in disbelief, the weight of leadership pressing down on him as the oppressive Texas heat does on a sunny day. He shook his head as he pondered the best way to rally his friends. They don't see it yet. "The weapons give us an edge against Black Arrow's aggression and whatever might come from the North. We can't back out now."

Kincaid turned to Derrick, an annoyed scowl on his face. "I can't believe you guys won't go," he snapped. "Are you *scared* to stand up against our enemies? You'll want those weapons when another arrow hits one of our own or the northern army rolls south with artillery—and that day may be coming soon. You've heard the US military is fighting some rogue fighters in Minnesota. If *they* lose, the conflict will surely come to us."

Logan nodded, his expression firm. "Don't forget—they *killed* Edmond just days ago," he said. "Do you think the attacks will stop? We have the opportunity to prepare, before we lose everything—our families, friends, and this town."

"I know, all right," Derrick said with a heavy sigh. "I just wish there was some other way. Conflicts always lead to people dying."

Logan fixed him with a hard look. "An alternative path never came, though. We've lost too much already, he thought—Edmond, those who starved, and our freedom. "Derrick, we'll never forget all that's happened, but now we can do something about it."

Derrick scratched his head, nodding slowly, as the tension in the room began to ease. "Yeah, you're right," he said.

Kincaid slapped his hand on the truck's hood with a resounding clang. "Good. So, Logan, what's our next move?"

"Well, I mentioned to Derrick before you two returned with the fuel that, while Travis and I were hunting one day, we stumbled upon an old farm with a large barn about three miles from here," Logan said. "Should be a perfect spot to store them, after we get permission. We ought to check it out before heading to Oklahoma. We'll drive there and test the truck—make sure it's up to the task."

"It's up to the task, I promise you," Derrick said with a confident nod.

"Then what do you say, guys? Want to drive out there tomorrow and see if that old barn will serve our needs?" Logan inquired, scanning their faces with renewed energy.

"*Drive* out there tomorrow," Derrick echoed, a grin breaking through. "It's been ages since I heard those words strung together."

Logan grinned back at him. "Well, maybe times are changing."

"Sounds good to me," Randall said, nodding with a determined glint in his eye.

Kincaid shrugged, a smirk cracking his stern facade. "You know I'm in—been waiting for something to happen."

"Yeah, me too," Derrick replied, his earlier doubts fading

Logan stood before them and gave a firm nod, his mind already mapping the risks ahead. This could be our turning point—securing those weapons before Black Arrow strikes again. We can't fail, he thought. "All right, let's meet here tomorrow morning, early. We'll give that truck a go."

Chapter 9

The restless mare snorted, stamping her hoof as Reilly Brewin looped the reins around a low branch. He gave her neck a quick, reassuring stroke before slipping away into the night.

He quickly found a sturdy drainpipe and a young sapling that bent under his weight but held as he pulled his way to the top. In moments, he was on the flat roof, easing the bow from his shoulder to settle into position. The town square lay spread below him: lanterns lit among the laughter, the soft strum of a guitar.

I need someone to point out a leader, he thought, gazing at the crowd.

A patrol of archers watched from the rooftop opposite him, their backs turned for now, eyes fixed on the festival crowd. Bows strung, quivers full.

Reilly could only assume they had heard about his attack at Pattonville and prepared for another. But what if there was a mole inside his camp giving away Black Arrow's secrets to other factions? Brody will want to know they were watching in case they came.

The security team's presence made his shot far riskier. The distance itself rendered accuracy uncertain, and any miss would draw them directly to him. Still, he remained resolute in fulfilling his objective.

A portly man finished a short speech, and applause rippled through the crowd. Others handed out homemade medals and certificates—none of which mattered if Reilly couldn't locate a target.

Time was slipping away. The risk? Growing by the minute.

The guitar continued its passive melody, and the security archers focused on the streets below. Reilly nocked an arrow, preparing to hit his mark as per Brody's instructions: kill one of their leaders, sow fear, and show Black Arrow's formidable power. He only needed a moment to strike and then be gone.

Brody had promised all three assassins leadership roles within Black Arrow, but Reilly didn't need such a dangling carrot to do his job—despite the boss's assurance.

He noticed that someone had arranged the townsfolk into clusters of five or six. One table of gray-haired elders clearly held no interest for him. Another was ordinary citizens. The third group rose when a middle-aged brunette in formal attire moved down the line, shaking hands with them.

The woman may be someone high up, a leader, he determined—*she means something to them.*

Reilly dropped to one knee to steady himself and drew the bowstring to his cheek. The brunette paused to speak with a man at the end table.

Three arrows suddenly thudded into the roof tiles beside Reilly almost simultaneously, forcing him to withdraw. He twisted toward the sound, spotting movement on the next rooftop, and fired on instinct. His projectile struck one of the security guards in the thigh—the man dropped with a sharp cry. Two more arrows hissed past Reilly's ear and chest, close enough to send a gust of wind across his face.

Too close, he thought.

He swung back toward the crowd, already drawing back the bow. The brunette had turned at the commotion, eyes wide. He aimed and released it.

Pain exploded in his left hip, sudden and white-hot. One of their arrows had found him. He staggered, reached down, and felt the shaft buried deep.

"Ouch!"

Blood soaked his trousers instantly, warm and slick. Gritting his teeth, he snapped the arrow in two, leaving the head embedded—*better than pulling it free and bleeding out*, he resolved.

Boots pounded across the adjoining roofs. The team was maneuvering for a better chance at him.

Unable to check whether he had hit his mark, he limped toward the edge, each step a fresh stab of fire, awakening memories of his bullet wounds from Afghanistan. He gripped the sapling, lowered himself over the side, and dropped the last few feet just as another arrow ricocheted off the metal ledge where his head had been.

His injury pulsed as he hit the ground hard, vision swimming. The mare waited where Reilly had left her, ears pricked at the distant shouts, tense amid the confusion. He slung the bow across his back, grabbed the saddle horn, and hauled his weakening body up. Despite a wave of pain so intense he almost fainted, he pushed his intact foot into the stirrup and directed the mare away.

They vanished into the dark before the next flight of arrows could find them.

★★★

"Someone's coming on a horse!" Travis called out. "Looks like one of your people."

"The one we saw yesterday," Wren said, peering through the trees.

The horse thundered toward them, snorting, sweat foaming white beneath the saddle. The rider slumped forward, barely clinging to the mane.

Travis stepped into the animal's path, arms raised to slow it. Wren lunged for the reins and pulled the mare to a halt. "Easy, girl. Easy."

The rider lifted his head, face gray as ash, and managed a faint smile. "Wren. Perfect timing."

"Reilly," she said flatly, "you have an arrow in you."

"And there may be some angry people behind me."

Wren gave the reins a sharp tug. The mare tossed her head, snorted once, then settled and followed.

Travis hurried after her. "Wren, where are you going? I thought we were only trying to slow the horse. He just told you that angry people are coming behind him." *Helping an assassin? I can't believe it*, he thought. "This man's done something, and they'll blame us for it. Send him on and let's go."

"I can't." She glanced back without slowing. "You want to leave, Travis—go ahead. I'll get Reilly somewhere safe and pull the arrow out before he bleeds to death."

"I got plenty of blood left, Wrenny," Reilly mumbled.

"Be quiet and save your strength."

Travis crept behind, his mind racing. He figured the man was from the Black Arrow camp—same as her, but an assassin. He shouldn't be an immediate threat, given his injury and half-conscious state. "Fine," Travis replied at last, his voice laced with frustration. "But I'm coming with you. For the record, this is a terrible idea."

He shouldn't be an immediate threat, given his injury and half-conscious state.

Wren led them through dense thickets until they reached a creek, where they traced its rocky bed for miles, the shallow water concealing their tracks as they navigated the twisted vines. The only sounds were the creak of saddle leather and the horse's labored breathing.

"Wait," Travis said, gazing up to the rider. "He's leaving a blood trail anyone could follow. We have to stop it." He shrugged off his pack. "Wren, reach into the side pocket of my pack and grab the blue shirt."

She unzipped his pack, took the shirt, and tore it into long strips. Working quickly, she packed the cloth against the wound inside Reilly's trousers, slowing the seep of blood, then urged the mare onward.

Miles later, the creek narrowed. They climbed the western bank and followed deer trails through the forest.

In a while, Wren halted where the undergrowth grew thickest. "Travis, check behind that foliage—there should be a cave."

Knife in hand, he pushed through the vines and bushes, slicing and pulling until a dark opening appeared behind a jutting boulder. "I see it. Let me make sure nothing's living inside."

He wrapped a strip of the torn shirt around a stick, struck flint from his pack to spark it alight, and held the makeshift torch high. Cautiously, he stepped to the entrance and peered in. "Looks clear."

"Good. Let's get him inside," she said.

They eased Reilly onto the cool stone floor. Wren knelt beside him while Travis held the torch steady. She cut away his jeans, parted the skin, and probed carefully with her knife as fresh blood oozed. Reilly, unconscious, flinched.

"Hold on, mister," she muttered. "Got it." The barbed tip dropped to the rock floor.

She pressed the last of Travis's shirt against the wound to slow the blood flow. "Travis, put your hand here," she urged. "Keep pressure on it." From a small pocket in her own pack, she withdrew a needle and a small coil of thread. In minutes, the wound was closed, the bleeding stanched.

Travis observed in silence, then remarked softly, "You're good at that."

She gave a tired shake of her head. "I hope I never have to again."

"The cool weather's in his favor. Less chance of fever."

"Getting shot with an arrow isn't what I'd call a favor," she replied.

"Only in the case of the wound."

Wren leaned back against the cave wall, exhaustion plain on her face. "He's lost a lot of blood and could still take a fever."

Sitting nearby, weariness tugged at Travis, but questions pressed harder. "All right. Time you told me more about your 'friend.'"

"Not tonight," she replied faintly. "And Reilly isn't my friend." *I've said too much already*, she realized. "Let's just gather some wood, build a fire, and sleep, please. I'll tell you everything in the morning. Promise."

He studied her for a moment. "All right."

They collected dry branches, kindled a modest fire near the mouth of the cave, and lay down beside its subtle warmth. Soon, the only sounds were the crackling flames and the exhausted, sleeping breaths of three weary travelers.

Chapter 10

As morning light filtered into the cave, a few coals still glowed faintly in the fire pit. Travis slipped outside to search for dry wood. He gathered an armful of branches and returned.

Wren waited at the entrance, arms crossed. "I'm sorry the fire nearly died. I must have dozed off."

Travis kneeled and arranged the wood over the embers. "We ran out of fuel, and we were both exhausted."

She nodded toward her pack on the cave floor. "There's deer jerky in it if you're hungry."

He retrieved a few strips, tucked them into his pocket, then let his gaze drift toward the unconscious stranger. Curiosity still tugged at him.

Wren saw him looking. "His name is Reilly Brewin. Once, he asked me to marry him," she said.

Travis raised an eyebrow. "But you said you weren't friends."

"We aren't. Not anymore."

"What changed?" he asked.

She gave a faint grin. "Let's just say Reilly grew too insistent—like most men who think they know what's best for me."

"I'm sorry," Travis said, studying the wounded man again. "Have you considered what he might have done to earn an arrow in the hip?"

"I'm not sure I want to know. Reilly has a talent for making enemies. Even among our own people, he's... different."

"Different how?"

"He doesn't forgive easily. Compassion isn't in his nature. He can be pleasant company until he leaps to judgment and tears someone down without knowing the full story. People resent it."

"I checked out his gear last night," Travis said, recalling the day his friend Edmond died at the hands of an assassin in Pattonville. "He seems like more than a common hunter, and it's hard to ignore that arrow you took from his hip."

Wren paused, choosing her words with care. "He's one of our Black Arrow fighters. We all use bows for hunting, of course—I've told you how exceptional he is with one. We keep about ten horses. Brody likes to have them ready when we need to reach somewhere quickly."

Travis sensed she was withholding something. "So every Black Arrow fighter carries weapons?"

"Bows, knives—yes. Reilly is among our best in hand-to-hand combat. He learned it during the war."

Travis's voice lowered. "Sounds like a man who could eliminate a council member whenever he chose to."

Wren's eyes narrowed. "Travis, do you think he killed your friend?"

"I'm only saying he has the skill, the tools, and a wound that suggests someone is hunting him. We know something went wrong somewhere. I'd like to know what happened before we end up in the same trouble."

"Everything will be fine, Travis. If Reilly's presence bothers you, you can leave. I'll take care of him."

She doesn't want me here, he believed. "Leave you alone with him? You said he was an assassin and a bad man."

Her eyes bore into him. "I'll be all right. Once he wakes, you'll see he can be decent when he wants to be. Obnoxious, yes—but he won't harm me. Right now, he needs my help. When he's strong enough, I'll take him and the meat back to camp."

Travis exhaled. "I'll stay until you go."

"That's fine," Wren said quietly. A flicker of regret crossed her face, a sudden realization of the unforeseen complications that arose from befriending someone from another faction.

Travis sat, turning her words over in his mind. If Wren got injured because of this man, he would never forgive himself—especially with one unanswered question: were Reilly's pursuers still out there?

That man had better not bring danger to her, he pondered.

Travis stood. "I'm going to scout around—make sure no one's closing in," he said.

"Sounds like a good idea," Wren replied, relieved for a moment alone to think. "Just be careful. I don't want to patch more wounds today."

Travis stepped outside and checked on the mare, seeing that Wren had already watered her. He followed the trail back toward the creek, eyes scanning for tracks or broken branches.

Snowmelt rushed over the rocky streambed. He moved through a shadowed stretch of forest, senses sharp. A buck burst across the path, paused to stare, then vanished into the underbrush.

Beyond a low rise, Travis sat on a log, pulled out the jerky, and ate slowly. Reilly's presence gnawed at him. He stayed mainly for Wren—not only to protect her, but because he had enjoyed her company until the assassin arrived. His father would despise both the killer and any Black Arrow woman associated with him.

Why else would men hunt Reilly unless he had taken a life? Perhaps a personal quarrel that turned deadly. Or rival hunters had felt threatened.

His instinct insisted the man was a murderer—possibly Edmond's murderer. Combined with his Black Arrow allegiance, it left Travis confident that Reilly posed a significant threat.

Then a chilling realization hit him: Wren was also Black Arrow. Could she secretly be an assassin? Nothing in her manner matched the stories he'd heard, yet she had shielded Reilly. Perhaps old loyalty compelled her, or maybe she and Reilly were closer than she admitted. He wanted to trust her, but trust felt fragile amid unresolved questions.

As midday neared, Travis had not returned. Wren stepped to the entrance and scanned the trees. When she turned back inside, she found Reilly had rolled onto his side and lay watching her with open eyes.

"He lives," she murmured. "A miracle, after all the blood you lost."

Reilly's voice was rough. "Because you found me."

She gave a short huff. "You're so grateful. Care to tell me what happened back there?"

"They ambushed me. I climbed a roof in Deport. We had a source inside—he told us that the town was holding a festival and when. Didn't expect they'd be waiting. Perfect shot from the rooftop."

"For what? To murder someone?" she pressed.

"To remove an enemy," he replied. "That was my orders."

"So now innocent people are our 'enemies.'"

"Speak to Brody or Cohen if you object. I won't argue about orders with you." His voice gained strength. "Mine came from your father."

"You don't have to obey them!" Wren shouted. "What happened to you? Are you all about killing innocent people now?"

"We're at war. And what about you? With your skill, you could make a difference for our group."

"I will never take an innocent life. I'll defend myself if I must, but killing for no reason? How do you live with yourself?"

Reilly's lip curled. "I'm fine. But listen to you now. You were ready to kill those men who grabbed you at camp a while back. Does your father know you've changed, Wrenny?"

"He knows I refuse to murder innocents—the very reason I'm not at camp. I overheard him and Brody discussing your orders, so I left." Her voice sharpened. "And don't call me Wrenny!"

"You know, I pledged to follow orders," Reilly said, "because that's what makes Black Arrow the strongest faction group."

"The orders are the problem," she added. "We could have found peace with the other groups a long time ago. But Brody and my father only want to turn this forest into your kind of Afghanistan.

Our wilderness may be all we ever have, but there's no reason to turn it into a war zone."

"Brody doesn't see it that way," Reilly replied.

"Oh, how I know." She handed him her canteen. "Let's stop fussing. Drink—you need some water."

She watched as he took the canister. "When I found you, another man was with me. Remember?"

Reilly drank the water. "Yeah. Who was that?" he asked.

"A friend I met while hunting."

"What side?"

Wren rolled her eyes. "Must everything be about sides? Not whether he has food or shelter?"

Reilly fixed his eyes on her. "So you don't want him joining us. Afraid he'll turn into another me?"

"Something like that. Leave Travis alone. He'll choose his own path."

A knowing look crossed Reilly's face. "There's more. He's why you've lost interest in our cause."

"What do you mean?"

At the entrance, Travis paused just outside. He hadn't meant to eavesdrop, but their voices carried.

Reilly could see in Wren's face that he had struck a note. "You have feelings for him."

"What if I do? Why should you care?"

"Because you know how I feel about you," he responded.

Wren stepped closer, eyes blazing. "I am not yours, Reilly. I never was, and I never will be."

Travis decided he'd heard enough and stepped inside. "Wren—I didn't see anyone out there."

She turned quickly. "Yeah… that's good. I was starting to worry. You were gone a long time."

"I waited and listened for movement. Looks like your friend is awake."

Travis extended a hand, but Reilly only stared at the cave ceiling.

Wren offered a tense smile. "Don't mind Reilly's manners. He's not big on gratitude. Unfortunately, he *will* live. Reilly, this is Travis. Travis, Reilly," she introduced.

Reilly shook his head slightly with a wry grin on his face. "That's no way to treat an old friend, Wrenny. I'll live—I always do."

"I told you we're not friends!" she snapped.

A smirk formed on Reilly's face, which reminded her that he didn't easily give up.

"I'm taking you to camp in the morning so the doctor can treat you," Wren said. "Can't let Black Arrow's favorite assassin die, can I?"

Travis slipped outside again, not willing to hear them fuss. Moments later, Wren joined him.

"He doesn't like me," Travis said, turning toward her.

"Reilly doesn't like anyone," she replied, drawing closer.

"Will he keep picking fights all night?"

"Not if he wants my help getting home."

"Do you think he tried to take someone out?" Travis asked.

"I don't know," she said, not wanting to assume. "Anything is possible with one of my father's soldiers. I'll find out more on our way home tomorrow. Let's eat and rest. We'll need our strength."

"Sleep should come easy enough," Travis said dryly, "if he stays quiet."

"He will," Wren replied with a fierce grin, "or I'll make him."

They turned and walked back into the cave together.

Chapter 11

The evening was marked by awkward silence as they searched for something meaningful to discuss. Travis sensed from Wren's manner of speaking that she had no interest in divulging his connection to the People of the Faith, but the longer they stayed together, the higher the chances that the assassin would stumble upon the truth.

On the morning of the second day, Wren packed her things in preparation to head back.

Travis watched her gather her few belongings. "Wren, I'm not coming with you. Reilly looks better, and you have the mare. I plan to hunt a little on my way home."

"We'll manage," she answered. "We should reach camp by nightfall."

"I'll refill my flask before you go," Travis said.

"I'll come with you," Wren responded. "Reilly, we'll leave as soon as I'm back."

"I'm with you, girlfriend," Reilly uttered, his voice dripping with mockery.

Wren shook her head in frustration and followed Travis down to the stream.

They kneeled side by side on the rocky bank. Travis uncorked his flask and let the clear water spill in, though he scarcely needed it.

"I wish I were riding with you instead," Wren said quietly. "Anything would be better than another day of Reilly's nonsense. So, you really plan to hunt?"

"Maybe nearer home," Travis admitted. "Mostly, I wanted a chance to speak with you alone before you leave, and I hope we'll see each other again."

Wren had the same sentiment, but returning to camp now was her only option. She rose to her feet. "I'm amazed Reilly hasn't guessed your connection to the POF. That's exactly why I think it's best if you head in a different direction."

Travis stood, meeting her eyes. "Will you come back this way to hunt?"

She found herself glaring at his piercing cobalt eyes, unable to look away.

He brushed his fingertips lightly along the curve of her cheek, tracing every line as if memorizing her. The pull between them was too strong to resist. He leaned in and kissed her.

Wren met him without hesitation, all caution swept away by longing. Their hearts pounded in unison, the world narrowing to the space between them, each moment stretching toward forever.

At last, Travis drew back, resting his forehead against her shoulder. "I don't want you to go."

Wren's voice was barely a breath against his ear. "I will come back and hunt near that creek."

"Get home safely first," he murmured. "And remember—you're always welcome at my house."

"I might come after dark so your father doesn't see me," she said, stepping back with a sigh. "Travis, be careful. If Reilly stirred up trouble, whoever's hunting him could still be in these woods. Don't let yourself get tangled in his mess."

He offered a small smile. "I'll be all right."

"I mean it. Trouble follows that man like lightning in a storm."

He nodded. "I'll stay sharp."

They walked back up the slope to the cave. Wren tossed the saddle onto the mare and tightened the girth while Travis went inside to fetch Reilly.

Reilly greeted him with a lazy grin. "Hey, lover boy. Decided not to tag along after all? I was looking forward to introducing you to some of *my* friends."

Travis forced a smile and shook his head. "I'm sure you two will do *just* fine without me."

"No doubt. Though I'm still not sure about the story you told her."

"What story?"

"You know—the one about who you really are and which side you're on."

"I only told what was truthful. I was hunting, and we met and became friends."

"Right. Just friends."

Wren's voice cut through from outside. "Travis, hurry him up, please. I want to reach camp before dark."

Travis slipped an arm around Reilly to steady him and guided him out as Wren waited, reins in hand.

"What's wrong, darling?" Reilly smirked as they reached the horse. "Afraid to spend another night alone with your old pal?"

"Oh, stuff it," Wren snapped. "You're lucky we found you. You owe me big."

Reilly smiled and said, "I guess you won't let me forget it."

Wren gave him a shove into the saddle, then turned to Travis, her expression softening.

"I'll follow if you need me," Travis offered.

She shook her head, gathering the reins again. "We'll be fine, perhaps a little late, but we'll make camp tonight."

Reilly threw one last triumphant glance over his shoulder as they started down the trail.

Travis watched until they vanished among the trees, a quiet ache settling in his chest. He wondered whether he would ever see her again. He had done all he could to help bring the injured man to her camp. Now their safe return rested in her capable hands—and he trusted her completely.

Chapter 12

"Crank baby, crank!" Logan shouted.

"Nah, the battery's shot," Derrick muttered, slapping the fender with enough force to make the metal ring like a dull bell.

The battery wouldn't hold a charge, so they trudged back through the junkyard for another. They soon discovered a cracked vacuum line. Then water seeped from the brittle radiator hoses, sending them back yet again.

Nearly half the day bled away before the repairs held. Logan turned the key. The engine coughed, then settled into a low, uneven rumble that vibrated through the seat.

"Now we just need to drive her," Derrick said, almost whispering, as if speaking too loud might scare the sound away.

Logan eased the hood down. "Except for that one time, I haven't heard the song in twenty years."

"Isn't it a beautiful melody too?" Kincaid murmured. "I just hope she sings long enough to get us there and back."

Derrick gripped the wheel. "Ready to see if she still remembers the road?"

Logan pointed down the overgrown road, where weeds rose like a garden on a sunny day. "Let's find that farm."

The truck ran smoothly until fallen limbs and toppled trees blocked the way. They stopped, dragged them aside, their sweat mixing with the dust that rose. Over the years, the road had shrunk to a path—used now only by wagons and those on foot—its edges softened by time and weather.

They cleared debris again and again while the engine sang like a persistent heartbeat. After an hour of slow progress, they rounded a familiar bend. A rusted iron gate sagged on its hinges beside the driveway, the name SALISBURY still legible on its panels.

"Logan, you remember Dan Salisbury?" Derrick asked.

"I do. Haven't laid eyes on him in years. Lived here alone after his wife passed."

"That's right," Derrick replied. "Wonder if he's still breathing."

"We'll know soon enough."

The driveway vanished into a quarter-mile tunnel of thorns and scrub bushes, branches scraping the truck's flanks with dry whispers. At its end stood the old farmhouse—paint peeled but walls straight—somehow having outlasted the storms. The outbuildings had not been so lucky; their roofs gaped open to the sky. Chickens scratched and squawked in the yard. Laundry swayed on a line between two posts, moving gently in the warm air like slow white flags.

Fifty yards beyond the house rose the big barn—tall grass brushed its lower walls. Beside it sat a tractor and other equipment, shrouded in rust, untouched since the Separation.

As the men climbed out, a mule ambled over and regarded them with mild, ancient eyes. A woman in a pale blue apron stood near the corner of the house, one hand shading her eyes. She tucked a loose strand of graying hair beneath a checkered headscarf.

She studied the strangers' faces, weathered, clothes patched—then spoke, voice soft but steady. "May I help you, gentlemen?"

Logan stepped forward. "Yes, ma'am, maybe you can. We were wondering if anyone still uses that barn."

"Not since I came here," she said. *Better keep my reasons to myself,* she decided. "Why do you ask?"

Logan hadn't rehearsed the words, but he knew truth was the only coin that still had value. "Ma'am, I'll be straight with you. We need a place to store some weapons out of sight."

"Store weapons?" Her brow lifted. "What kind?"

"Rifles and ammunition. We mean you no harm. We thought the place might be empty. We remembered Dan Salisbury owned it."

"Mr. Salisbury did own it. My husband and I bought it from him several years ago, for next to nothing. He said he no longer needed it after the Separation and was moving to Georgia to be near family." She paused, gaze drifting across the fields. "I'm still learning things about this farm myself. And you are…?"

"Forgive me, ma'am. Logan Weston." He gestured to the others. "These are friends from Pattonville. I didn't catch your name."

She offered a small, tired smile. "Gaela Woods." A sadness crossed her face. "My husband, Jerry, passed last year—may he rest in peace. We never managed to live here while he was alive. A few months after he was gone, I came back to see if I could make something of the place."

"I'm truly sorry for your loss," Logan said quietly.

Kind eyes. Strong shoulders, too, she thought. "Thank you. Jerry suffered for a long time with the rheumatoid. But he's in a better place now."

She weighed his earlier words a moment longer. "Mr. Weston, does storing weapons mean we're heading toward a war?"

"No one knows for certain, ma'am. But we have a chance to reclaim some guns the North hid years ago. We just need somewhere close to store them before we bring them in. If trouble comes, having easy access could matter."

Gaela nodded slowly. "I understand. Use the barn. This farm's as hidden and quiet as any you'll find." She glanced at the truck. "That's a fine machine. How did you find fuel?"

"That's a long story, Mrs. Woods. Maybe another time."

Her eyes brightened. "You mean you'll come again, Mr. Weston?"

Logan felt warmth rise in his face. "Please—call me Logan."

"Then call me Gaela." She smiled fully now. "It gets lonely out here. I only see folks when I walk to town to trade—and those walks are few."

"I'll make a point to come by."

"Good. Before you leave, would you like to see inside the barn?"

"We'd appreciate that."

"Take your time. Stay for lunch even—I can put together meat and bread."

"Thank you, but we should head back soon. Maybe next time?"

"Then plan on supper next visit, Logan."

He grinned. "I will."

"One more thing," she said. "Hunters pass through these woods regularly. When you bring your weapons, you'll want a guard."

"Thanks for the warning," Logan said, stepping toward the truck.

The men climbed in and eased over the cattle guard toward the barn.

Derrick smiled sideways. "That woman's taken a shine to you."

"She's just being neighborly," Logan said.

"Neighborly enough to invite you to supper. You ought to go."

Logan allowed himself a small smile. "Maybe I will."

"She's right about hunters," Kincaid said from the back.

"Right. Travis and I have seen several in these woods," Logan answered. "Nothing in the barn is worth bothering—yet. I hope you boys will take turns guarding once we have something to guard."

"No problem there," Derrick said.

"Oh, yeah," Kincaid replied. "If we get weapons and ammo back safely, count me in for guard duty."

They stepped down and approached the barn. Logan gripped one of the big sliding doors and hauled it open. Sunlight spilled through translucent panels in the roof, revealing a clean concrete floor and seven rolled bales of hay.

"This place is huge," Randall said, voice echoing softly. "We could hide a mountain in here."

Logan nodded. "Roy Wayne said the cache is big, but we'll know once we see it."

Kincaid walked to the nearest hay roll. "We can stack the crates behind these."

Logan glanced out the door. "Wish that tractor still ran."

"Where would we get diesel?" Derrick asked.

Logan chuckled. "Same question I had. Maybe we can use the truck and chains to drag the hay where we need it."

Randall studied the rolls. "Should work."

"Remember to bring chains on the next trip," Logan said, sliding the door shut.

Derrick sat behind the steering wheel. "So—we're doing this?"

Kincaid settled into his seat. "Sooner the better."

Moments later, the truck rolled down the driveway, thorns whispering along its sides, and turned toward Pattonville beneath a quiet sky.

Chapter 13

At the halfway point, Wren eased the mare to a stop beside the familiar creek. The water ran clear and cold over smooth stones, its murmur the only sound in the expanding dusk. She filled her canteen, giving some to Reilly and handfuls to the horse, watching the liquid catch the last glint of sunlight before it flowed down their throats.

When we reach camp, she decided, *I will finally be able to breathe.*

They crested the final ridge just as the sun vanished, leaving a bruised violet sky. Below, the campfire rose in bright columns, flames snapping against the dark. The scent of roasting venison drifted upward, rich and savory, laced with the sharper scent of pine smoke that always clung to this place like a second skin.

A mob of people surged forward the moment they entered the gate. Hands reached to steady Reilly as someone shouted for help, easing him to the ground. His face had gone gray from the long journey, pain jarring like a dark accusation.

"Take him to my quarters—the second room," Broderick Holmes ordered, his voice cutting through the murmurs.

Brody Myles pushed through the crowd, eyes wide. "Wren—what happened?"

"Ask Reilly," she answered flatly. "I found him half-bled-out with an arrow buried in him."

Cohen Daniels appeared, parting the onlookers with quiet authority. When he reached her, he pulled her into a brief, intense embrace. "Wren. I've been half-mad with worry."

"You needn't have been, Father." She stepped back, weariness sharpening her tone. "Save your concern for your assassin. He nearly didn't make it."

Cohen's mouth tightened. He glanced around, then lowered his voice. "Inside, now."

Reilly's mission was secretive, as Wren could tell from the flicker of caution in his eyes. Hidden assignments rarely stayed concealed in a camp this small, but the pretense still mattered to the men who gave the orders. She had overheard enough days ago—Cohen and Brody dispatching Reilly and two others to remove the leaders of rival groups. Quiet, precise, final.

Inside her father's quarters, lamplight cast a low glow across the worn couch and scarred coffee table. The faint trace of wood smoke lingered in the air, carried on their clothes from the fires outside. Wren set her backpack and bow on the table with deliberate care, the familiar weight of the yew stave anchoring her. She sank onto the couch, crossed her legs, and waited for the lecture she could recite by heart.

Cohen closed the door, then stood over her, arms folded. "I'm glad you're home safe, daughter. But you scared me half to death, storming off like that and staying away twice as long as usual."

She offered no reply.

He exhaled slowly. "I saw you listening outside the tent. You heard us give Reilly's orders. We sent him and the others out to begin the work."

Her gaze lifted to meet his. "No matter who you send, Father, it's still murder."

"Wren, we are at war!" he declared, his voice rising.

"With people who simply believe differently?" she replied, her voice level, sharp with an icy edge. "I don't remember the People of the Faith—or any other faction—ever raising a hand against us. They live and let others live."

"You wouldn't understand even if I explained," Cohen said.

"Try me. For once, trust that I might."

Cohen studied her for a long moment. Something shifted behind his eyes—resignation, perhaps regret. He dragged a chair closer and sat.

"Okay, you want to know the truth?" he asked.

He reached beneath his shirt and drew out a slender chain. Dangling from it was a small, tarnished oval medallion, its coin-like frame etched with a cross, now rubbed smooth.

"A lot of people wore these to signify our faith before they drove us south of the thirty-sixth parallel—the periphery." He turned it over in his fingers, tracing the emblem's faded edges. "Your mother wore hers until the day she died, praying for a miracle that never came. You won't remember the endless ration lines or the scraps of food we lived on—the death of her and so many others. Due to hunger, a few tried to slip back north, only to be hunted down by the military drones within hours."

She gazed at the cross. "Why do you still wear it?"

"To remind me that we survived that foolishness."

After a pause, she said, "Go on."

He let the chain and cross drop against his chest. "Well then," he continued, his voice growing rougher, "their representative finally got word to us, backed by their soldiers. They offered a way home—if we renounced the faith we once held and proved our loyalty by eliminating the believers whom they blamed for the Separation."

He stood and began to pace, the floorboards creaking softly under his boots. "Hunger had already burned the faith out of most of us. It took years to muster enough strength and resolve to act. The People of the Faith became our primary target because theirs was the strongest—and therefore the greatest obstacle to the deal. Eradicate them or shatter their beliefs, the North said, and we could all go home."

Wren's fingers tightened around the edge of the couch. "How will the North even know you're doing your part? Are their drones watching us?"

Cohen gave a short, tired shake of his head. "Nothing's crossed our sky in years. No planes, no drones—they aren't watching."

"And if they never come after all that blood is spilled?" she asked quietly. "Or decide the bargain is off?"

His shoulders sagged, the first crack she had ever seen in his certainty. "Then we will have done a terrible thing for nothing."

She let out a slow breath. "Right."

He turned, eyes earnest in the lamplight. "We aren't monsters, Wren. We just want our families safe—our elderly and our children. One chance to cross back over that line. Do you understand?"

Wren held his gaze. Candlelight carved deep shadows across the lines in his face, the exhaustion that had settled there like dust on old photographs.

"What I understand," she said slowly, "is that someone in charge made a cruel bargain, and instead of considering another path, staked everything on this one—blood for a promise."

She shifted, fingers brushing the bow in front of her. "We could have joined them. Stood together. Combine our strength and protect each other."

Cohen gave a short, bitter laugh. "The North's terms left no room for that. Years of deliberation went into our plan. Trust that we considered every alternative."

Silence stretched, thick as the smoke in the room. Wren felt its weight pressing against her chest. Her father preferred war to concession, death to compromise. Friends would die. Families would shatter. And for what—a promise from people who had already exiled them?

Cohen watched her, waiting for something she could not give. At last, he turned away. "Say nothing of this to anyone," he murmured.

He stepped out onto the small rear porch. Night had fallen completely—the campfires dotted the dark camp like low stars. Cohen leaned against the rail, breathing in the cool, smoke-tinged air.

How did my daughter come to stand so firmly against us? he wondered, heartache as sharp as any knife. *Where did I fail her?*

Somewhere in the dark beyond the camp walls, an owl called once—low, mournful—and was gone.

Chapter 14

Travis moved through the woods with the slow, deliberate steps of a hunter who had learned long ago that haste scattered game. His eyes swept the forest floor for any flicker of movement, but the only life stirring was a pair of gray squirrels chasing one another along a high oak limb—too quick for an arrow. The late-afternoon light slanted gold through the canopy, laying long fingers of shadow across the leaf-littered ground.

Soon, the faint trace of an old lane appeared, choked with honeysuckle and young persimmons. Vines had woven themselves into a living curtain—few boots had broken through in years. Anyone searching for Reilly Brewin would pass it by without a second glance.

Fatigue settled into his bones after hours of empty walking. Then, deeper among the trees, the shape of an abandoned house rose like a memory someone had tried to bury. Most shingles had slid from the roof, leaving raw pine boards exposed to decades of weather. The last rays of the sun painted the ruin in faded purples and lengthening shadows. Travis paused at the edge of the clearing, weighing whether the place might offer shelter against the coming night.

He called once, twice. Only wind answered, threading through broken windowpanes with a low, mournful note. The front door sagged on a single rusted hinge, mouth open to darkness. He crossed the creaking porch and stepped over the threshold to the inside.

The rooms were stripped bare—no furniture, no curtains, nothing left of the lives once lived here except faint rectangles on the wallpaper where pictures had hung. Dust floated in the slanted light like pale ash.

In the kitchen, a gray squirrel darted across the sill of a shattered window, paused to scold him with a sharp flick of its tail, then vanished into the trees outside. Travis exhaled a quiet regret. Should have seen you earlier, he murmured to himself.

He eased onto the dusty counter, set his bow and pack aside, and let the stillness settle over him. Thoughts drifted, unbidden, to Wren—her hurried stride as she guided the wounded assassin toward home, the tight line of her mouth that said she wanted this ordeal finished. Had she reached the camp yet? Was she safe?

He understood her drive was not pleasure but duty—perhaps only to satisfy her father, Reilly's commander, possibly to prove something to herself. She had knelt beside a man who carried out lethal orders without hesitation, yet she had chosen mercy. They had spoken, in stolen moments, of forging some fragile bridge between their sides. But peace felt like a child's wish spoken into a storm. Could words sway men who saw compromise as betrayal? Would anyone even listen to two young people who had dared to trust across faction lines?

Wren had been his first contact from Black Arrow, and she was nothing like the cold killers he had heard about. Reilly Brewin, on the other hand, carried the hard edge of a lifelong soldier.

After a brief rest, Travis scanned the area for signs of hunters while gathering dry branches. He started a small fire in the porcelain sink, striking the flint until flames licked upward, casting restless shadows across the empty room. He chewed strips of dried venison, tasting smoke and salt, then stretched out his exhausted body on the counter. Sleep claimed him quickly.

★★★

Morning arrived with voices in the air.

Travis snapped awake, heart pounding. He lay motionless, eyes fixed on the pale gray sky through the broken window. The voices rose again—closer, unmistakably real.

Not a dream, he thought.

He rolled silently from the counter, snatched bow and pack, and eased into the hallway's deeper shadow.

"Check inside," a rough voice ordered.

The words were clear enough, but the tone revealed nothing—friend or foe? If these were the men hunting Reilly, curiosity could cost him his life. Bootfalls thudded on the porch. Travis slipped through the broken kitchen window and pressed himself flat against the exterior wall, breath shallow.

"The room smells of smoke," the coarse voice reported.

A second man brushed fingers over the sink's warm ashes. "Fire's recent."

"Look out back," the first commanded.

Travis felt the house at his back like a trap closing. Running forward would expose him to the open porch; running sideways would tangle him in briars. His gaze fell to the base of the fence, wrapped in vines and thorns, where a low, woven tunnel formed—a game trail, narrow but passable.

A distracting tremble seized his hands—one he'd seen only once before when his father thought he was having a heart attack.

He dropped to his belly and crawled, bow thrust ahead like a blind man's cane. Branches scraped his shoulders and backpack, and damp earth filled his nostrils. After an eternity measured in heartbeats, he emerged at a narrow creek glittering under early light.

His short boots wouldn't keep his feet dry, but a fallen oak spanned the stream like a bridge. He sprinted toward it.

"Hey, you—hold up!" came a voice.

Travis spun. A heavy man in a faded plaid coat sat astride a horse midstream, reins loose in one hand, eyes sharp.

"You might want to wait, mister!" he shouted.

Travis sprang onto the log, bounded across, and plunged into the dense trees. Behind him, the rider's shout cracked like a whip: "Here he is—into the woods!"

Only then did he hear the dogs—deep-chested baying rolling through the valley, echoing closer.

He ran.

Two creeks, three clearings, another stretch of timber—he pushed until his lungs burned and his legs trembled. At last, he broke onto an old highline right-of-way, power poles long fallen, the corridor choked with blackberry and young pines. A narrow deer trail threaded the tangle. Briars clawed his sleeves and cheeks as he fought upward to the ridge crest.

His mind raced faster than his feet. They had set out as Good Samaritans and stumbled into a hornet's nest. Wren's parting warning echoed in his head: Please don't get caught up in Reilly's mess. Yet here he was, running like a guilty assassin.

Four, perhaps five miles since the house, and still no sign that the pursuit had broken off. Over the next rise, he spotted another creek glinting to his left. Water might throw the dogs off the scent, he thought. An ancient barbed-wire fence lay rusted and flattened nearby. Beyond it, open hardwoods sloped to the stream.

The creek proved shallow but icy. He waded south fifty paces, doubled back, waded north, then south again—crisscrossing until even he lost track—before scrambling onto the far bank and sprinting away, water streaming from his trousers, boots, and soaked socks.

A logging road offered firmer footing. Travis paused, chest heaving, straining to hear—nothing but wind sighing in the treetops.

The silence felt more ominous than pursuit, as if unseen eyes tracked his every step.

He had done nothing criminal—only helped Wren save a life. Yet if these men believed him complicit with Reilly Brewin, innocence wouldn't matter; they'd hunt him down like a fugitive. Perhaps he should have escorted her all the way to camp. Perhaps—no. Enough second-guessing. One wrong move now could end everything.

He struck a steady jog along the road. Miles later, he climbed a high hill overlooking a bridge and another creek below. The water tempted him again, a desperate chance to confuse any lingering scent before the dogs caught up.

He started down the steep slope—and his boot skidded on hidden ice beneath the dead leaves. The world tilted violently. He wind-milled for balance, fingers brushing but missing a sapling, then slid faster, gaining uncontrollable speed. Sharp thorns raked his palm, drawing blood, while a low branch clipped his temple with stunning force, stars exploding in his vision. Shoulder over heel, he tumbled, crashing through the underbrush until the ground struck with jarring impact—breath knocked out, body battered.

Then only darkness.

Chapter 15

A sharp jolt of pain shot through Travis's left side, as if a boot had driven into his ribs. *I hit the ground hard*, he thought, eyelids fluttering open to the chill of damp earth against his cheek. Through the thinning fog, the hound's dark eyes fixed on him. The dog pushed closer and dragged a warm, wet tongue across his mouth.

Ugh—slobber. Travis scrubbed his lips with his sleeve.

A rough voice shouted from behind, "Get up, you murderer!"

Travis pushed himself upright, still wiping drool from his face, to three men looming over him—knives flashing, bows drawn. A moment later, a broad-shouldered man in faded overalls stepped forward, his shadow swallowing the others.

"On your feet," the big man said. "We've *got* you now."

Travis rose slowly from the ground. "Why are you following me?" he asked.

The man from behind stalked closer, jabbing a finger at Travis's back. "Don't act like you don't know what's going on, mister. We *know* what you did."

"What exactly do you think I did?" Travis inquired.

The big man answered, voice low and steady. "Night before last in Deport, someone shot an arrow and hit our mayor from a rooftop."

"I've never been to Deport," Travis remarked.

The youngest of them, with blond hair brushing his shoulders, snatched up Travis's bow and quiver. "Oh, you're funny. You've got a bow, *ain't* you?"

"My bow's for hunting," Travis said, nodding toward it. "Had it since I was ten. Never loosed an arrow at anything I couldn't eat."

The big man fixed him with a stare sharp enough to cut pine bark. "You're lying. We tracked you straight to that empty house. Boot prints matched yours perfectly. Found another set, too, smaller, and a horse led slowly, likely carrying a wounded man or a deer. Where'd that one get to?"

An icy dread coiled in Travis's gut at the thought—if they linked him to Wren, no amount of talking would free him. He breathed a silent prayer. "I saw someone leading a horse through the forest. The rider looked hurt."

The young man turned to the big man, eyes bright. "Told you, Marius, I wounded him. *Knew* my aim was good."

Marius grunted, unconvinced. "I don't know, Timothy—there were lots of tracks."

Timothy pressed on. "This one ain't *bleeding*. The shooter limped off that roof with an arrow in his hip. Only other possibility is that *this* fella was hiding somewhere nearby."

Marius faced Travis again. "You claim you've never been to Deport. How do I know you weren't part of the hit—as Timothy said, hiding, and watching?"

"Someone came to our town, too," Travis said. "Pattonville. Killed a council member with an arrow. What would I have to do with your mayor?"

Marius's brow furrowed. "Someone had a problem with her."

"I wouldn't kill anyone unless they're trying to kill me," Travis said quietly. "That's the truth."

The third man lunged forward, face twisted. "Marius, we can't just let him *walk!* We followed his tracks. It's *him!*"

"What if we're wrong, Kade?"

"*Wrong?*" Kade spat. "He's the one!"

Marius exhaled slowly through his nose. "We'll take him to Deport. Send word to his people. If they swear he was home that night, we have to turn him loose."

Kade's mouth twisted, anger warring across his features. "Lindy and her husband were close friends of mine. *I* expect justice."

"Oh, we'll get justice," Marius answered, "but it has to be for the right man." He watched Kade pivot sharply and stalk a few paces away, boots crunching on frosted grass. Marius shook his head, then fixed his gaze on Travis. "So, mister, what's your name?"

"Travis Weston." The words came out rough, as if his throat carried the dust of miles he'd run. "My father is Logan Weston. He'll tell you I've been hunting these woods. Brought deer meat home a few days ago—he'll remember."

A faint breeze stirred the branches overhead, scattering a handful of dry leaves that spiraled down like pale warnings. Marius studied the prisoner a moment longer, listening to the distant, restless shifting of the dogs chained to the wagon, their earlier frenzy cooled to low growls. Somewhere farther off, a crow called once—sharp, singular—then fell silent, leaving only the creak of leather and the slow exhale of horses.

Marius nodded once. "All right, Travis. I hope for your sake he does."

They pressed on through the rest of the day beneath the soft glow of a waning winter sun. Travis walked untied, by Marius's choice, while the others rode horses in his trail, their eyes never leaving his back.

At dusk, they reached an abandoned highway rest stop, its cracked concrete bathed in pale silver. Marius reined in. "We camp here."

After a quiet supper of jerked meat and hard bread, Marius settled on a weathered bench beside Travis. The moon hung high in a velvety indigo sky, its silvery rays spilled over the picnic table.

"We'll reach Deport by mid-morning tomorrow," Marius said. "I'll send a rider to your father."

"Thank you," Travis answered. "Can you tell me again what happened?"

Marius gazed at the low fire. "We hold an annual gathering—honor the council, bring folks together. The town's grown—-can't know everyone anymore. We'd just finished eating, music had started, when an arrow came down out of the dark. Struck near the head table, grazed the mayor's arm. She'll heal.

"Word had come days earlier that one of your council members took an arrow—Edmond, wasn't it?" he added.

Travis nodded, throat tight.

"Sorry for your loss," Marius said. "We figured Black Arrow might try something in our town. We put our best shooters on the rooftops. As things went along, Timothy spotted a figure across the way and loosed an arrow—so did others. Whoever that man is quickly returned fire—good training, I suppose. He got the shot off at the mayor just before Timothy's landed."

"Did Timothy see him?" Travis asked.

"Too dark for clarity," Marius admitted, "but his build matched yours, and the bow work was clean and quick."

Travis stared at the campfire. "Edmond was also a friend. Do you think Black Arrow is trying to pull us into a war?"

"It looks that way," Marius said, his voice dropping to a confidential murmur. "Between you and me, Deport's got fighters prepared to tangle with them. Alliances south of us, too. We may not match their archers, but we won't sit quiet."

The words landed heavy in Travis's chest as moonlight slipped across the broken concrete like spilled mercury—cold, bright, and impossible to gather back.

"We're all the same people, aren't we?" Travis asked barely louder than the dying fire's crackle. "Them, us. Isn't it time we stopped fighting each other?"

Marius let out a slow, tired breath that hung white in the chill air. "Haven't heard anyone speak like that in years. I tried once—pushed our council to sit down with Black Arrow, talk it out. Only made our folks angrier."

"I know," Travis said softly. "All anyone expects is fighting. A major disaster could change minds."

"I know the feeling," Travis said softly. "Everyone's waiting for the next arrow in the night. And it might take something truly terrible before they choose the way of peace."

"I'm afraid you're right." Marius rose, joints creaking like old timber in the wind. "These old bones cry for rest."

"Mine too."

***

Travis drifted into uneasy sleep on the cold floor of the decayed restroom, moonlight striping the cracked walls through broken windows.

He woke to a rough hand clamped over his mouth, fingers digging into his cheeks. He thrashed, but the heavier body pinned him to the floor.

In the thin silver wash spilling from above, Kade Keating's silhouette took shape—eyes fierce, the skinning knife in his fist catching the moonlight in a single, deadly gleam.

"I didn't believe a word you fed Marius," Kade whispered, his breath sour and hot against Travis's face. "Old fool."

Travis tried to answer, but only a muffled sound escaped beneath the crushing palm. Kade eased his hand away, inch by inch, the knife hovering like a promise.

"One sound," he breathed, "and I'll open your throat."

"Mr. Kade," Travis murmured, voice barely louder than the wind in the broken panes, "I didn't harm your mayor. I swear it." Escape routes flickered through his mind like sparks in dry tinder.

"My name's Kade *Keating*," the man snarled, waving the blade close enough that moonlight flashed along its edge. "Up—slow. If you run, I'll *shoot* you."

Cold, unyielding iron pressed hard between Travis's shoulder blades. Travis rose, every motion measured, heart hammering against his ribs. The window of escape he had glimpsed only moments ago had slammed shut.

"Sidewalk," Kade ordered, prodding him forward. "To the right."

Moonlight covered the cracked sidewalk in a pale, unearthly glow, every fracture gleaming like a vein of frost. Travis's eyes slowly adjusted—the dying coals' faint crimson pulse marked the path ahead like a heartbeat in the dark. He prayed a silent plea that someone—anyone—would stir in the camp.

Kade shoved him forward, convinced his justice was more fitting than Marius's mercy.

"Mr. Keating," Travis whispered, voice barely louder than the night wind, "you don't want this on your conscience."

"Quiet," Kade answered, the words trembling with certainty. "They'll turn you loose in Deport, and you'll kill again."

"I didn't kill anyone," Travis said, the plea soft but urgent. "Don't you want to see the right man caught?"

"Shut up." Kade's prod at his back sharpened. "Behind that tree."

The moon's shadow swallowed them.

"Now, on your knees."

Travis sank into the frost-stiffened grass. "You're going to end me here—no trial, no chance to speak for myself? What will Marius say?"

Kade stepped behind him, the knife rising until its flat pressed cold against Travis's throat. "Lord, forgive me for what I'm about to—"

A sudden dull muffled thud cut through the night. The knife drifted downward—Kade's weight sagged against Travis's shoulder, then crumbled to the ground with a ragged gasp that quickly thinned to silence. Moonlight, slipping between the branches, caught the silhouette of the arrow's shaft buried deep between Kade's shoulder blades.

Footsteps pounded the ground closer. Timothy dropped to one knee beside the body, bow still in hand, eyes wide in the silver light. "You hurt?"

"No," Travis breathed, the words trembling out on a rush of relief. "Thanks to you."

Marius stepped into the moonlit clearing, drawn by the voices, his face carved deep with regret beneath the silver wash. "I'm sorry, Travis. I should've watched him closer. Kade was off all evening."

"I tried reasoning with him," Travis said. "He wouldn't hear a word."

Timothy remained on one knee beside the body, staring down at the friend he had just felled. Moonlight caught the wet shine in his eyes. "He was one of us."

Marius rested a heavy hand on his son's shoulder, then met Travis's gaze. "I hope your folks speak for you tomorrow, son," he said quietly. "I truly do."

Chapter 16

The knock echoed through the small cabin like a distant rifle shot. Brody Myles set his coffee mug on the scarred wooden table and crossed the living room.

"Yeah, wait a minute. I'm coming."

He opened the door to the chill morning air and the familiar figure of Broderick Holmes.

"Come in, Doctor."

Holmes stepped inside. "Sir, you asked me to keep you posted on Reilly's condition."

"Yes. How is he?"

"He'll live," Holmes said, standing inside by the door, arms folded. "Arrow dug deep into the hipbone—pain's going to dog him for weeks—but in a few days, he'll be on his feet. Limping, maybe. Reilly's stubborn enough to hide it if he does."

Brody exhaled through his nose, the faint bitterness of coffee still on his tongue. "Good. Any word on the other two?"

"Not a thing, but I've been busy treating cuts and bruises all morning. Some of the men hunting hit a briar patch."

"I understand. Give me a heads up when you do. I'm worried for them after what happened to Reilly."

"Of course." Holmes pointed his thumb outside. "Well, I have patients waiting."

The door closed with a soft thud, leaving the room quieter than before. Brody returned to his chair, cupped the mug, and let the steam curl against his face like a question he couldn't answer.

When Reilly had first arrived at the Black Arrow camp, he brought more than a bow, arrows, and a rucksack. He came with extensive combat experience and valuable hand-to-hand skills, honed in the military. Most of the other fighters Brody trained had their limitations. But watching Wren lead an injured Reilly into camp two nights ago had unsettled him more than he cared to admit.

He and Cohen had chosen their targets carefully: mayors and council members to instill a measure of fear in the groups. Arrows in the dark—the first stage of the plan. If this failed, the subsequent phases would be far harder to execute.

Reilly was not only the best sharp-shooting archer in camp, but he also shared the same vision, which made his injury a deeper cut than the arrow itself. And the absence of the other two archers—men who should have returned by now—gnawed like a splinter under the skin, impossible to ignore.

Who tipped Deport off about setting an ambush? Someone had talked. The thought settled sharply in Brody's chest.

A second knock—sharper this time—cut through the quiet.

Brody took another slow sip of coffee and stayed seated. "Come in."

Cohen Daniels stepped inside, bringing with him the aroma of campfire smoke. "Morning, sir. How are you doing?"

"Well enough." Brody pointed to the pot on the cast-iron stove. "Coffee?"

"Don't mind if I do." Cohen poured himself a cup and settled into the chair opposite. "How much of this do we have left?"

"Enough for a while. Thank goodness for that abandoned town and the supplies we found." Brody cradled his mug, letting the warmth seep into his palms. "I missed this more than I care to admit."

Cohen gave a quiet laugh. "I drank coffee by the gallon before the Separation. Went without so long afterward that I finally broke the habit. I still enjoy an occasional cup."

Brody studied the dark liquid in his cup. "What's on your mind, Cohen?"

"Just wondered about Reilly."

"Doc just left. Says he'll pull through."

"Good," Cohen nodded, eyes on his cup. "And those other two?"

"Nothing." Brody's voice dropped. "Deport was ready, Cohen. They learned he was coming."

Cohen's gaze flicked up, sharp. "You're thinking, traitor."

"I'm thinking someone talked."

Cohen stiffened and set his mug down. "Our men don't break."

"I trained them. But people often trade stories when they trade supplies." Brody turned the cup in slow circles, watching the dark liquid cling to the sides. "But if one of ours is selling us out, they won't enjoy what happens when I find out."

Cohen was quiet long enough for the fire to pop in the stove. "The other two are good. Best archers we have and will return soon."

"They'd better." Brody's eyes drifted to the window where gray light pressed against the glass. "Cohen, I keep thinking about that representative. Do you remember the price he named for our path home?"

Cohen's mouth tightened. "Eliminate the people responsible for the Separation."

"I was angry enough to agree. Still am." Brody's fingers tightened on the mug, and he gave a humorless smile. "Friends walked away after that meeting. That's why the woods are crawling with splinter groups now. Twenty years on this side of the periphery, and the bitterness remains." He tapped the rim of his cup. "Like this coffee—burnt if you let it sit too long."

Cohen's gaze softened. "Your sister—"

"Even now, her face remains etched in my memory from that moment at the crossing. You lost your wife not long after. We carry it differently, but we carry it."

Cohen looked into his own cup as if answers might float to the surface. "I remember more about how she died than the day itself. First, no food, then the fever took her down slowly. No medicine left to steal," he paused. "But then we built something. Cabins from scavenged lumber. Men who can fight. A plan taking shape."

Brody met his eyes. "We were the smallest faction once. Won't be for long."

Cohen rose, setting his empty cup on the table. "Men will be headed to morning drills soon."

Brody reached for the pot, already thinking ahead. "Later, we'll talk about phase two."

Cohen paused at the door. "Just say when."

The door closed. Brody sat alone again, the faint scent of coffee lingering. Outside, wind moved through the pines, carrying no answers, only the long wait for the footsteps of the two that hadn't yet returned.

Chapter 17

The rider swung down from his lathered horse and made his way across the dusty street to the open-fronted shop. "Sir, do you know Logan Weston?"

Derrick Griffin dragged a rag across his grease-blackened hands. "Who's asking?"

"Name's Kyle, from Deport. We've got a man in our jail who says he's Logan Weston's son."

"You mean Travis? In jail?"

"That's the one. Our security team arrested him yesterday," Kyle said.

Derrick tossed the rag over his shoulder. "What did he do?"

"I'm only cleared to tell Mr. Weston himself."

With a short nod, Derrick replied. "Then get your horse and follow me. Logan's place is just up the road."

He led the younger man past a weather-beaten fence and several dilapidated buildings until they reached a small house set back beneath a pair of huge oaks. Derrick knocked on the door.

Logan appeared, wiping water from his forearms. "Derrick, what's up?"

"Someone's here from Deport to see you."

Kyle touched the brim of his hat.

Logan studied the stranger in the midday light. "What's this about, son?"

"I'm Kyle, sir. We're holding your boy, Travis. He's shot an arrow at our mayor."

Logan's hand froze on the doorpost. "Travis? That's nonsense."

"All I know is the tracks led straight to him. They sent me to fetch you—see if you'll ride back and help sort it out."

Logan exhaled through his teeth. "Of course I'll come. Let me grab my gear. I'm without a horse, though."

Derrick gestured toward town. "I'll speak to the council while you get your things."

By the time Logan stepped onto the porch with a bedroll and a bag of supplies, Derrick was returning with a saddled chestnut mare. A small knot of council members and curious neighbors trailed behind, like smoke behind a fire.

Logan eyed the crowd. "What's all this?"

"They're concerned for Travis," Derrick said quietly, tying the mare to the post.

Logan lifted both hands. "Folks, listen. Whatever they're holding Travis for, it's a mistake. My son doesn't shoot arrows at people."

Desmond Devan pushed forward. "We believe you, Logan, but his skill with a bow—it don't look good."

"They're wrong," Logan said, voice steady. "Pray for him, people. Don't judge him till you hear the facts."

Pastor Greyson Parker stepped up. "We will pray, Logan."

"Thank you, pastor."

Logan swung into the saddle and rode out beside Kyle, dust rising in soft swirls behind them.

***

Dusk had settled into full night by the time they reached Deport. Candles glowed along Main Street, guiding them to the jail. They tied the horses to a gnarled elm and climbed the steps.

The jailkeeper stepped out on the porch and saw a shadow move out front. "Kyle?"

"Yes, Mr. Caldwell. I have that man, Logan."

"Good. Take the horses to the stable, Kyle. Mr. Weston, step inside if you're a mind to."

Logan followed the jailer to the porch and a soft glow of candlelight. "My son—is he in there?"

"He is, sir, but you'll need to speak with Marius Nevins first, our head of security," Caldwell replied, then spun to the other jailer. "Jody, go find Marius.

Jody vanished into the dark as Logan settled on a bench beneath the overhang, the night air carrying the scents of pine smoke and distant rain. Minutes stretched long until hoofbeats announced a heavyset man riding up.

"Logan Weston?"

"That's me. I came to see about my son?"

Marius Nevins dismounted with a creak of leather and climbed the steps. "Let's go in and sit."

Inside, firelight danced over plank walls lined with faded photographs of better days. Marius lowered himself behind a broad desk.

"I'm Marius Nevins. I suppose Kyle told you that four nights ago, someone attempted to assassinate the mayor. We followed their tracks straight to an old house in the woods where your son spent the night. One set of boot prints from the trail matched his."

Logan's jaw tightened. "That doesn't sound like Travis. The night you mentioned, he was home—Pattonville—brought in deer meat."

Marius leaned in, a faint smile on his face as he noted the silence in Logan's account—no second person, no mention of a horse. "Your version lines up with most of what Travis told us," he said. "The council made it simple: prove he was somewhere else that night, and we'd release him. After returning, we learn of Black Arrow's mark on the projectile. Travis told us it matched the arrow that killed your councilman." Marius paused, letting the words settle.

Logan nodded. "If everything is cleared, then please let me see him."

Marius nodded. "Sure. We had to be certain, you see." Marius rose with a key in hand. "I'll fetch him."

Moments later, Travis stepped into the firelight, shoulders squared, eyes wary. Marius offered them both a bed for the night, and they accepted.

★★★

At Marius's table, candles warmed the room and softened the tension. The two older men spoke of memories, then of darker times—Black Arrow's shifting tactics, the slow erosion of hope in the wilderness.

Marius set his glass down. "Logan, you strike me as a man willing to make bold choices for the sake of his people."

"Some things are worth doing," Logan said.

"I'm weary of this endless scrub and struggle," Marius admitted. "We all are. Black Arrow's latest boldness could put us all under their control unless we find a way to stop it—peacefully if possible, by force if necessary."

Logan chewed slowly, studying his comment. "Peace won't come easily with them. Their leader's hands are stained with our blood and yours."

"Yet retribution only breeds more graves."

"If it comes to that," Logan said, "our people will fight."

Travis cringed as if slapped. The thought of his father marching men to war twisted something sharp inside him. He quickly pushed back his chair. "Father—what are you saying?"

Logan turned, confused. "You've heard me speak of this before."

"Not this," Travis responded. "Not about war against another faction—our own people." Color rose in Travis's face as he strode toward the door.

"We'll talk later," Logan called.

Travis paused, touching the door handle. "I've heard enough about fighting." The door shut softly behind him.

Marius watched the empty doorway. "I take it your son prefers peace."

Logan sighed. "I guess I should have expected as much. That's why I knew he could never fire an arrow toward your mayor. I owe him a better explanation than I've provided—we never talk much anymore."

Marius gave a chuckle. "I see his point of view. I'm no war-monger, but Black Arrow leaves little room for soft words. My people will fight if they must, yet we'd all choose another path if one appeared."

Logan leaned an elbow on the table. "Our real challenge is the North. Until every fragment of us stands as one, we'll continue to suffer slowly."

Marius's eyes sharpened. "You're thinking of going beyond the periphery—against the North."

"That day may soon come," Logan said. "I'm working on a new venture—too soon to disclose, but it could change our odds. If the undertaking comes to pass, would Deport stand with us?"

Marius studied him in the candlelight, a grin forming. "You've brought out a measure of curiosity, Logan. Send someone with particulars when you're ready, and we'll talk."

"I'll plan to."

"And Logan, don't fret over Travis—he'll come around. Maybe the details of your project will do the trick." Marius rose and gestured with his hand. "Take the bedroom down the hall, first door on the left. Hope you rest well."

Logan stood. "Thank you. I'm ready for it."

Chapter 18

Wren moved silently along the narrow hallway of the old quarters. She paused at her father's door, easing it open just enough to peek inside. As she had expected, Cohen lay on his narrow bed, deep in sleep, his chest rising and falling in the stillness before dawn.

She slipped away as quietly as she had come, returning to her small room to lay an arrow across her bed. The gesture was unmistakable: gone hunting. Cohen would understand, though hunting was only the cover she needed for leaving.

Easing her arms through the straps of her backpack, the familiar weight settled against her spine, lifted her bow from its peg, and started toward the door.

The pre-dawn air carried the sharp tang of pine resin and musty, wet earth as Wren stepped beyond the sleeping quarters. A faint ribbon of wood smoke still drifted from last night's campfires, but the camp itself lay silent—no creak of doors, no murmur of voices, only the soft crunch of frost-brittle grass beneath her boots and the occasional drip from the eaves.

She moved quickly along the inner perimeter until she reached the familiar place in the barbed-wire fence, dipping downward from years of her escapes. Ducking between, she felt the rusty barb snag briefly at her sleeve before she was free.

The eastern path began just beyond: a narrow trail worn smooth by countless boots of hunters, bordered by thick stands of shoulder-high thickets and scattered clumps of blackberry brambles now bare and brittle with winter. Cedar needles carpeted the ground in a moist, fragrant mat that muffled her footsteps as she slipped into the deeper darkness beneath the trees.

As she followed the narrow southern trail, leaves cushioning each careful step and releasing their rich, earthy scent into the cool air, Wren's thoughts drifted to Reilly. Two and a half weeks had passed since she and Travis had found him—half-conscious, blood-soaked, clinging desperately to the saddle of a lathered horse. It still felt like a miracle that they had come upon him at all.

The memory of her father's ordering that mission—Reilly's part in the death of an innocent man in Travis's hometown—tightened her throat with fresh anger. When did Cohen become the kind of man who could sanction such things?

She traced the shift to Brody Myles' poisonous notion: eliminate the Christians blocking the way, and the North would make a safe way for them. In truth, it was Brody's cruel pretext for the war he craved. Wren wondered if distance from camp was the wisest course until her fury cooled. Time alone with Travis might quiet the storm inside her.

The trail dipped toward a narrow creek, its water murmuring over smooth rocks. She kneeled on the mossy bank, the cool mist rising from the flow carrying the clean scent of wet rock and leaf mold. She uncapped her canteen and dipped it into the current as the first golden spears of sunlight pierced the canopy, scattering light across the rippling surface.

A sharp crack of a branch cut through the morning hush—heavy, too deliberate for deer or squirrel. *Human.*

Heart quickening, she slipped silently into a thick stand of dense buckthorn bushes and young alder saplings that gathered beside the creek's edge, their damp frond brushing cold against her sleeves. Crouching low, she parted the leaves just enough to see.

Through the screen of trunks and undergrowth, she caught the glint of a bow, then the familiar dark hood of a camp coat.

Someone from home. *Who is it?* she questioned.

The figure halted twenty feet upstream, boots sinking slightly into the soft, mossy bank as they studied the muddy margin of the creek—searching, Wren realized, for the faint crescent prints of deer. The soft gurgle of water over stones and the rustle of a light morning breeze through the alder leaves were the only sounds.

Then he turned toward the deeper woods, and the pale shaft of sunlight caught his profile.

Reilly Brewin.

A chill unrelated to the morning air prickled across her skin. His hip had been torn open by a broadhead only weeks ago—*he should still be favoring a crutch, not stalking through the woods,* she thought.

Memories surged involuntarily: the dim cave where she had cleaned and bound his wounds, the long hours of wary conversation, the way his gaze had lingered too long, or his false accusations jabbing at her.

Since returning to camp, she had kept Reilly at arm's length, limiting contact to terse nods when they passed.

Now suspicion blazed into fury. Had Reilly followed her all this way just to coax out what she knew of Travis—and the POF? If that was his game, he already suspected how deeply Travis was entangled with them.

I have to lose him.

Reilly was one of the best trackers in camp; shaking him would not be easy. Her plan to reach Pattonville would have to wait until she broke his trail.

He moved closer along the bank, eyes lowered, scanning the damp earth and scattered leaf litter. Wren's pulse pounded in her ears, loud enough—she feared—he might hear it over the creek's quiet rumble. She pressed deeper into the thick underbrush and slender alder, their petals brushing her cheeks and releasing a subtle essence.

Whatever direction he chose, she would take the opposite.

Reilly paused again, crouched, and brushed aside a layer of soggy oak leaves with careful fingers, studying the ground beneath. After a long moment, he straightened and started northward, his limp barely noticeable in the deliberate, measured stride.

Wren remained calm among the bushes until the soft crunch of his footsteps faded into the rustle of distant branches. Only then did she draw a slow, steadying breath, rise and turn south, the direction her father had drilled into her when trouble loomed: 'put solid distance between yourself and pursuit.'

Reilly's fixation on Travis felt deeply unjust. If she could draw him away long enough, perhaps she could safeguard Travis from whatever Reilly intended.

Their shared history pierced like a thorn beneath her skin. They had been best friends from the day Reilly first walked into camp. Somewhere along the way, though, his friendliness had soured into possession as he began to speak and act as though she belonged to him.

The thought tightened her jaw. But Reilly would soon realize he had taken the wrong turn at the creek. A tracker of his caliber would waste no time doubling back, reading the faint signs she could not fully erase.

The thought propelled her forward. She moved faster, boots pressing through the thick carpet of pine needles and scattered oak leaves, the air sharp with the loamy smell of humus. Every few strides, she glanced over her shoulder, straining for the snap of a twig or the rustle of undergrowth that would betray him. Even when nothing appeared, she felt Reilly's presence like a shadow at her back.

The trail narrowed into a dense stand of young pine trees and scrubby hawthorn, their springy branches whipping lightly at her coat as she pushed through. Loose needles rained down in soft patters, catching in her hair. When the growth finally thinned, she had reached the old fence line—a drooping stretch of rusted barbed wire half-hidden by tangled blackberry vines. The dry thorns snagged at her sleeves as she carefully lifted one leg, then the other, over the sagging strand.

If the wound in Reilly's hip slowed him even a fraction, it might buy her the chance she needed. Yet she knew his stubbornness too well; the fact that he had pushed this far on a torn leg meant he wouldn't easily abandon the hunt.

Wren slowed at the edge of the meadow, chest heaving, the cold air tasting of frost and trampled grass. She swept her gaze across the open ground behind her—nothing yet—then forward again.

Beyond the clearing, the land dropped into a shallow gully she knew well. She had hunted its rims many times for deer, though no one from camp had come this way since one of the men claimed to have seen fresh mountain lion signs scraped into a pine trunk.

A small ridge of mountains loomed ahead—a daunting climb if conquered—and promised an end to Reilly's pursuit. She angled downhill, boots skidding on loose gravel and slick stone until she reached the bottom of the gully. The ground here was a jumble of broken shale and exposed rock, sparse tufts of bunchgrass clinging in the crevices—terrain that would frustrate even Reilly's eye for sign.

On the far side, a dense thicket of young pines stood tall and straight like arrows, forming a green barrier twice her height, their lower branches a tightly woven tapestry. Wren plunged in without hesitation. Needles scraped against her cheeks and showered down in fragrant bursts, while brittle twigs snapped underfoot with sharp, betraying cracks she could not silence. She pushed forward, arms raised to shield her face, the resinous scent thick until, abruptly, the growth thinned, and she stepped into open air again.

Finally.

She stood at the edge of the pines, breath still ragged from pushing through the dense trees, and fixed her gaze on the mountains a hundred yards ahead. From this vantage point, the slope looked almost manageable—a dark rise of rock with scattered juniper breaking through thin soil—but she knew the truth: the pitch would sharpen quickly, the holds would crumble, and the wind would slice through like a blade at higher elevations.

Well, I've come this far.

She crossed the open ground in long strides, boots crunching over dried bunchgrass and loose shale that shifted underfoot with dry, gritty rasps. The air carried the clean, mineral scent of exposed stone warmed by the sun's first real touch, laced with the faint, sharp tang of crushed sagebrush she bruised against passing.

At the base, she paused only long enough to steady her breathing, the cold burning in her throat. As she began the climb, her fingers searched the cracks between mossy-covered rocks, her boots tested each narrow ledge before she trusted her weight. Loose gravel rattled downward in small avalanches; the wind funneled up the slope, tugging at her coat and carrying the distant cry of a raven overhead.

She moved deliberately, muscles already trembling from the morning's ascent, every sense attuned to the sounds of the mountain—the scrape of her own palms against rough granite, the soft clatter of dislodged pebbles, and the low moan of air flowing through a cleft above.

Then, a sudden voice cut through the thin air. "Wren, where are you?"

The words bounced off the rock walls, sharp and unmistakable.

Her stomach lurched. How had he closed the distance so fast?

Again, louder, edged with certainty: "Wren, I'll find you!"

The echo placed him nearer than she dared believe—somewhere just below the first steep pitch, pushing hard despite the torn hip that should have slowed him to a limp.

Wren paused on a narrow ledge, palms stinging from the rough granite, and studied the wall above. The route narrowed sharply, the holds growing sparse and treacherous under a thin layer of loose slate. Yet surrender was not in her. She shifted her bow higher across her back, cinched a strap tight around it, and reached for the first solid crack.

One deliberate move at a time, she ascended—fingers curling into shallow pockets, boots scraping for purchase on tilted slabs that shed dry grit with every shift of weight. The wind funneled colder now, carrying the balsamic scent of the distant trees. Her breath came in measured pulls, audible over the soft clatter of pebbles tumbling into silence.

Midway up, the cliff bulged outward in a massive boulder the size of a small cabin. The detour around it looked impossible—the only path was over or back down. She chose over.

She stretched upward, palms flattening against the boulder's cold, pebbled surface. A fist-sized chunk broke free beneath her right hand, spinning away into empty air with a sharp clack-clack-clack that echoed too loudly. Her body lurched—for a heartbeat—only her left hand and the desperate press of her boot toe held her weight. Breath caught in her throat.

Steady.

Muscles trembling, she lunged for a higher edge, fingers scraping over loose flakes until they found a solid seam. Adrenaline flooded her veins, sharpening every sense. Reilly's voice had been too close moments ago—there was no time left.

She slithered sideways across the bulging face, weight distributed carefully over crumbling plates that shifted and groaned beneath her. One wrong move and the whole section might shear away, sending her sliding down the long, jagged slope to the rocks below. Finally, her searching hand closed around a knob of granite.

She hauled herself upward, boots scrabbling, until she cleared the danger and collapsed briefly against a safer shelf.

Reilly's voice rose again, clearer now. "Wren, I'm getting warmer! I won't stop until I find you!"

The words bounced off the stone, close enough that she could hear the faint rasp of his breathing between them.

Heart hammering, she eased her head around the boulder's edge. Far below, Reilly stood at the base, eyes fixed on the debris that had fallen during her near-miss. He ran his fingers over the freshly disturbed rocks, then tilted his head back—scanning upward.

If Wren had scaled this unforgiving face, then he had no choice but to follow. Shale scraped his palms as he reached for a hold, the cool, mineral scent of the cliff rising around him like a warning. Dust drifted down in thin veils, settling on his tongue with the faint taste of old rock.

He gripped a jagged outcrop of rock and hauled himself onto the lowest rung, loose fragments skittering past his shoulder to clatter down the face beside him. Pain flared white-hot through his injured hip, a fresh surge that drew sweat from his skin in rivulets beneath the jacket. Each breath tasted of dust and the faint tang of stone.

The cliff rose steep and unforgiving above him. His body, already weakened, protested every inch. Yet doubt gnawed harder than the pain pulsing from his hip: *perhaps she had never climbed at all—only made it appear so, a deliberate misdirection to buy time.*

After a long, trembling moment—scarcely three feet above the ground—he eased himself down, fingers slipping from the crumbling hold. His boots struck the leaf-strewn earth with a thud that drove a piercing spike through his injured limb. Breath hissing between clenched teeth, he shifted weight to his good side and began a slow, uneven limp along the foot of the cliff—thoughts focused on a new search path.

Each step ground pain deeper into his joint, yet he kept moving, eyes fixed on the place ahead where the terrain dropped away into the shadowed throats of the ravines. *She must be there,* he thought.

Wren watched Reilly changing paths from the mountain's ridge. *He doesn't know if I climbed up, and his body won't let him,* she resolved. *So be it.*

Relief found her fragile and brief, amid the cold bite of the wind against her sweat-damp skin.

Reilly's sudden departure left her unsettled, a flicker of doubt curling in her gut. Was he circling the ridge to intercept her on the far side?

I must hurry, she decided.

The broken terrain at the mountain's base sprawled for miles—jumbled boulders, deep ravines, and thickets of scrub oak and madrona that would slow a healthy man. If Reilly took that route, he would veer away from her entirely—but for how long?

Only when the crunch of his footsteps faded completely did Wren move. She reached overhead, fingers closing around a solid knob of granite veined with quartz, and hauled herself upward. One final pull, boots scraping, and she rolled onto the narrow summit, chest heaving, the thin air sharp and cold in her lungs.

She eased to the edge and peered down. The cliff face fell away in shadowed folds; no movement stirred below. Whether Reilly had chosen the long southeastern traverse or given up, he had vanished from sight.

Wren turned to survey the small plateau. Wind-whipped bunches of wiry grass clung between slabs of weathered stone, and near the center, a shelf of rock overhung a shallow recess—more alcove than true cave, but deep enough to break the wind.

"This might work," she said with an agreeing nod.

She shrugged off her pack, rummaged for a short, dry branch of mountain shrub, and wound one end with the remaining strip from Travis's old shirt. A few strikes of flint sparked the cloth alight—the faint, smoky glow revealed bare stone floors dusted with old pine needles and a scatter of rodent droppings, but no ominous signs—no claw marks, no matted fur, or lingering musk of mountain lion. Satisfied, she propped her bow against the wall and let the backpack thud softly to the ground.

Night settled quickly at this height, the temperature dropping until her breath plumed white. She chose not to risk a fire—even a modest campfire—that might betray her position. Instead, she drew the thin blanket left from her mother's things, wrapped it tightly around her shoulders, and settled against the cold rock.

Rest tonight—tomorrow is my descent.

Guardian

Yea, though I walk through the valley of the shadow of death, I will fear no evil: for thou art with me; thy rod and thy staff they comfort me. Psalm 23:4

Chapter 19

As Travis and Logan rode toward Pattonville, a heavy silence wrapped around them, broken only by the steady clop-clop of hooves on the crumbled pavement and the occasional creak of saddle leather. The air sharpened with the scents of humus, pine resin, and the faint horse musk.

Logan drew a slow breath. "Travis, we can't keep pretending nothing's wrong between us," he said.

Eyes fixed on the trail, Travis said, "You mean the war you're brewing with your friends?"

Logan asked quietly, "Looks like there's no better way than fighting it out?"

"There has to be," Travis shot back. "Humans talk. Sit 'em *down*—tell them we reject their tactics and want it stopped. Then find common ground and *move* forward."

Logan's voice hardened. "Think talk'll *sway* Black Arrow? Or maybe you mean the North: those above the periphery? These are two different beasts—can't approach them the same way."

Travis glanced back. "Black Arrow's the trouble."

"Yes," Logan said, "and they must answer for what they did. When they murdered Edmond—" He broke off, jaw tight. "I lashed

out in anger—words I regret. But sending an assassin to take a life…
is a declaration of war."

Confusion shadowed Travis's face. Logan caught it, mellowing.
"Son, Black Arrow's a thorn for sure—but our wounds run much
deeper. Hoped they'd stay neutral until we're ready, but that hope's
fading."

"So, you're saying the North's the bigger threat? We're miles
from them," Travis said.

"But they are."

Travis's mind reeled. His father had never spoken of war against
the North—only quiet bitterness over exile south of the periphery.
Yet it rang chillingly true: the North had banished them to this
hardscrabble waste, where winters gnawed deep and summers
scorched, all for clinging to faith. "Father, Wren's night over, you
were working on a truck—was it part of this?"

Logan nodded. "It was. You'll know soon enough—we're hauling weapons and ammo in it soon."

Travis's gut knotted. "Weapons? I thought you sold yours years
ago—you had no bullets, right?"

"I hid that 25 mil pistol to take it across, but when we were
starving—" he paused. "It's different now. My friend in Oklahoma
knows where there's a cache of weapons—rifles, ammunition, and
maybe other firearms. Enough to make a difference. The Pattonville crew and I prepped the truck for the first run, before this
happened with you."

"I'm sorry," Travis said, staring at the saddle horn. So the tools
and the truck's secrecy hadn't been idle pastimes. "You're truly
preparing for war."

"Maybe," Logan said. "I know it's not what you thought. Our government abandoned us here because we wouldn't bend to the new rules. We've scraped for every mouthful, every blanket—and that's no life. You were born just before the Separation; you don't remember what we gave up. I nearly lost you that first winter after crossing." His voice roughened. "There's much I should've told you sooner. I'm sorry."

Travis listened without responding.

"America was once a nation under God," Logan went on. "Then they chose another creed and punished dissenters. They cut us off from medicine, fuel, seed—everything—for clinging to faith. God's kept us alive despite it all."

Travis shook his head, struggling to take it in. "There's more to it, isn't there?"

"In time." Logan's gaze sharpened. "My turn now. You've got something to confess, too."

Travis exhaled slowly. "It's Wren, Father. Please don't be angry. She's Black Arrow, but she didn't kill Edmond."

"I'm glad to hear that," Logan said calmly, "but what makes you so certain? Her arrow markings matched the one that killed Edmond."

"Spend time around her, and you'll see," Travis said. "Wren wants peace, just like me."

"I figured you two had something in common."

"You're not angry I'm friends with her?" Travis pressed.

Logan grinned faintly and nodded. "No. Relieved, maybe. Now that I know for sure, I'd like to speak with Wren. Perhaps she can open a door to their leaders."

"What if she's unwilling?"

"It's her choice. But I'd like to ask," Logan said, keeping an eye out for a camping spot.

Travis noticed the dense wall of leafless oaks, green pines, and holly berries passing by. "Why tell me all this now?"

"Partly because Black Arrow attacked us—though they've raided other camps for food and supplies before. It angers me, and it must stop. Still, they're people who split from us years ago. The fight that matters is with the North." He took in a deep breath. "You remember my friend Roy Wayne Sam?"

"The Indian with the loud laugh?"

"The same. Roy Wayne heard credible reports of foreign invaders slipping into the North through Canada, forcing the government to intercept. They think we're weak now with the recent changes in government. If they push south across the periphery, we'll need a way to confront them. Crossing the line's always been suicide unarmed. I pray Roya Wayne's wrong, but I know he wouldn't lie."

Travis lifted an eyebrow, mind spinning. "So you plan to fight the North."

"Perhaps. We've dreamed of returning home for years, but those dreams can't come true without weapons to stand against the Northern military. When Roy Wayne brought word of the Oklahoma cache, I rallied friends who know how to fight. We've kept it quiet—except for what I mentioned in the shed that day."

"You wanted tools... to work on a truck."

"Yes, now that we have that truck, we're making plans to head to Roy Wayne's to pick up the weapons. I'd like you to go with us, son."

A sudden, violent tremor shook Travis. "I figured you'd fight Black Arrow one day, not make peace with them."

Logan flashed a weary smile. "Divided, we're prey. United, we've got a shot at reclaiming what they stole."

A fragile thrill kindled in Travis—Black Arrow reconciliation, Wren alongside them, suddenly within reach.

Sunlight bled through the trees as Logan reined in beside a clear creek lined with pin oaks and sweetgums. "Pattonville's too far to make tonight. Let's camp here."

Travis helped his father ease from the saddle, pain etched in every motion. "You shouldn't have ridden all this way in your condition, Father."

"You're my son. I needed to come." Logan loosened the pack. "Besides, they asked for me."

A sudden pang of regret struck Travis as the memory hit him—he was the one who'd told Marius his father's name. He should have asked someone else, sparing Logan this grueling journey.

He unsaddled the horse as Logan spread bedrolls over a thick pine-needle cushion. Nearby, the creek rushed over rocks while a woodpecker hammered a tall pine, echoes rippling through the hush.

By the small campfire, Travis sat dividing deer jerky. "Father, I held back with Mr. Nevins. That morning, Marius's men came to the old house. I figured they hunted the same assassin who hit our town. I slipped out a back window, tore through briars and dewberry thickets to the creek before they found me. Their dogs tracked me for miles."

Logan poked the fire with a stick. "Did you know who it was they wanted?"

"Yes, Reilly Brewin. Wren knows him—she saved his life, actually, pulling an arrow from his hip. He's one of those who kill mayors and councilmen. Marius's son and some others were waiting for him."

Logan's eyes narrowed. "I remember what Marius said. So, she's friends with an assassin?"

"She left her camp, couldn't stomach those kill orders. Reilly was ex-military before Black Arrow—had once asked her to marry him."

"He's older?"

"Between you and me."

"He's still carrying a grudge?" Logan asked.

"I think so, but she isn't."

Logan sighed. "Be careful around him, Travis."

"I will."

"I won't forbid you from seeing Wren, but find somewhere safer until we settle things with Black Arrow."

"Sure, if we can."

Logan stretched out on his bedroll, wincing. "I'm ready for some sleep, son. Bet this ground's no softer than it looks."

Travis grinned. "Imagine it's a bed of fresh cotton. You never know—might help."

Logan huffed a quiet laugh, the sound roughened by weariness. "At my age, imagination yields to the harsh reality of hard ground.

Goodnight, son—early or not, I need it." He eased onto the blanket, eyes drifting shut as he silently prayed that dawn would bring less pain.

"Goodnight, Father," Travis replied. The branches whispered secrets to the fading light, as if the forest itself lingered, reluctant to surrender the day.

Chapter 20

Early morning sunlight filtered through the canopy of trees as Travis stirred on the cool ground. The scent of damp pine and campfire smoke hung in the air, the same airiness that had wrapped their camp since they entered these woods. He remembered his father sleeping beside him and eased himself upright—then froze. Thirty feet away, half-hidden among the shrubs and tangled briars, a man stood with a bow drawn.

Who's that? Travis asked himself.

The stranger raised his weapon, arrow already nocked and aimed at Travis.

Travis tensed, his breath shallow, bracing for the fatal twang. Instead, a sharp whistle sliced the morning air. An arrow buried itself in the attacker's chest with a dull thud. The man's own shot flew wild, spiraling into the woods as he collapsed, letting out one final gasp—then nothing.

Travis leaped to his feet and snatched his bow in a single motion.

"Everything is fine," a calm voice drifted from the mist-shrouded trees. "I'm not here to harm you."

The figure emerged from the morning mist: tall and broad-shouldered, bow in his left hand, tattered pack slung low on his hip. He wore weathered fatigues, except for a green baseball cap and trousers the color of the trees. Olive skin, a short beard, and long golden hair tied loosely at the neck lent him a weathered, almost regal aura.

Logan woke to the voices and quickly rose from his bedroll to see the stranger standing near his son.

"Why did you kill him?" Travis asked the man.

"He was about to put an arrow in you," the golden-haired man answered. "Seemed the right thing to do."

A knot of worry tightened in Travis's stomach as he stared at the still form on the ground, then at the man responsible for its demise. "Who are you, and what are you doing out here?"

"Just passing through, looking for supper. I don't usually meddle in other folks' troubles, but that one wasn't giving you any chance."

Logan walked to where the young man's body lay. "Travis, is that Reilly?" he asked.

Travis made his way there and studied the dead man's face lying beside the bushes. "No, never seen him before."

"Then why did he come after you?"

"I don't know."

"This group doesn't need a reason," the stranger said quietly. "The marks on his arrows say Black Arrow."

Logan turned, eyes narrowing. "Mister, I don't understand why you stepped in, but thank you for saving my son. He might not be breathing if you hadn't."

"Someone above must be watching over him."

"That He is," Logan said. "What's your name?"

"Sacha Bourget."

Logan offered his hand. "You're not local—I hear an accent."

"I'm from the coast—outside of New Orleans."

"I'm Logan Weston. This is my son, Travis. Thank you again, Mr. Bourget."

"Pure chance I was here. So, you truly didn't know that man, Travis?

"Never laid eyes on him."

"I take it you've heard of the Black Arrow," Logan said.

"Oh yes," Sacha replied. "Not a likable bunch."

"Would you share breakfast with us, Mr. Bourget—some jerked deer meat? A simple meal—we've enough."

"I'd be grateful. My supplies ran dry yesterday. I was tracking some game when I saw him draw his bow on your son."

Travis had turned to gather dry wood from the forest's edge, listening as they talked.

Sacha spoke of losing his wife and young daughter when military units opened fire on civilian cars near Missouri's southern border. Several rounds struck them, and his car veered into a ditch. He buried his family near the site, then fled into the woods and began the long walk south. Months ago, starvation along the southern coast drove him north again, where he heard accounts of Black Arrow's assassins, their marked arrows left as signatures—leaving whole settlements terrorized.

"Have you had dealings with them before today?" Sacha asked.

"One of them killed a friend back in our town, Pattonville," Logan said, passing him a strip of jerky. "He shot him as he left the church. The coward fled before anyone could catch him."

"What do they hope to prove with such displays?" Sacha asked.

"Word is the North struck a bargain: take out the believers, and Black Arrow gets safe passage home. Nobody knows why they waited this long to instigate their plan."

Sacha gave a faint, bitter grin. "If they believe it's a good plan, they're fooling themselves. The way home will only come through facing the North, who are happy to waste lives like ammunition to thin the numbers—a deed they should do themselves, but are too cowardly."

Logan's brows raised, and the thought struck him like fresh kindling catching fire. "That angle never occurred to me. Might be enough to turn some of them, make them see they're being used."

"Turn them toward what?"

Logan glanced at Travis feeding the fire, sparks rising into the cool morning air. "Not ready to share that," he said softly. "Time isn't right. Maybe later."

"I understand," Sacha said. "You owe me no explanation."

Travis settled near them, uneasy. Something about the stranger's sudden arrival gnawed at him. He remembered another town that welcomed a wounded hunter, nursed him for weeks, only to find a hidden quiver of Black Arrow's marked projectiles and a bow. The man had been a spy searching for food stores. Travis studied Sacha's easy manner, the calm eyes, and wondered if his kindness was a facade for something more sinister.

When they had eaten, they dug a shallow grave beside the creek, covered the young archer with humus of leaves and needles, and set off toward Pattonville—Travis and the golden-haired stranger walking together and Logan riding the horse.

Chapter 21

They arrived in Pattonville under a pale sun that offered little warmth. Logan's exhausted body begged for sleep, and his friends urged him to postpone the weapons run until he recovered. They needed him sharp—only his friend Roy Wayne Sam knew the location of the hidden cache.

As Logan settled into a restful slumber, Travis made his way to Pastor Parker's humble residence, nestled next to the church. A nostalgic aroma of pine smoke swirled from the chimneys, a scent that seemed to weave itself into the very fabric of the town, wrapping the whole place in a warm, familiar embrace.

Andy, a young man, greeted Travis. After his mother's death, Pastor Parker had taken Andy in.

Is Pastor Parker here?" Travis asked.

"Sure, I'll go get him," Andy said.

Greyson Parker stepped into the doorway a few moments later. "Hello, Travis. What brings you here?"

"Have you heard about the visitor at my house?"

"No, I haven't."

Travis sat on a chair and shared what he knew about the incident involving Sacha Bourget showing up out of nowhere and killing the young archer.

"Travis, have you ever challenged the accuracy of your instincts?"

"Pastor, all I can tell you is I have a terrible suspicion that this man is hiding something."

"I'm unacquainted with him, but I see you're concerned. Let's look beyond what you're feeling and consider other possibilities. Sometimes people hide their past: a previous experience, shame over something they did. Each of us carries memories we want to forget."

"All I know is, he won Father's trust so quickly."

"Maybe, or your father has similar feelings to yours but prefers to know more."

Travis exhaled, "So what should I do?"

"Give it time. The truth usually finds its own way out. And remember—Sacha saved your life. There's good in that, whatever else he might be."

The weight lifted lightly, and Travis met the pastor's eyes. "May I share another matter in confidence?"

"Always."

He fixed his gaze on Pastor Parker. "I recently met a girl in the woods while hunting—a little creek I like to go to, and it turns out she is Black Arrow."

"Black Arrow. Indeed, that's a matter that should stay confidential."

"We've only met a handful of times," Travis said, voice low, as if the walls themselves might carry his words beyond the warm room. "I know the risk, but for some reason, I trust her. She speaks of peace between our groups with such quiet conviction that I believe her. Our people call Black Arrow the enemy. I've heard father and his friends, Derrick and Kincaid, speak of them—I know they see them as adversaries. But when I'm with Wren, those words feel wrong—like a coat that no longer fits."

The pastor gestured to the chair beside him. Travis sat back down.

"Years ago," Pastor Parker said, "a young woman sat right there and told me almost the same story. She was expecting a child; the father was from another town. Our council wanted them kept apart—old rules, old fears, some hatred. I talked to the elders until they eventually saw the cruelty in it. They were married in this church and still live among us."

Travis leaned forward. "Who are they?"

The pastor gave a small, protective shake of the head. "Some stories are safer left sleeping. But listen, son—two things matter here. First, what you've found with this Black Arrow girl is rare and precious. We're not meant to see them as enemies. In God's eyes, we're the same, even if not everyone understands that yet. Evil endeavors create a greater gulf between allies."

"I know," Travis said, the voices of the town echoing in his ears. "But when people talk—"

"I hear them too." The pastor's gaze held steady in the firelight. "And about Sacha—maybe the Lord brought him here for a reason."

Travis frowned. "You think so?"

"There's purpose in what God does. I'm not asking you to trust the man blindly, Travis. Watch him, weigh his words, follow your gut until it feels right. Just leave room for the possibility that he is part of a larger design of God."

He reached for the Bible on the side table. "Hebrews reminds us: 'Be not forgetful to entertain strangers: for thereby some have entertained angels unawares.' Maybe Sacha's sent; maybe he's just a flawed man God can still use. Either way, something may be moving along with God, and we can't see it yet."

The stove popped softly, the only sound for a long moment as the words settled over Travis like quiet snow. "I hadn't considered that."

Pastor Parker smiled faintly. "I've prayed for years that God would send help our way, and I believe he answers, but often in ways we don't expect."

Travis felt the weight shift again, lighter now. "Maybe one day I can trust Sacha," he said.

"You will, when the time is right. Remember that instinct is a valuable asset, but fear can often distort it. Better if you season each one with prayer."

"I do pray," Travis admitted. "Maybe not enough."

"What brought you here today? Parker asked gently. "Maybe a prayer that's in progress already?"

"I see what you mean," Travis said, rising, the scent of pine smoke following him as he headed slowly toward the door. "Thank you, Pastor. I'll see you at church."

"I'll be looking for you," Pastor Parker replied, and closed the door gently behind him.

Chapter 22

After a day of rest, Logan felt well enough to travel. Before his departure, he entrusted Sacha Bourget with overseeing things at home while he was away and urged Travis to keep their mission confidential. Logan hoped this forced proximity would ease his son's wariness of Sacha, believing familiarity is the best way to bridge the suspicion.

They took the narrow farm road from Pattonville—broken pavement edged with tall broom sedge and wild blackberry runners that clawed at the truck's sides. Two miles out, the land seemed to have swallowed the road. Massive oaks and hickories lay across it, their bark scarred and moss-covered, roots clawing at the sky. The air smelled sharply of damp earth and decay, mixed with a faint resinous scent of pine.

Derrick eased the truck to a stop. "Well, Logan. Ideas?"

Logan stared at the barricade of fallen trees. "We'll clear only enough to squeeze through," he suggested.

Randall shook his head. "Some of those trunks are nearly as wide as the truck."

Kincaid was already out, boots crunching in the branches. "That's not a problem, fellas." He slid a chainsaw from under a tarp in the truck's bed.

Derrick raised an eyebrow. "Does that thing even run?"

"Started yesterday."

Kincaid primed the bulb, set the choke, and yanked the cord. The two-stroke engine snarled to life, a raw, hungry sound that scattered a flock of crows from the treetops. Sawdust and the oily smoke of chainsaw gasoline filled the air.

Logan's pulse quickened at the roar. "I don't believe it," he muttered, then caught himself and grinned. "Let's get to work."

They fell into a steady rhythm: Kincaid slicing through the trunks with the saw, the others dragging the cut sections aside. Sawdust and bark chips flew like yellow snow, and the sharp scent of freshly cut oak and hickory clung to their coats. Hours passed, and the road slowly opened before them like a reluctant wound.

When they finally clambered back into the cab, the cool air brushed against their skin, and sweat cooling beneath their jackets, Logan broke the silence. "I've never seen the roads in such disarray. We've hunted these woods countless times, but this—"

"Only seen it once before," Derrick said as he shifted the truck back into gear. "It was during that huge hurricane that triggered a tornado swarm. We were without power for days, but the Gulf Coast suffered most of the storm's destruction."

"That's right," Logan recalled. "The power was out for days in some states."

Kincaid's voice, sharp with impatience, cut through the cab. "Bad as it was, it's nothing next to what's coming from the North. Let's stay focused on why we're out here."

Logan sympathized with Kincaid. He still carried his own ghosts: the long, desperate journey south with Travis strapped to his back, each mile weighted by the grief of losing his wife at the periphery. An image flashed in his mind—the frantic search for shelter from the cold rain, accompanied by the smell of dampness on his clothes.

Silence settled inside the truck until Derrick broke it. "Logan, what do you make of this Sacha character?"

"He seems fine, though it's hard to know for sure yet. A man like that could prove helpful if we clash with the North. I held off telling him about the weapons cache until we learn more—Roy Wayne's word is all we have for now. I trust him, but things could've changed since he mentioned them."

"I think that's a good idea," Derrick said. "But my gut tells me he's the real thing."

Logan nodded. "I wouldn't want to face him. Can't figure out why Travis distances himself from the man ever since our return from Deport. Sacha saved his life."

"Trust issues, maybe?" Randall asked.

"Not usually. By the time we get home, I'm betting they'll have sorted it." Logan paused. "I like him."

"Maybe Travis feels crowded," Derrick offered.

"That's not Travis's way."

Kincaid leaned forward and spoke in a low voice. "Former Special Forces. I'd stake money on it, if I had any."

Logan twisted in the seat, his eyebrows raised. "Based on what? You caught one glimpse of the guy."

Kincaid's gaze stayed fixed on an open field along the road, as though he could still see the stranger's silhouette there. "I ran with enough Green Berets to recognize the type. Get past the hair, the clothes, and the fit shoulders, and you'll notice it. Those eyes watch every movement."

He tapped two fingers against the tattered seat, tracing an invisible design. "Most of them wear ink on their bodies somewhere. Crossed arrows, dagger if they're feeling dramatic, and underneath in block letters: 'De Oppresso Liber'. That's Latin for *liberate the oppressed*."

Logan let out a slow breath, the sound almost lost beneath the truck's rumble. He glanced toward the outside at an old highway sign, bent like an ell from past storms, then looked back inside to them.

"Yesterday in the yard," he said quietly, "Sacha worked on his martial arts forms. Took his shirt off. There it was: tattoo with crossed arrows and the motto exactly where you said it would be."

Kincaid gave a single, satisfied nod. "Told you."

Derrick's eyes flicked to the rearview mirror.

"So a man built like that, a soldier," he murmured, "trained well to slip into places and vanish again... what exactly is he doing in Pattonville?"

Randall's tone took on a more serious edge. "Maybe Travis has a good reason to be cautious. Maybe we do, as well. We *don't* know anything about him."

Kincaid tapped Logan on the shoulder. "Want to turn around, Logan?"

Logan looked ahead at the narrow path through the trees, an uneasy sinking feeling in his stomach. "No. My instinct says he's on our side. Remember, he already proved it when he protected Travis. An act of saving someone speaks volumes to me."

The engine growled as they pressed on, the scent of freshly cut wood still clinging to their clothes and uneasy questions trailing behind like exhaust.

Chapter 23

Wren paused at the ridge's edge, scanning the slopes below for any trace of Reilly. There was no flicker of movement, no telltale snap of a twig, and no glint of metal. She exhaled slowly, the sharp, aromatic scent of loblolly pines filling her lungs, and began her descent toward Pattonville. Every few paces, she glanced over her shoulder in case he lurked just out of sight among the underbrush.

As she followed the narrow game trail, her thoughts drifted to her father. Had Cohen dispatched Reilly to spy? The notion gnawed at her. Her father had an uncanny gift for predicting people's choices—almost as if he could read their future. Yet how could he have anticipated her predawn departure? She tightened her jaw and veered onto a secondary path, letting the thick carpet of pine needles muffle her footsteps and hide her trail.

She reached the outskirts of Pattonville several hours later, her legs heavy and breath ragged. Her pulse hammered against her ribs, and a familiar knot twisted low in her stomach as a memory surfaced—the last time she had waited at this spot while Travis readied the shed for her to sleep. His house stood at the far edge of a wide grass field, perhaps a hundred yards away. She settled among the low cedars and sweetgum saplings, waiting for full dark to fall.

Her mind turned to Travis. Had their sudden parting after she cut the arrow from Reilly's hip changed how he felt for her? The farewell had felt amicable enough, yet what if someone—his father, perhaps—had reminded him that her group was their rival? She would learn the truth soon enough.

As the final thread of violet light faded from the sky, a barred owl's low, mournful hoot drifted across the open field. Wren rose quietly and stepped forward, placing each foot carefully to avoid the telling snap of a twig or the dry rustle of fallen needles.

Through the house's broad front window, candlelight spilled in a soft, amber glow, pulsing against the encroaching dark like a living heartbeat. The unmistakable scent of wood smoke—rich, warm, and faintly sweet—drifted on the night air, curling from the chimney.

Her pulse quickened, a sudden and insistent drumbeat beneath her ribs.

Was Travis's father inside?

She edged forward until her breath misted the cold glass, the porch boards giving a faint, protesting creak beneath her weight. Inside, low voices drifted toward her—Travis's familiar cadence mingling with another she could not yet place.

Wren leaned closer, heart thudding against her ribs, fingers already lifting to tap the pane and announce herself.

Then a figure rose smoothly from an armchair just out of her line of sight. A stranger—tall, measured in his movements—crossed the room and disappeared down the dark hallway.

Wren froze, hand suspended in midair, the impulse to knock dissolving into sudden, sharp uncertainty.

That's not Logan, she determined.

Adrenaline flooded her veins in a white-hot rush. Wren jerked back from the door—only to feel a hard, unyielding hand clamp around her upper arm while seizing her backpack in an iron grip. A second palm slammed over her mouth, broad and calloused, smothering the sharp cry that surged up her throat before it could escape.

Her back collided with the solid wall of a man's chest. She twisted and thrashed against him, but his hold tightened like a vise—immovable, relentless—pinning her in place with terrifying ease.

The man bound her with brutal efficiency, his arm like a steel band across her chest as he drove his boot against the door in a single, resounding kick. Wren's muffled protests echoed uselessly against his palm; her body twisted and bucked, but he absorbed every frantic movement without yielding an inch.

"Who's there?" Travis's voice cut through from inside.

"Open the door!" the man barked.

The latch gave a metallic click. The door swung inward.

"Sacha, what are you doing out there?" Travis demanded, his gaze shifting from the man to Wren. Fury darkened his features the instant he recognized her—eyes narrowing, jaw tightening.

"I thought perhaps they returned to finish you," Sacha answered, calm and unhurried. His palm remained clamped across Wren's mouth like a steel latch, fingers pressing just hard enough to silence any sound she might attempt to force past them.

Her cheeks burned with heat, eyes blazing with fury in the dim, flickering light that spilled from the open doorway.

Travis's gaze fastened on her, awareness flashing across his face. "No! That's the woman I told you about. Let her go—please."

Sacha's grip loosened at once. He eased his hold and lowered the slender woman gently to the floor.

Wren spun toward them, face still flushed a deep crimson, every line of her body coiled as though ready to explode. "Travis Weston!" she shouted, voice trembling with anger, "that is no way to welcome a friend at your door!"

Travis raised both hands in a cautious, placating gesture. "I... I see you're upset," he said, choosing his words with deliberate care. "But how were we supposed to know you were coming?"

"I told you I would," she snapped, whirling to face Sacha. Her eyes locked onto his with unyielding intensity as she jabbed a finger firmly against his chest. "This brute crushed my supper before I even reached the door."

Sacha lifted one broad shoulder, the faintest curl tugging at the corner of his mouth. "My apologies for embracing you so tightly. Old habit from my training."

Travis cleared his throat, choosing not to tell her that wasn't what she had said. "Wren, this is Sacha Bourget, a friend of mine and my father's. Sacha, meet Wren Daniels."

Sacha's gaze lowered, pausing for a moment on the arrows tucked into her quiver—the dark fletching, the carved insignia etched into the wood. "You weren't kidding. She *is* Black Arrow." A broad, genuine smile spread across his face as he extended a large, steady hand. "A pleasure."

"Nice to meet you—I think," Wren answered, her tone still edged with wariness as she grasped his palm.

Sacha's fingers closed gently around hers. With a subtle tug, he drew her forward a single step and bent to press a brief, courteous kiss to her cheek. "A custom among my people," he murmured, his words soft and unhurried.

Wren blinked, a flicker of hesitation crossing her features. "Maybe… we should hold off on customs until I know you better."

She turned to Travis, rose onto her toes, and pressed her lips to his in a brief, deliberate kiss.

When they parted, Travis held her gaze as he gently brushed away an insect that had ventured too close to her cheek. "You caught me off guard," he murmured, a faint, rueful smile tugging at his mouth.

Wren cast another glance toward Sacha, her brows drawing together in a subtle frown. "Clearly, I've missed a lot since we last parted."

"Not as much as you think," Travis replied calmly. "Come inside."

She hesitated, her eyes darting toward the shadowy interior beyond the threshold. "What about your father?"

"He's away for a few days."

"That's good news," Wren murmured, relief threading through her voice.

They stepped across the threshold into the small living room, where the fire in the hearth cast a steady warmth across the worn wooden floors and simple furnishings. The scent of oak smoke lingered, comforting now rather than ominous.

Travis gestured toward the chairs near the hearth as he spoke. "Sacha found Logan and me in the woods. One moment, we were waking up; the next, an archer had his bow drawn at me. Sacha took him down before he released his arrow." He glanced at the tall man with quiet gratitude. "He saved my life. Strange way to meet someone, isn't it?"

Wren nodded slowly, absorbing the weight of his words. "I would have arrived sooner," she explained, "but Reilly trailed me from the moment I left camp. I had to change my route—swing wide through the foothills, then climb into the mountains to lose him."

Sacha's dark eyes settled on her. "Do you know why he followed you?"

Wren's gaze dropped briefly to the fire before lifting again. "Reilly believes I belong to him—has for a long time. Perhaps he thought I'd lead him straight to you, Travis. He became suspicious after we removed that arrow from his hip, and he hasn't trusted you since."

"Travis mentioned the incident," Sacha said, his voice low, carrying a quiet authority.

"I hope he doesn't show up here," Travis added, the faintest edge of unease threading through his tone.

Wren shook her head, firm and certain. "He won't. I made sure of it."

Sacha rose from the chair. "Well, young ones, I'm heading to bed now so I can wake up early for a morning workout."

Travis dipped his chin in acknowledgment. "Good night, Sacha. See you tomorrow."

They waited in silence until the steady rhythm of Sacha's footsteps receded down the hallway and a distant door clicked softly shut.

Only then did Travis reach for her, taking both of Wren's hands in his. "You're certain Reilly didn't follow?"

Wren met his gaze. "He's an outstanding tracker on ordinary ground, but the mountains have always confounded him. Where I hid, the terrain was mostly bare rock—little soil to hold a print, no pine needles to give away my steps. He would have lost the trail long before nightfall."

"Maybe we have a little time together," he murmured, his voice lowering. Then a thought seemed to come to him, and he tilted his head slightly. "But I haven't even asked about your plans."

She shrugged. "I didn't come to hunt, but I can't stay long. Father grows uneasy when I'm gone for too many days. I don't want him wondering why I keep slipping away from camp."

Travis exhaled, a crooked smile forming on his lips despite the disappointment in his eyes. "I'd hoped for more, but I'll take whatever time you can give."

Wren's gaze drifted across the room. A modest bookshelf stood against one wall, crowded with worn volumes. In the center of the room, a small coffee table bore a collection of keepsakes: faded photographs, a carved wooden box, and more books with edges that had softened from years of handling.

She turned back to him, her expression sharpening. "So, Travis," she said, "who was it that tried to kill you?"

"I don't know his name," Travis said quietly. "He wore a hooded coat like Reilly's—same markings etched into the arrows."

Wren's eyes narrowed. "You think he was one of ours?"

"His gear certainly suggested it."

"Was there a horse nearby?"

"Not that we noticed."

Her frown deepened. "Three men had kill orders, Reilly among them, but I was never told their targets. Describe him."

"Rust-colored hair, coppery beard, a jagged scar across his forehead." Travis traced a line just above his right eye.

Wren drew a sharp, involuntary breath, the sound cutting through the quiet room. Her gaze locked on the space where his finger had moved, as though she could see the scar itself hovering there.

"Grady Henderson," she whispered. "One of our best archers."

"Grady would have killed me if Sacha hadn't intervened," Travis said, the words carrying the quiet weight of a truth.

Wren studied him for a moment. "Tell me about Sacha. Something about him stirs a memory, but I can't place it."

Travis shook his head slightly. "I barely know him. I never heard him approach—never even suspected anyone was near. When I asked Pastor Parker about it later, he said God sometimes sends help in disguise—like an angel when we're in desperate need."

Wren's lips curved in a faint, wry smile. "He doesn't look like any angel I've ever imagined," she said, "but I've never seen one. Still, you can tell by watching him move that he has major skills."

"I agree," Travis replied softly.

They sat in the firelight, voices low, unaware that the walls were only thin drywall—poorly insulated. Down the hallway, Sacha lay awake, hearing nearly every word they spoke.

Chapter 24

Reilly stood at the open door, the cool air brushing his face as he peered inside and caught Brody's sour expression in the dim glow of the candlelight.

"Come in, Reilly," Brody said.

Reilly stepped inside and found a chair directly across from his leader, the wooden seat creaking faintly beneath him.

"What's the story behind you tracking Wren?" Brody asked, his voice edged with curiosity.

Reilly felt the familiar tightness in his chest. *Why does he* probe *me like this?* he questioned. "Sir, do you recall I mentioned a man was with her?"

"Of course. But how does that connect to you trailing Wren from camp?"

"Sir, that's the point. I believe he's from the POF. I thought she would—"

"Your report was clear: a single hunter with no visible ties to any group."

"Yes, sir, but I have changed my mind since then," Reilly explained. "Why would Wren be anywhere near the enemy. At the cave, she became defensive when I asked her questions about him."

"Defensive how?"

"When I pressed her on which group he belonged to, she became angry. It didn't sit right. Then the other night I saw her slip out of camp. Something felt off, so I followed to see if she was meeting him again. That's all, sir."

"Did she meet him?"

"She kept just beyond reach, then vanished somewhere near the mountains." The memory cut sharp: shattered rock scattered where Wren must have climbed—and his own agonizing attempt to follow, hobbled by a throbbing hip.

Brody let the silence stretch. "Here's a thought, Reilly. Would an enemy have pulled you from harm's way and stayed with her when Wren cut out an arrow from your hip the way he did?"

"I don't know how to answer that."

"Oh, cut it out, soldier!" Brody's tone hardened, the scent of burning candles sharpening in the close space. "You knew exactly what you were doing. Your decision to pursue one of our own was reckless and irresponsible. Wren's father is my oldest friend and my first officer—I've trusted him since the days right after the separation. She would never betray Cohen or me. Your story sounds absurd?"

"You weren't there, sir. You didn't see the way they looked at each other."

Brody studied the younger man, distrust simmering beneath his calm. He could not afford to let this exaggerated tale ripple through camp—Reilly already carried himself with the quiet confidence of someone who believed he deserved a command. "So you threw it all away just before dawn, watching her leave, fully aware Wren's one of our finest hunters and practically family to me—like my own blood."

"I understand why you'd think that."

Reilly realized Brody had shut down his complaint, despite his presenting information that could protect the camp. Masking the discomfort that burrowed inside, he replied, "Maybe so, sir."

For a moment, the thought of getting back at Brody for dismissing him flickered through Reilly's mind as a sharp knock rattled the doorframe.

"Who is it?" Brody called.

"Cohen, sir."

"Come in, Cohen." The first officer stepped inside, settled into a chair, and leveled a piercing stare at the archer.

"Reilly, you're dismissed," Brody said. "But mark this: you do not leave camp without permission from Cohen or me."

"Sure," Reilly muttered, rising.

Once the door fell shut behind him, Brody shifted his attention to Cohen. "Is your daughter back at camp yet?"

"No, sir. I expect she's out hunting again."

Brody saw no reason to bring up Reilly's suspicions. He remained certain of her loyalty. "What do you have, Cohen?"

Cohen sat on the edge of a chair. "I've had a thought that may cast light on our earlier discussion concerning the leak."

"Oh?"

"Do you recall the man we took in several months ago—Sacha Bourget?"

"The fellow from New Orleans."

"That's him," Cohen said. "Well, he's missing. Raines hasn't seen him in three or four days and assumed I'd sent him hunting. I asked around the camp, but no one could pinpoint when they last saw him."

"He's not on assignment?" Brody asked.

"He is not, but I was going to send him out to hunt for game—he's done well for us before."

"What did you mean by, 'possibly clearing something up'?"

"It occurred to me he might be the source leaking information to those other towns. I've mulled it over for days and can't come up with anyone else who would. Our people are devoted to our cause. We welcomed this man on his word alone, right before we began sending our archers on special assignments. He stands out as a plausible candidate."

Brody braced his palms on the desk's edge, the wood cool under his skin. "A reasonable suspicion, but don't lock onto him too tightly—we risk missing the real culprit. People change, Cohen, even those who've been with us a while. He might have been injured while hunting. Or he moved on. I hope neither proves true, because the man was a special fighter. We could use him in our endeavors."

"I agree."

Brody turned, leaning once more against the desk. "While you're here, there's another matter we should discuss. I want to launch phase two of our plans—and soon." He crossed to the map pinned on the adjacent wall. "We should begin striking towns within the next few days. Surely, the fear we instill will compel them to surrender control of their groups."

"Might work—that's what we want," Cohen replied. "How many men?"

"We can't leave the camp bare and exposed. Twenty should suffice to inflict enough damage."

"I hope you're right," Cohen said.

"Count me among them. I want to lead the first strike."

"Are you certain, Brody?"

Brody traced a finger along the map's worn lines. "Yes, I will join them. We'll start with Pattonville, then DeKalb and Clarksville. Soon, these camps will know Black Arrow is the strongest and the one to lead."

"Will be a powerful persuasion," Cohen declared. "They'll understand right away that we mean business. I'll see to the supplies and have the men ready to move out." He started toward the door, then paused and turned. "Should we include Reilly in the fight?"

Brody hesitated only a moment, staring out the window at a red bird perched on the fence. "No. Keep him here making arrows. That suits him best."

"Yes, sir." Cohen stepped through the door and was gone.

Chapter 25

Logan and his friends finally arrived at the outskirts of Lawton, Oklahoma, where old buildings stood abandoned. The sight of electric poles scattered across the roads, structures overtaken by overgrown vines, and trees penetrating roofs resembled a city devastated by war. Once vibrant houses lay in ruins, neglected streets showed clear signs of drainage issues. Placards hung askew on the few remaining businesses, while parking lots exhibited a chaotic maze of shattered glass.

"This place looks like a ghost town," Derrick said.

"Or a combat zone," Logan added.

"Yeah, I thought our little township looked bad," Randall replied gazing out the front window. "This is awful."

The days of the separation came flooding back to Logan. "I figure the cities couldn't handle the influx of people. When they came here, they needed provisions and probably turned to the woods. Nothing else matters if you're out of food. We are fortunate, it seems."

"The North worsened the problem by forcing people to the South," Derrick explained.

"Yeah, we are part of those people."

"And our homes were barely north of the thirty-sixth parallel."

Logan responded, "It didn't matter to them where we lived. They came with force to make sure we left one way or the other."

The exchange brought back memories of the day Kincaid lost his family, a day he wished to someday erase from his mind. "Logan, how far is it to Fort Sill?"

"Only a few miles, I believe. This highway should lead us to it."

Thirty minutes later, they drove past the front entrance of the abandoned army post.

"Keep driving, Derrick," Logan uttered. "Roy Wayne lives on the backside of the base."

Ten minutes later, they arrived at an old house. The disheveled neighborhood was impossible to ignore; the shingles were aging, and the decaying wood beneath the peeling paint showed years of neglect. Broken window frames and shutters lay strewn across the ground.

A man of Indian descent stepped off the porch wearing an old cowboy hat and a well-worn, light blue, Texas-style checkered shirt.

Logan hurried from the truck. "Roy Wayne, how are you?"

"Logan Weston, my friend, you made it!"

"The place looks so different. I couldn't be sure you still lived here."

"This has been home since the separation?"

Logan extended his hand to shake.

"I guess you're here about those weapons," Roy Wayne stated.

"Yeah, we want to look inside that bunker before settling for the night. We'll load up in the morning. You wouldn't believe the shape of those old roads?"

"Oh yes, I would. Don't forget, I visited your place. Along the way, I came to some rough places."

"Please come meet the guys." Logan led his friend to the truck and introduced him. "Roy Wayne, would you show us where those weapons are?" he asked.

"Sure, just drive the way you came in," Roy Wayne remarked as he joined the others in the truck. "There's another old entrance on the backside of the base. That's where the refuge is."

They spotted a sign for the Wichita Mountains Wildlife Refuge about three miles down the road. In a while, Derrick steered the truck toward the locked gate.

"I have a key," Roy Wayne said as he got out.

"How did you come to have that?" Derrick asked.

"The army left the gate open, so I put my lock on it," Roy Wayne replied, walking away.

"So they left it unlocked?" Logan asked when his friend returned.

"I came across the building while I was out hunting. Since the government owns the land, they can build whatever they want. After I found the weapons inside, I decided to lock the gate because if my people knew about them, they would have taken them all and started their own war. Drive on through. I will keep it unlocked until we come out."

They arrived at the large metal storage building and exited the truck.

"I believe the army thought it would look empty after they pulled out," Roy Wayne commented.

"Secrets are the government's specialty," Kincaid said. "They concealed the weapons because they believed that if we discovered them, they would give us a better chance to win our country back."

Logan responded, "Leaving them behind might backfire on them."

Roy Wayne gestured towards the building as he walked on. "Inside the sliding door is a hidden staircase. You'll want to head down to the lower level." He pulled open the metal door until it banged against a stop. "Alright, it's over there," he said, pointing to a distant location.

When they reached the spot, Roy Wayne showed them a peculiar iron door flat on the floor. "Just pull it and toss it towards the back of the building."

Derrick grabbed hold, yanking it open to reveal stairs leading downward.

Roy Wayne stepped into the dark stairwell and paused. "I forgot how dark it is down here. I put a generator outside with a small can of fuel next to it. Could someone please find it and get it started?"

"Leave that to me," Kincaid said, rushing towards an exit. Within a few minutes, the generator rumbled.

Roy Wayne raised a lever, and the lights came on. "Okay, follow me."

They stepped inside the bunker and found hundreds of government-issued handguns and M4 carbine rifles, along with a considerable stockpile of .223 and .30-06 caliber rifles. They saw .22 caliber rifles and handguns, hundreds of .30-30 Winchesters, and an assortment of models of shotguns. Many of the crates contained weapons confiscated from gun owners. The original tags from the pawnshops and gun stores still hung on guns inside the second group of crates. They also counted seventeen rocket-propelled grenade launchers in separate containers, with the warheads placed beside them.

Randall asked, "I wonder why they have rocket launchers sitting with the guns?"

"The only thing I can think of is they ran out of room," replied Roy Wayne.

"This is strange, though I bet you're right."

Once they finished assessing the array of weapons, the men drove from the refuge to Roy Wayne's house.

When they reached his driveway, Roy Wayne stepped out of the truck. "Logan, I have something else I need to talk to you about before you go. Can you please come inside for a moment?"

Logan turned to the other men. "Sorry, guys. Just wait for me." He got out of the truck and followed Roy Wayne through the doorway.

He found a straight-back chair and sat, gazing at his friend. "Roy Wayne, what's going on?"

"Logan, our people are worried. Once, we lived free alongside the wolf and the eagle. Our ancestors hunted the buffalo and the deer for food, and we made clothes and blankets with our hands and survived well. But as you know, the white man took most of our land, killed the buffalo, and through the years, we became dependent on the white man's ways. Twenty years ago, they forced us from our homes. My people came to Lawton, while others scattered to other places. Now, my people all want to leave Oklahoma. The elders said to ask Logan about moving to his town."

"Your people want to walk all the way to Pattonville?

"Some have their horses."

"Okay, but why come that far from your home? I'm sure there are other places closer."

Roy Wayne turned and gazed out the window, his eyes narrowed. "Maybe I shouldn't tell you, but I will. Some of our men crossed the parallel line into the northern zone early in the year."

"Wow! That's dangerous."

"I know. The men met some of our people in the night for supplies. But they saw something that frightened them: the North fighting rebels from another country. The men overheard them speaking in Arabic. They must have crossed the Canadian border and are here to take our country from us."

"We heard how they came."

"Our people are worried that a war might escalate and reach Oklahoma. Our tribal elders hope we can move to Pattonville since it's farther from the danger. We believe it will be safer for the women and children away from here." Roy Wayne sighed. "Logan, I hope you can forgive me. I mentioned your town to them and hope you don't mind that I shared my thoughts about you. The elders now trust you just as I do."

"I appreciate that, Roy Wayne. So, does this mean *your* family will also move away from Oklahoma?"

"Yes, all of our people will go there if you allow us. They have asked my wife to help the elderly and the children. If we like your town, we might stay for a long time and help protect you from the other white men." Roy Wayne chuckled.

"I should mention that there aren't a lot of empty homes in our town. Many have fallen into disrepair over the years. Until you can build your own place, most must rely on tents or makeshift structures. We might have a few shelters available, but there won't be enough for everyone. Some land is available."

"The important thing is the safety of our children and the elderly. Our ancestors lived in tepees for centuries, and if necessary, we can do it again."

"I don't see any reason you can't, but the guys and I won't be able to wait for you. They're eager to get back and unload the weapons. You might have to rescue us if our truck has any issues," Logan said.

"Take all the weapons, Logan, because you might need them someday. We'll get to Pattonville on our own. If you run into trouble, we'll pull you with the horses." Roy Wayne laughed. "It's nice to know we're welcomed and needed."

"Sure, you're a US citizen and can live anywhere you choose."

"Thank you. We'll pack tonight and leave right behind you."

"How many people are we talking about?"

"Maybe four hundred, including women and children."

"Four hundred, huh? I suppose the more, the merrier."

Chapter 26

Travis pressed his forehead to the cool glass, breath fogging the pane. A sparrow swept past the window on silent wings, then dropped to the damp earth. It scratched once, twice, unearthed a shiny seed, and picked it up with its beak. In a flutter of brown feathers, the bird vanished into the gray sky. He sensed the familiar verse rise unbidden: *"Look at the birds of the air… Are you not of more value than they?"* A soft smile touched his lips. "God has truly blessed us."

Limited by resources over the years, but they never went hungry. "Thank You, Lord, for watching over us," he whispered, his words warm against the chilled window.

Yet God's steady presence did not ease the urgent knot in his chest. His father and the others should have returned days ago; Logan had promised four or five at most. Travis's eyes followed the muddy lane that disappeared between the trees. No truck. No friends of his. "Lord, keep Your hands on my father and those guys," he murmured. "Protect and shield them from harm."

He turned from the window, his thoughts shifting to Wren. She had stayed an extra day, then left with the promise to return soon. Already, the house felt emptier without her smile and laughter.

Sacha's unexplained absence weighed on him as well. The steady rain offered an easy explanation for hunters caught in a downpour—but his father had taken a liking to the man. Travis owed it to Sacha to at least ask around. As the last drops pattered against the roof and faded, he lifted his bow from the corner, slung the quiver over his shoulder, and stepped into the cool, damp air.

The trading post wrapped him in familiar warmth the moment he pushed open the door: the rich scent of honey nectar, the low murmur of voices, and the soft brush of cards across a scarred table.

Jacoby Meyers and his friends sat at their usual table near the window. He took a sip of his drink and spotted Travis coming inside. "Hey, Buddy, I don't see you much anymore," he said, glancing back at his hand.

"Yeah, I know. How are you guys doing?"

"We are fine," Jacoby answered with a nod, still focusing on the game.

Travis shifted his weight, boots squeaking on the plank floor. "Hey, I'm looking for the man who has been staying at our house. His name is Sacha Bourget. I need to find him."

Terrence Jones leaned back. "I know him. Met him a few days ago, but haven't seen him but the once."

"I saw him yesterday," Jacoby offered, turning to gaze at them. "Where?"

"On the road north of town. Looked like the man was heading out to hunt. He was looking straight ahead for the game."

Travis's fingers tightened around his bow. "Yeah, that's what he told me, but he hasn't come in. I'm worried something might have happened to him." He turned toward the door.

"I wouldn't worry about your friend," Jacoby said with a grin. "He looked like he could take care of himself."

"Thanks, Jacoby," Travis replied, his words carrying a faint edge of doubt and worry as Sacha's intention gnawed at him.

"Where are you going, Travis? You should stay and play cards."

"I'd love to, but I really need to find Sacha."

"Okay, another time."

Travis pressed on along the north road until a familiar, rusted gate marked SALISBURY came into view, leaning crookedly against a gray, weathered post—just as his father had described. He walked through an opening and followed the winding lane, where overgrown bushes brushed his sleeves with damp leaves. At the end stood a weather-beaten farmhouse, its porch planks creaking under his boots. No one stirred. No voices sounded.

Then the door swung open, revealing Sacha beside an older woman, both staring out at him.

Sacha stepped forward with a wide grin as he leaned his bow against the house.

Travis glanced between them, struck by the stark age difference. *Surely not,* he thought. "Um, I've been looking for you, Sacha," he said.

"Come in and sit at the kitchen table, fellows," the woman said. "I'll bring you some water."

"Thanks," Travis replied, "but I'm not thirsty."

"I'm really sorry about this, Travis," Sacha responded with a curious expression. "How did you know I was here?"

"Father reminded me of this place."

Once they were seated, Sacha fixed his eyes on him. "I know what you're thinking. Maybe you thought we're together. Well, you can put that out of your mind. Her name is Gaela Woods, and I know her well. This farm belongs to Gaela, and she and your father have already met."

Gaela reached for some dry wood and shoved it into the wood cook stove, then set a pot of water atop it. "I'm glad to meet you, Travis," Gaela offered, rising. "Maybe someday you and Logan will let me cook dinner for you."

Travis shifted his gaze to her and nodded. "That would be fine. I remember my father mentioning you. He told me this was the place they planned to—" He paused, not wanting to spill too much of Logan's plan.

Sacha leaned forward with a slight grin. "Travis, I'm already aware of the weapons. I know Logan will bring them to this farm. You see, Gaela and your father have already discussed an arrangement."

The words settled over Travis like the last pieces of a puzzle, filling in the empty spaces. Still, a thread of discretion remained heavy in his mind—who was Sacha Bourget?

Sacha yearned to tell Travis that Gaela's skills surpassed those of any simple farmhouse woman—but what if this group wasn't right for what lay ahead? One wrong move could spoil everything.

"Travis, it's a long story," Sacha continued. "Maybe I'll tell it someday. Just know that Gaela and I once worked together."

"Oh, okay—that's a relief," Travis replied, so they might stop staring. "I'll have questions later, but maybe we should head home now." His chair scraped back as he stood. "Father and his friends haven't returned, and I'm worried."

Sacha nodded and rose. "Then what are we doing here?" he answered with a grin. "Gaela, we'll see you later." They gathered their gear and headed toward the door.

"Bye, fellows," she replied. "I'm sure I'll see you again soon."

The door closed behind them, and the two men started back toward Pattonville, the air much cooler now along the sodden path.

Chapter 27

The forest held an unnatural stillness as Sacha and Travis drew nearer to Pattonville.

"Something is wrong," Sacha said.

Travis listened as he scanned the trees. "No birds chirping."

A woman's cry suddenly echoed in the wind.

Sacha raised his bow an d pointed toward the town. "We'd better hurry."

As they ran, more screams sliced through the air from the direction of town. They reached the edge of the woods and looked toward the town.

Travis's sharp gaze took in the scene before them. "Our people are being attacked and there are a lot of them."

Sacha nodded. "That's got to be Black Arrow. I see at least a dozen." As Travis shifted farther to the right, Sacha said, "let's disrupt their assault."

Travis slipped behind a thick tangle of vines and shrubs, grabbing a handful of arrows, eyes searching for a target. He inched forward for a clearer view, his footsteps sinking softly into the carpet of damp leaves and pine needles as the sharp screams continued.

An attacker had seized a woman by her dress, dragging her down the street.

Oh, no. Can't let them take her, Travis thought.

Raising his bow, arrow notched and string drawn taut, he searched for a clear shot, careful not to hit the woman. Moments later, she yanked herself free, creating space between them. Travis released the arrow, striking the man in the side. The attacker grasped the shaft and crumpled to the ground as the woman fled.

Another assailant loosed an arrow that felled a young man. Travis quickly drew the bowstring again, aimed at the intruder's upper back, and watched as he dropped to the ground. A second attacker, seeing his companion fall, turned to fire an arrow toward Travis, but Sacha's keen eyes caught the movement and sent a projectile into the man's chest.

When he had scanned the area once more, Sacha signaled for Travis to edge farther right, spotting two figures half-hidden behind a cluster of pines. As Travis advanced, an arrow whistled past him and thudded into a tree just inches away. He quickly fell to the ground, taking cover behind a rough-bark pine, while scanning for the archer. Where had he gone?

About thirty yards away, a clump of sage rustled. He noticed an assailant crawling through the tall grass, trying to slip away. Another archer waited in the opposite direction, watching from behind a small thicket near a large oak, only twenty feet away.

Travis charged him, his eyes fixed. The attacker hearing a sound, pivoted, bowstring drawn, and released his arrow just as Travis closed the gap—the projectile narrowly missed his head. He snatched the man's weapon and flung it aside, but the assailant reached for a knife. Without hesitation, Travis kicked it away and drove his fist into the side of the man's head. The attacker stared blankly at the trees for a moment before collapsing onto the ground.

Sacha released an arrow from forty yards, hitting another scaling the side of an outlying building. He then dashed across the road and, in only a few heartbeats, brought down two more attackers.

More screams rang out, drawing Sacha's gaze toward an older woman. A man with a bow in one hand had his other arm locked around her, dragging her toward the woods. As arrows whizzed by from two more intruders, Sacha sprinted forward. In one leap, he planted a foot on the attacker's head, forcing him to release her. She reached for Sacha, and he pulled her to safety behind the nearest building. Gazing into her eyes, he said, "Stay down until this is over."

"But they shot Sarah, my neighbor. I saw her on the ground crying," she wailed as tears flowed down her face.

"You can't worry about her right now. We'll help her in a while."

He turned when he heard a motor growing louder. Just ahead, Logan and his friends sped past in a truck. *I don't believe it. A truck?*

They came to a stop amidst the chaos, and Kincaid and Derrick jumped out of the vehicle, weapons in hand, firing several rounds at the intruders. Three archers fell, sending a wave of panic through the Black Arrow entourage. They bolted to the woods, disappearing into the undergrowth without a trace.

Travis and Sacha held their weapons high to show the others they were not enemies.

"Travis, is that you?" Logan said, gazing their way.

"Yes, and Sacha," Travis replied as they jogged down the street to where his father and friends waited beside the truck.

Derrick watched them as they drew closer. "What are you men doing out there?" he asked.

"Just a minute," Sacha replied. "There are injured people who need attention. Several townsfolk took arrows."

Logan looked around, taking in the scene. "Travis, find Doc Duggan and make sure he attends to those who need him the most first."

Derrick continued to stare at Sacha, "Okay, now tell us what happened here?"

"Travis and I were on our way back from the Salisbury farm," Sacha explained. "As we got closer, we heard people screaming. We stopped on the outskirts of town and spotted Black Arrow's men positioned on the edges of town, launching arrows toward the street and the people. We counted about a dozen archers."

"How many of our folks are injured?" Logan asked.

Sacha shrugged. "I don't know—I saw some go down. Others helped carry the injured away. A few people brought out bows and returned fire, but most seemed terrified."

Kincaid laid his rifle in the back of the truck. "Well, it looks like Black Arrow has upped the ante. One person dying at a time wasn't enough."

"They'll probably head toward their camp now," Sacha said. "Should we try to track them?"

Logan gazed toward the trading post, where volunteers were treating some of the wounded. "If we face Black Arrow again, we'll be better prepared. However, these weapons may not stop them from attacking. If only we could convince them to end this foolishness and work with us."

Travis ran up to Logan and placed his bow on the hood of the truck. "Some of the injured are being treated by Doc Duggan—others are helping at the trading post. I heard arrows struck four or five people, and one of them might not live."

Derrick ejected the last few bullets from his weapon. "Logan, let's talk to the witnesses and see if they know anything."

"Hold up on that," Logan replied, shaking his head slowly. "We can do that later. Let them get treated first—we have other things to take care of." Sacha stood nearby, looking into the truck bed. "I suppose you heard the guns when Derrick and Kincaid fired at 'em?"

A faint grin crossed Sacha's face. "Guns firing are hard to ignore, Logan."

"I apologize for not mentioning our plan earlier. I only met you a few days ago. But since you've helped to safeguard our people, you deserve the truth."

"I'm afraid I haven't been completely honest with you either," Sacha replied with a sheepish grin on his face.

"Oh, really? Well, I am curious that you mentioned the Salisbury place."

"Yeah, maybe we should talk."

"Good," Logan agreed.

Sacha gave a half-nod. "How about setting up a meeting and include your friends? I have information you all should hear."

Logan gazed at him with a curious grin. "I'll set it up."

Chapter 28

Logan had called his friends to the old church for the meeting, while others helped the wounded. The air inside carried a comforting scent of aged pine pews and the faint trace of candle smoke from years of use.

When the last stragglers settled, Sacha stepped into the thin beam of afternoon light that slanted through the stained-glass windows. He cleared his throat softly, as though testing the silence.

"First, let me clear something up about myself. New Orleans is my hometown. I never meant to deceive any of you, but I had to protect my cover until I knew how to move forward." He paused, cracking his fingers as he looked at them. "A few months back, I joined Black Arrow."

A heavy hush fell over the room, thick as the dust motes drifting in the light. Every man held his breath—the only sound was the distant creak of a settling beam overhead.

"I sure wish we'd known that," Logan said.

"I ask you not to judge until you've heard the full story," Sacha continued. "I assumed a false identity, hoping not to raise alarms. Getting accepted was a gamble—I half expected them to turn me away at the gate."

"Or shoot you," Kincaid replied with a grin.

"They allowed me to enter their camp, but I never felt a sense of belonging. Inside the camp, there is another woman I'm associated with. Her name is Coco. She entered ahead of me to keep suspicion low and is still gathering information. I had hoped we'd find fighters willing to help us against the North. Once I realized Black Arrow's true aim was to betray the other camps, I found no reason to stay. I slipped out and started searching for other groups. A few days later, I crossed paths with Travis and Logan in the woods."

Travis nodded. "That was the day he saved my life."

Sacha then lifted his chin. "May I explain why I'm really here with you?"

He observed each of them as they conveyed their consent with a nod.

"Many in the North quietly oppose the new laws and the government's grip on things," Sacha added. "These are honest, red-blooded Americans who still love their country, even if they can't say it aloud."

"You mean there are Christians who refused to leave when we did?" Derrick asked.

"Yes, quite a number, and many now make up our alliance. They stay hidden, but stand as one. We call ourselves the Patriot Endeavor. Most members lead ordinary lives while working secretly against the rogue government. After two decades of patient, grinding effort, we have built what we have today."

Logan raised a hand. "So the people you're describing—they aren't the ones who came armed to the teeth and drove us from our homes and fired at us across the line?"

"Some of them might have been," Sacha admitted, meeting Logan's gaze without flinching. "But many disagreed with their orders and followed them only because their families were under government surveillance. What you may not know is these Christians live every day in fear."

"I figured there were some, but it sounds like many stayed," Logan said.

Sacha nodded. "They refused to leave during the Separation, holding onto hope that circumstances would improve. Now, life in the North feels like a third-world country. They are stuck in jobs they are untrained for, receiving almost no pay for endless hours of work. After enduring this for years, bringing them into our fold wasn't difficult."

"Sounds like some are worse off than us," Derrick murmured, rubbing the callused edge of his thumb against his knuckles.

"Many have died trying to keep our secret, but the government learned about us a few years ago and is trying to break the alliance. Old prisons are used for those who let slip they were involved."

"Oh, no," Derrick said.

"Sacha," Logan said softly, "how does any of this help us here in the South? We're hundreds of miles from the periphery. Maybe they've suffered some hard times, but have they felt the same losses we have? Our numbers have declined from starvation alone."

"There is death everywhere," Sacha replied. He exhaled slowly. "But there may be more survivors in the South than you might think. I've traveled around the lower states and spoken with groups hoping for change and ready to stand with us."

"You mean they will fight too?"

He gave an assuring nod. "Yes, and hopefully we can soon add Black Arrow to the mix. Like you, Logan, I believe it's wise to gather as many allies as we can before confronting the North. Black Arrow has seasoned soldiers who are battle-tested. With help from this group and others, I believe we can reach their leader, Brody Myles, and show him that a united front can give us a chance to reclaim the nation and set it right. Brody has a thirst for conflict, and I would rather he direct that energy toward the North."

"Amen to that," Derrick said.

Kincaid rose abruptly from the pew, his boots scraping against the floorboards. "I'm sorry, but I'm not convinced that Black Arrow will ever join us. Ever since they sent an assassin after my friend Edmond, all I've wanted is to confront them face-to-face. Then today, they attacked the town without warning, claiming another life. How many other towns have they assaulted?"

He walked toward the door, opened it, and paused, resting his hand on the frame. He could still see Edmond lying just outside the church, wailing in pain as blood poured from him. Then he shook his head and stepped out into the gray afternoon.

Logan fixed his gaze on Sacha. "Please forgive Kincaid. He lost his family before he came here. Edmond was one of his closest friends. We'll pray for Kincaid."

Sacha lowered his gaze and then looked back at the others. "Yes, we will. Black Arrow is certainly behind these raids, and people are dying. But hear me: if we unite, we can become something almost unstoppable. It's a chance to set the country right. The South may once again see supplies return—food, various things you need. Towns will thrive again."

Logan leaned forward in his seat. "Just to be clear—you're saying the Patriot Endeavor will stand with us against the government?"

Sacha's mouth curved in the smallest, rueful smile. "They know what's coming for them if they don't. Thousands wait—police, soldiers, patriots across every walk—ready for the signal. Will you join us?"

"Yes. I will," Logan said, his voice steady and assured. "Because I want my son, his wife, and my grandchildren to have the same opportunities I once had."

Sacha's smile flickered, warm and brief. Low murmurs of agreement rose around the room like a shared breath, as every man felt the hope in Logan's simple truth.

Derrick lifted a hand. "Sacha, is there a timetable for heading north?"

"Another good question. Nothing's carved in stone, but time is pressing. Islamic rebels are moving across the Canadian border into Minnesota. The sooner we act, the better our odds of rooting them out. Let me be clear, though, our fight is against both the government and the insurgents."

"This is hard to wrap my head around," Travis said. "I was so young when we crossed into the southern zone—I don't even remember it. Never knew my mother because they took her life. But I do know what it's like to hunt for a rabbit when you're hungry or pick wild berries because you haven't eaten in days. I'm not complaining—Father somehow kept us fed. Still… when you talk about a conflict with the North, I look around and see older men—like my father. Some can't run or carry a heavy pack. Are you sure we have enough able fighters to make a difference?"

Derrick grinned and gave Logan's shoulder a light, proud tap. Logan sat straighter, a faint flush of warmth gathering in his cheeks.

Sacha looked down at the floor, gathering his thoughts, then met Travis's eyes. "Not with only one group. Members of the Patriot Endeavor haven't walked your exact road, but they understand the challenges you faced and stand with you. I hope the other southern groups will join us as well."

Logan's smile broke wide as he turned to his son. "Glad you're thinking of me. Listen—there are always things we crippled old men can do in a fight. We'll offer ourselves if it means getting the country back."

"He's right," Sacha added. "Sometimes the task is as simple as driving a team to a drop point. Or observing in an undercover operation."

Derrick stood slowly. "So you're saying we really have no choice—we gotta move against the North?"

"There's always a choice," Sacha replied. "You can stay out of it, but not if you want your country back." Heads nodded around the room; he could sense the shift, the slow kindling of interest. "For now, let's set that all aside. Our immediate task is to stop Black Arrow from taking more lives and to bring them along with us. We'll need every group for what lies ahead."

Logan eased his weight in the pew, the wood giving another soft creak. "Sacha, I'm grateful that we're not alone in this fight. But there's one question you still haven't answered."

Sacha tilted his head. "What question?"

"What were you really doing at the Salisbury farm?"

Sacha smiled, turning to him. "Not what you're imagining. I told you—the Patriot Endeavor has been making plans for a long time, and others in the South are working to make it happen—including Gaela Woods. She's one of the covert operatives for the Endeavor—handles radio messages with our friends in the North and passes them on. The day I went to the Salisbury place was to provide her with an update on my findings regarding Black Arrow. She was supposed to send that information out. That's all."

Logan's heart thudded as his fingers tightened on the pew's arm. "Gaela is part of your Patriot Endeavor?"

"Yes—all of you could be." Sacha looked slowly around the room. "What do you say, men? Will you join us?"

Travis felt a surge of excitement at the thought of Black Arrow and their people working side by side—and at the opportunity to see Wren more often—if they could convince them. "But what if Black Arrow declines?" he asked.

"We'll proceed without them. If we can explain our position like I did today, perhaps they will consider our invitation. Despite what Brody Myles claims, he wants to go home. The Patriot Endeavor offers him the most straightforward route—far better than the empty promises the North dangled."

Randall's brow furrowed. "What promise?"

Sacha's expression darkened. "So, you haven't heard?" The blank looks on their faces assured him they were unaware. "The North promised Brody and his people they could return home—if they eliminated most of the Christians in the South."

The room erupted, voices overlapping in sharp bursts of outrage.

"No wonder they want to kill us!" Derrick shouted.

Randall shook his head. "How can this be happening. They made us targets."

Logan raised his hand, his voice cutting through the chatter. "Fellows, fellows—this is our government's oldest trick. To pit us against each other so they don't have to dirty their own hands."

"Exactly. That's the main reason Black Arrow came for you," Sacha said. "But Brody's chasing a delusion. They can never trust the North."

"Okay, back up, Sacha. You mentioned radios," Logan said, leaning forward again. "You said Gaela receives messages at the farm. I saw no tower—just a barn, outbuildings, the house, and—"

"What else?" Sacha prodded, a knowing glint in his eye.

"The grain silo? The antenna is up there?"

"Correct."

"And power?"

"After she settled in, our people brought her a solar generator. Enough power for the radio and a few small items—like a coffee pot."

Logan chuckled. "I do enjoy coffee, but I haven't had any in ages."

Sacha raised his hands to calm the group. "Gentlemen," he continued, "our next step is to gather every willing and able fighter you know. Bring them here tomorrow. They need to hear what I've just told you and decide for themselves if they want to fight." He scanned their faces. "I know this can work."

"We'll spread the word," Logan said. "Can we unload the truck now? I could use some rest."

Sacha nodded in agreement. "Sure, I want to see those weapons as well."

"Come on." Logan pushed himself up, wincing slightly. "I reckon that's where Kincaid went. I need to get him sorted out."

Travis watched them file out of the church, the heavy door groaning shut behind them. His thoughts drifted northward, already tracing the long foot trek that awaited. They would first try to persuade Black Arrow to join their cause. Then, memories of those who perished at the periphery drifted through his mind like smoke that refused to clear. The realization that close friends, and even his father, might face death in a confrontation with the North sent a chilling twist of dread through his gut.

The church now stood empty, its silence broken only by the fading echoes of boots. He realized the others had already reached the weapons and the truck, but what cost would they pay for collecting them? Yet deep down, he understood that if a conflict arose, they would need every piece of iron and every bullet to tip the odds in their favor.

"Lord, I fear only that some friends and family may succumb in this confrontation. Please keep us strong and protect Father."

Chapter 29

A gentle breeze stirred as Reilly Brewin pressed his foot against the dirt, extinguishing the fire. He gathered his gear and left the camp, still troubled by the accusations Brody Myles had made against him. Perhaps it was time to remind him of what he is capable of.

The observations he made about Travis Weston—the well-used bow and his extensive knowledge of the woods—confirmed that he was one of their enemies. Years earlier, they had received word that the POF and other groups had skilled archers among their ranks. This realization aligned with the conversations between Travis and Wren in the cave that day. He had considered asking about his affiliation, but chose to listen to their discussion instead. As he expected, Travis avoided mentioning any of the factions.

More evidence of Wren's connection to Travis surfaced two mornings ago when she left camp. When he noticed her departing, he decided to follow, suspecting she intended to meet him. She somehow sensed his presence and slipped away before he could catch up to her. But she would see him soon, face-to-face with Travis, and they would determine who the better archer was.

Defying Brody's orders might bring harsh repercussions, yet wasn't the entire purpose of the plan to eliminate leaders from rival factions? Merely catching Travis and Wren together would prove beyond doubt that she had been consorting with an enemy. The other fighters back at camp would then see that he could meet any challenge Brody set before him—and prevail. He was, after all, a master archer; why should he wait for permission to select his own targets? Soon, he would pick up the trail that led to their enemy camps—and eventually, straight to Travis.

But first, he needed to help a fellow fighter. Solomon Warner never made it to Clarksville to complete his assignment, so he would finish the job himself. He would find a worthy target—perhaps a mayor, a council member, or another person of high importance—and take them out. If Travis is there, he would deal with him immediately.

Exhausted from hours of walking, Reilly spotted the bent, weathered sign for Clarksville next to the road. Knowing he was close, he slipped into the woods to hide and observe.

The town buzzed with activity. People chatted while some haggled over goods on the opposite side of the road. Beneath an overhang on a porch, a group of men exchanged jokes and hearty laughter. Just behind them was an open doorway to a trading post.

At the end of a narrow lane, overgrown with years of bushes and wild shrubs, he noticed two men on horseback, their voices resonating softly. He knew that ordinary townsfolk typically did not have access to horses, which were mainly used for transporting supplies, meaning that at least one of these men must be his target.

After they finished their conversation, the men rode toward the other end of town. As they neared a group of people chatting on the porch, Reilly spotted a badge on the chest of one, suggesting that he might be more valuable than the man beside him.

It was unfortunate that Travis wasn't one of these. *I still have a choice between two,* he thought.

The distance forward was still too far, but how could he resist the urge to support their mission? He moved forward, carefully maneuvering through the dense underbrush and trees, stopping behind a large oak to avoid detection. When he sensed that the riders were still unaware of his presence, he reached for an arrow and notched it. Their horses stopped near the porch as they chatted with those who had gathered.

One of the horses whinnied, and he wondered if it sensed his presence. Wasting no time, Reilly lifted his bow, drew the string taut, and took careful aim at the man with the badge. He released the arrow, watching as it struck the rider's upper body. The man buckled and fell to the ground.

Now that he had completed his task, he quickly moved away from his position, navigating through thick vines and shrubs as wails and screams echoed behind him.

Reilly knew the town might have men capable of tracking him, just as they had when they shot him with an arrow at Deport. He fought against the pain in his still-healing hip, determined to put distance between himself and his pursuers.

Adrenaline surged through his veins as he broke into an unnatural sprint, hoping to escape before they could catch up to him.

Chapter 30

Cohen Daniels stepped into Brody's quarters, the faint scent of campfire smoke clinging to his coat. He eased onto the old couch beside the leader. "The men just finished the first round of exercises," he said.

"Good," Brody said.

Cohen sighed. "We have a problem, sir. We can't locate Reilly this morning."

Brody's head snapped up, and he tossed his notebook across the room. "Are you kidding?" he said.

"No, sir. I spoke with all our people. He never slept in his bunk last night."

Brody exhaled sharply. "That man." His right fist bore into his left hand. "Cohen, we may have to lock him in the cell if he keeps this up. His defiance—I cannot abide it." Pointing his finger across the room, he said, "I told him straight: no one leaves camp without orders from you or me. And what does he do? He slips off to wherever he pleases?" Brody's face reddened as anger gripped him. "That contemptible—"

"Surely he'll come back soon," Cohen offered, trying to smooth things over. "He'll probably drag in some deer meat to smooth things over."

"No." Brody's voice hardened, the faint creak of the couch springs audible as he leaned forward. "This doesn't smell like a hunting trip! It feels like he's gone against us on purpose. I think it's time to make an example of him—reprimand him publicly so the others remember who gives the orders."

Cohen's thoughts drifted to a young man from a few years ago, found lifeless in his cell. He firmly believed in discipline, yet he drew a clear line: it must never descend into torture. Nevertheless, he wasn't the boss.

Brody's eyes narrowed toward the window. "Gather a small group of our men. Make sure you include some of our best archers and one of our better trackers. I don't want this dragging on—we've got another town to hit soon. Find him, Cohen. Bring him back! Tie him and drag him if that's what it takes."

"Yes, sir. I'll go along to make sure they get—."

"No." Brody cut him off with a raised hand. "I need you here. Reilly's rebellion can't stop our work. Keep the training moving." He studied Cohen for a moment longer, then asked, "Did your daughter leave again? I haven't seen Wren around camp."

Cohen hesitated, his head turning toward the window. The only sign left was the single arrow she'd laid on the bed in her room—a sign for him—but it told him nothing about her intentions. "No, sir. I'm sure she's out hunting again."

"Maybe so." Brody stood, the floorboard creaking as he walked to the window, staring out. "I hope this time she's not the reason he left. Too bad she's not here to help track him. Wren's got the best nose for the trail among us."

"We've got other men who can track just fine," Cohen replied.

"I know. Just bring him back, Cohen!" Brody said, turning back toward him.

"Yes, sir. They will."

Chapter 31

Seventy men from the town and the surrounding countryside gathered for the meeting. Sacha repeated the details he had shared with Logan's group, and the words sparked an excitement among them—a sense that things were finally changing. When he finished, most drifted back toward their homes, while Logan and his friends stayed behind to refine their plans.

"Do any of you have ideas for dealing with Black Arrow?" Sacha asked.

Kincaid raised a hand. "We go in as one solid force and make them listen. Black Arrow won't change unless we force the issue—and we have the proper weapons now."

Sacha shook his head and crossed his arms. "If we truly want them as allies, showing up heavily armed will only breed resentment. I understand they've taken lives from you, but overwhelming them with firepower will only invite more bloodshed. That's a poor foundation for a lasting alliance."

"I refuse to face them on uneven terms," Travis said, eyes fixed on the floor, Wren weighing on his mind. "They only have the bow and arrow. The risk of killing many of them with guns is too high."

"But we can't pretend they didn't murder Edmond," Kincaid shot back, his hand striking the old wooden pew.

"Edmond was also my friend," Travis replied, leaning forward to meet Kincaid's gaze. "I was there the day he died—the memory hasn't faded. Still, if we want them on our side, forcing them at gunpoint makes no sense."

"I just don't trust them."

Sacha scanned their faces, noting the concern. "Folks, we're only laying out possibilities. Anyone else want to weigh in?"

"It may not earn their trust at first," Derrick said, setting down a weathered plastic mug of water. "What if we took their leader? Brody would have no choice but to hear us out."

"Kidnap him?" Sacha questioned, pacing slowly in front of them. "Yes, he probably would listen. But I've been inside that camp. The gate is always guarded, the watchtower is never empty. Brody rarely steps beyond the perimeter without his finest archers at his side—and they are deadly accurate with a bow. So, getting him in a spot where we can easily snatch him may not work."

"Wasn't Brody part of the group that hit the town?" Logan asked, leaning forward. "I'm almost certain I saw him in the woods when we rolled in with the weapons shipment."

Travis's head snapped toward his father, eyebrows rising in surprise at Logan's recognition of the leader's face. Was there a history he hadn't revealed?

Logan met his eyes briefly, then glanced away.

Sacha paused in front of him. "If Brody was there, I never saw him."

"Hey, there might be another way," Logan said with a half-smile. "Travis, didn't Wren mention her father opposed using their archers as killers? That he only went along because Brody ordered it?

Travis crossed one leg over the other. "Sounded like Brody holds the reins, and Cohen heeds his word. But even if that's true, their old friendship might keep him loyal."

Logan nodded. "You don't know him, but you know Wren. From what she's shared, do you believe he could sway Brody to step outside the camp—or at least agree to a meeting?"

"I don't know. We'll have to ask her."

Logan shrugged slightly. "Can you find their camp?"

"I've never been there," Travis replied, shaking his head.

"I can," Sacha said, reminding them of his short time in their camp. "I need to bring Coco out before they realize she's been feeding us information. But I can't just stroll back in after leaving without warning. Travis and I will slip in under the cover of night. Maybe I can spot her, too."

"I'm fine with your plan," Logan said, turning to them, "but both of you—move with caution. I can only imagine what they'd do if you're discovered."

"We'll take every precaution," Sacha promised as he spun to face Travis. "Let's collect our gear and move out.

"The door creaked open to the night air, carrying the low drone of crickets as the dry whisper of leaves skittered across the ground. Without a care, the two men stepped into the morning light, heading toward an enemy camp.

Chapter 32

The journey through the woods was brutal as they raced. About midway, the two paused to catch their breath. By sundown, they were watching the camp from a distance, just outside the Black Arrow gate.

As they looked through the fence, they saw several of Brody's fighters. "I don't see Wren. I wonder if she's hunting."

Peering from behind an oak, Travis said, "I hope she's not on the way to my house."

Sacha turned to him. "I wish you thought of that sooner."

Travis shrugged. "We were halfway here when it occurred to me."

"Wait! Is that her, Travis? Look, this side of that group of fighters?"

"That's her, but who's she talking with?"

"That's not Cohen. But, look, she's headed our way."

They crouched behind a cluster of trees beside the main trail, waiting for her approach.

"Wren. Hey Wren!" Travis muttered.

"Reilly, is that you?" she asked, pausing in the path.

Travis stepped out where she could spot him. "No, it's me."

"Travis! What are you doing here? Our hunters are due back soon."

"I'm not alone," he said, pointing toward Sacha.

Sacha poked his head into the opening and waved. "Hello, Wren."

"Travis, what's going on? How did you find our camp?"

"I led us here," Sacha responded. "It shocked me you didn't remember who I was when you came to Travis's house."

"I knew I had seen you before. Sacha, right?"

"Yes. I was in your camp for several months. I expected you'd remember me."

"Things have been chaotic around here. Travis, I was on my way to see you—wondered if I could stay at your place. But what are you doing here?"

"We came to ask if you would try to lure Cohen from the camp," Sacha explained.

"What? Why would I?" Wren replied.

"We really need to speak with him."

"That's a terrible idea. If my father suspects anything, he will send his men to search the woods over for you. He only needs to call out."

"We don't want any trouble," Travis said. "If you could coax him out, so we could talk to him, it would be great. We think he's the one person who might convince Brody Myles to listen to us."

"You're kidding, right?" Wren questioned. "Brody won't listen to you. He'll only arrest you and throw you in jail."

Travis crossed his arms in frustration. "Wren, there is much Brody doesn't know. He might reconsider joining us if he did. I'll share more details later: we just need to see your father for now."

"Wren, you can persuade Cohen to come outside the gate," Sacha said. "Invite him to go hunting with you."

Wren turned and looked out at the forest, wondering how much trouble doing this would cause her. Collaborating with the enemy was a surefire 30-day jail sentence—but what if the talks led to the peace between them she hoped for? She bit the edge of her lip, pondering it. "Maybe. I'll ask. It's been some time since he went hunting, so it could work. But I want you to know I hate lying to my father."

Sacha gave a nod. "We'll explain to him—just act like you knew nothing."

Wren let out a heavy sigh and turned back toward the camp. Cohen was chatting with a group of men who had returned from an unsuccessful hunt for Reilly.

"Father, go hunting with me," Wren asked as she drew close to him.

"Daughter, I have too much to do," Cohen replied.

"Just this once. We haven't hunted together in years."

"That's because I have responsibilities, and you're so good at it."

"Do it for me."

Cohen remembered the arguments they'd had recently. "Sure, we need some time together. Let me get my gear."

Moments later, they left the camp together and made their way down the main trail from camp.

Out of the brush, Sacha and Travis sprang, one of them ahead of Wren and Cohen—the other behind them.

"What is this?" Cohen barked.

Sacha stared into his eyes. "Today is your lucky day."

"Where have you been, Sacha?" Cohen questioned, remembering him. "So, you're the one giving away our plans."

"I don't know what you mean."

"Somebody leaked our intention to the other groups. You!"

Sacha cocked his head, staring at him. What happened to them could only have been coincidental. "Let's say I am responsible, which I'm not. Maybe we should compare your accusations to Black Arrow's violent actions against the innocent."

Cohen's jaw tightened.

"We're willing to offer Black Arrow some leniency for those actions, but right now, you need to accompany us to our camp to resolve some other matters. Come peacefully, and no harm will come to you."

"You'll be sorry for this," Cohen replied, casting a stern glance at him. He noticed Wren's expression and realized she was in on their plan to capture him.

After tying his hands in front of him, they led him away from camp toward Pattonville.

Chapter 33

They found the wood in the forest still soaked, so they camped without heat that night before pressing on through the brisk autumn chill, reaching Pattonville with Cohen Daniels in tow.

Some townsfolk gathered as they hit the center of town, questioning why the man's hands were tied.

Constable Antoine Fisher walked up beside Sacha. "You're Logan's friend, right?"

"That's right," Sacha replied. "We're just talking to him, then we'll let him return to his people."

Antoine eyed him with caution. "One of the Black Arrow?"

"That's right—not the assassin, though."

Disappointment clouded the constable's face. "If you need the jail, just say the word."

They took Cohen to a small room at the back of the church, while Sacha slipped out to fetch Logan and the others.

As the rest of them waited in the candlelit room, Cohen drew Wren aside. "Wren, when did you get mixed up with the POF?"

"Not long ago, Father."

"Have you been to this town before?"

"Yes."

Cohen's brow furrowed with disappointment. "I expected better from you."

Wren didn't flinch—just rolled her eyes. "I haven't spilled any secrets, Father, nor betrayed *the cause*," if that's your concern.

Her words lingered in the cool air. Cohen hesitated, loath to widen the rift between them. These men had dragged him from camp by force—yet Wren had to see how wrong this was. What more did they want beyond prying secrets from him?

He held her gaze. "But you know I'd never condone this. They're our adversaries—you knew that."

"Adversaries?" Her voice sharpened like a blade. "You rarely spoke of living with those from the other factions."

"Our lives were different back then. Years in this wilderness hardened us—the POF and others are enemies now. I saw no need to burden you with this."

She bared her teeth in a quiet snarl. "Father, does our survival truly hinge on slaughtering the innocent? The POF camp would never stoop to the depths Black Arrow has. Brody Myles is rotten with a sickness that has infected you. I hoped you'd find your way back. I clearly was wrong."

The accusation struck Cohen like an arrow through the heart. Those harsh directives had come from Brody, not him. But was she right, he wondered. Had he allowed the man to change him?

He thought of the cold, sodden forest they'd just traversed—the surreal, distant journey on foot, yet his captors had paused to let him rest, sharing water and food. They'd shown more "American" spirit than Black Arrow's camp ever had. Had his people lost that ember of compassion?

He turned back to Wren. "I confess the kindness these men showed was unexpected, and perhaps Sacha wasn't the leak." He paused, searching her face. "Wren, I haven't forgotten the harsh treatment you endured at camp. I regret raising you in that brutal, male-dominated place."

Tears glistened in her eyes as she examined him for truth.

Cohen offered a crooked, rueful smile. "Did you and Travis cross paths in the woods?"

Glancing up at Cohen, Wren said, "I appreciate how you raised me. We survived many challenges with what we had, but everything changed when you gave those orders."

Cohen fell silent. *The orders.* Brody Myles's cold, iron-fisted commands—the ones she'd heard him relay.

"To answer your question, yes," Wren said. "Travis and I met hunting the same spot. I got the only deer—he wasn't thrilled." She shot Travis a modest smile. "Didn't know anyone was there. We talked awhile and became friends."

"How long ago?"

"Weeks," she added, sensing his protective tendency. "Don't interrogate me, please. I'm old enough to choose my friends."

Travis offered a modest, sheepish smile from the table's end chair, listening quietly.

The door creaked open. Randall and Sacha stepped inside, the smell of old wood trailing after them.

"We're the only ones free to talk right now," Sacha said, glancing over at Travis. "Your father's not well. They've taken him to the Salisbury farm so Gaela can tend him. You should go if you need to."

Travis straightened and set his jaw. "I'll stay for now. We have business here."

Sacha turned to Cohen. "Mr. Daniels, I spoke briefly of the Patriot Endeavor on the journey here. May I share more?"

"Whatever you judge best."

"It's not just the North. Islamic insurgents are flooding over the Canadian border, turning northern cities into war zones. The government's compromised—infiltrated from within. Worse is the military cutbacks. That's why they need us so badly."

Cohen shook his head, face paling. "Rebels in the North? How could they allow that?"

"Because it's part of the plan," Sacha said, scraping a chair close and leaning into Cohen's space. "If the North falls, our enemies own the country. We'd offer little if those rebels hit here—but joining the Endeavor, we can make a difference against them."

Cohen's gaze softened with regret. "I didn't realize it was this dire."

"I know, sir—it's hard to grasp."

Cohen eased forward in his chair. "So you have come to rally the southern factions, to stand with the patriotic elements in the military?"

"You got it. I had a feeling I'd like you. Weren't you a Colonel?" Sacha asked.

"I was."

"Colonel, we need everyone who can fire a weapon or slip into the darkness and gather intelligence."

Cohen raised a hand in gentle protest. "No need for the title. I left the army long ago."

"You're still a colonel to me—and that's why I ask you to bear this burden," Sacha said. "I remember Brody as imposing and unyielding, yet he's your leader. We must sway him to our cause."

The room grew quiet as Cohen realized the weight of what they were asking. "You want me to talk to Brody?" he whispered.

"Yes, sir," Sacha replied.

Cohen's jaw dropped as he recalled fleeing the north with his pregnant wife. Near the periphery, he spotted Brody pinned behind a bullet-riddled car, under heavy fire from a young soldier. Creeping up behind the soldier, he knocked him out, earning Brody's gratitude. They parted ways after safely crossing over. Some time later, Cohen and his wife encountered Brody again. Remembering how he had helped him before, Brody invited them to join his camp.

"Good heavens," he said. "I've been friends with Brody for many years and still cannot predict his mindset. But this shift might intrigue him—impossible to say."

"Then you will try?" Sacha asked.

Cohen looked at Wren—the decision would affect her too, but change was overdue. "Yes, I suppose I must. When's the northern push? Brody will demand details."

Wren tapped Travis on the shoulder. "We must go too?"

"I don't know, we'll see," he muttered.

"If it were my decision," Sacha said, "we'd have moved already. The timing rests with operations, but current intelligence suggests two to three months—enough to ready the men."

"There's more you should know," Cohen added. "You must understand that Brody's patience frays quickly. And though I often disagree with his plans, it's my job to relay the orders."

"Understood, but hopefully you won't have to for long," Sacha said.

"Brody was once warm, even compassionate. Now war has made him distant and indifferent. Though we've both changed since the divide."

"If you objected to his ways, why stay with Black Arrow?" Sacha asked.

"It gave us safety when we had nowhere else to go."

"I tried to warn you about Brody, Father," Wren said quietly.

He nodded. "I know, dear. I should have listened." Then he turned to Sacha, "Tell me honestly—do you believe we can reclaim our country?"

"Yes, but not without great cost. Even victory will require years of rebuilding. If we delay much longer, that chance may vanish forever."

Cohen rose slowly. "I'll depart at first light and seek a private word with Brody—perhaps he'll listen."

"That is fine," Sacha replied. "We will pray he hears you."

The words resonated deeply. It had been many years since anyone had prayed for him. "Thank you," he said.

Wren rested a hand on Cohen's shoulder. "Father, I am certain Travis has room for us. There's a small shed out back."

Travis rose from his chair. "No need for the shed, sir. There is plenty of space inside." He glanced at Randall. "How's Father faring?"

"Logan was in a lot of pain when I last saw him—couldn't make another weapons run. I took him to the Salisbury place in the town's wagon. Derrick, Kincaid, and Jacoby took the truck to pick up another load."

Travis stepped forward, motioning toward the door. "Colonel, stay at our place as long as you need. Father's at the Salisbury farm—the house is available. You need a real bed."

Cohen nodded, the exhaustion visible in his eyes. "Rest would be welcome."

Chapter 34

The late-afternoon sun shone brightly over the open road, filling the truck's cab with warm light as Derrick, Kincaid, and Jacoby headed toward Lawton for the second time. The engine purred steadily, no hiccups, no complaints—except for the rough asphalt.

The key turned smoothly in the gate lock. Derrick eased the truck down the narrow lane, tires crunching gravel, until the building appeared like a forgotten bunker half-swallowed by trees. Inside, they moved quickly, stacking rifles and ammunition in their crates, and a few handguns into the bed until the suspension protested. When the last crate was shut tight, they backed out and set up camp right there in the clearing near the building.

Jacoby stood at the edge of the fire, eyes flicking toward the road. "I hope the military doesn't roll up," he said, his voice low, almost lost under the first crackle of kindling. "I'm not ready to fight."

Kincaid crouched, feeding dry oak limbs into the new flames. Sparks skittered upward like startled fireflies. "Somehow I don't think they're losing sleep over this place," he answered, the corner of his mouth twitching. "Not tonight, anyway."

Derrick dragged a weathered wooden crate from beside the building and sat on it, staring into the growing orange heart of the fire. Wood smoke sharp against the back of his throat. "We just need to think about getting these weapons home," he said.

Kincaid gave a slow nod of agreement. "Right, and right now Black Arrow is our only mission."

The fire popped, sending a small shower of embers drifting into the air. Derrick watched them fade into the deepening blue above the treetops. "Guess we'd better rest while we can."

"Yeah," Jacoby muttered, turning so the heat pressed against his back. "Soon as I warm."

He edged closer until the flames painted a shifting motif across his shoulders, and before they settled beside the fire to rest, the three of them sat, inviting the small circle of warmth as the night pressed in around them.

***

The first part of their trip home went smoothly. Later, the engine warmed up. A quick stop to tighten a fan belt fixed the problem. Ten minutes later, they were on their way again.

Forty miles from Pattonville, the road bent around a thick stand of oaks—and there it lay: a massive oak sprawled across both lanes, trunk freshly split, leaves still green.

Derrick eased off the gas, brakes singing. "That tree wasn't here yesterday," he said, eyes scanning the treeline.

Kincaid already had the passenger side door open. "I'll get the chain."

Before they could step out, hoofbeats thundered—sharp and sudden—stopping behind the fallen tree. Five riders burst onto the road, horses snorting steam, bows slung across their backs, faces shadowed under black hoodies.

"Back up, Derrick," Kincaid barked, hand grabbing the dashboard to hold on. "Black Arrow. Has to be."

Derrick threw the truck into reverse, tires spinning once before catching, backing them fifty yards down the straightaway. The riders reined up, milling behind the fallen trunk, horses sidestepping nervously.

"I bet they saw us yesterday," Jacoby muttered, peering through the windshield. "And they probably remembered attacking the town when you arrived in the truck with guns."

Kincaid's jaw tightened. "Doesn't matter what they remembered. We got to keep this load safe."

Two riders nocked arrows, drew, and released them as their horses stamped, impatient. The shafts arced high and fell short, clattering harmlessly on asphalt twenty yards ahead.

"Glad you backed up," Kincaid said. "One tire hit, and we're walking the rest of the way. We've only got one spare."

"They won't target the tires," Derrick replied, gaze steady on the group. "They want the truck and the weapons."

"They're not getting either," Kincaid said.

Derrick glanced at him. "So, you got a plan?"

Kincaid gestured his thumb toward the truck bed. "Shotguns won't reach them. But those .30-30s are sitting on top in one crate. They have a better range. The men's arrows will drop short, but that rifle won't."

He slipped out low, popped a crate lid open, and returned with a Winchester lever-action, brass gleaming dull in the overcast light.

He braced the barrel against the open window frame, worked the lever once, and lined up his shot.

The bullet snapped, echoing off the trees. A bay horse screamed, staggered sideways, legs buckling. It crumpled, rider tumbling free as the animal thrashed on the ground.

The others' mounts reared, eyes rolling white. One man clung desperately as his horse bolted toward the woods, while two others followed in a panic. The last rider hit the ground hard when his horse pitched him. He scrambled up and grabbed the reins, then hauled his downed companion onto the saddle behind him. They vanished into the darkened forest, hoofbeats fading fast.

Silence settled, broken only by the truck's idling rumble and a distant crow's call.

They dragged the heavy chain from the bed, hooked it around the thickest part of the trunk, and pulled the oak aside until the path was clear. Kincaid coiled the chain, threw it into the truck bed, and climbed back in.

Jacoby let out a long breath, staring through the rear glass as they accelerated away. "Man, that's the most excitement I've seen in years."

Derrick gave a short, humorless laugh. "You call that fun? Wait till the real shooting starts. Then you'll really know excitement.

Deep in the forest, several hundred feet from the road, Reilly Brewin crouched among bushes, watching the truck's taillights wink red and then disappear over the rise. The smell of exhaust still hung in the breeze.

Whatever it takes, Reilly thought, fingers tightening on his bow, *I'll get my hands on some of those weapons.*

Chapter 35

Reilly wondered if the truck's destination was Pattonville. Back at camp, he'd caught fragments of talk—whispers about the town and the heavy guns that brought down Black Arrow fighters during their assault.

He set a steady pace, boots grinding against the worn pavement, his aim to arrive before nightfall. The miles stretched on, and before he knew it, the day had surrendered to the night. He then stopped to eat some jerked meat, allowing the pain in his hip to subside, and settled for some sleep against a fallen log.

A few hours later, the wind woke him, tugging at his collar. Under the soft moonlight, he pressed on, feeling refreshed. *Someone,* he told himself, *would have spotted that red truck.*

Morning arrived in a slow spill of gold. He spotted a field with dry winter weeds as they whispered secrets to one another in the wind. At its far edge crouched a ramshackle farmhouse, chimney trailing lazy smoke. Closer to the road, a barn—its boards bleached gray and dipping like a bowl—and splintered livestock fences lay half-buried in the dirt. What had once been neat rows of crops had surrendered to a thick stand of young oaks and pines.

A brown-and-black hound materialized behind him, yapping in sharp, insistent bursts. It trotted closer, halting twenty feet away—hackles raised, teeth bared, ears pinned—with a growl that vibrated the cold air.

Reilly's hand drifted to his quiver. "I've no time for a barking dog."

For a heartbeat, he pictured it: bowstring taut, broadhead slicing air, the mutt's yelp cut short as his projectile punched deep. He could almost smell the copper tang of blood on the wind.

He exhaled, slid the arrow back into the quiver. "It's your Lucky day, mutt."

Stooping, he chose two smooth stones. The first sailed wide and low. The second, he thrust higher and struck the hound's foreleg with a dull thwack. A startled yelp pierced the air, then scrambling paws dashed across the field, his tail low.

"Sorry, buddy," Reilly said. "Have to keep going." He wiped dirt from his hand with his pants leg, watched the dog trot across the field, before continuing his journey.

Miles down the road, a faded sign greeted him: *Pattonville, Population 1172.* He chuckled. "Fifty, maybe, if the graves hadn't taken more."

From the next hilltop, the town unfolded below—main street lined with weathered buildings, a trading post crawled with people haggling in the open air, a white church steeple piercing the sky like a bone.

Reilly remembered the spot all too well—he'd taken out a man here before, moments after they exited the church. The next day, he returned to camp, and Brody raised the stakes: target bigger fish from now on, like a mayor.

He slipped into a cluster of young pines and bushes, needles sharp against his arms, and crouched to watch—no truck in sight. Doubt crept in. Maybe he'd guessed wrong.

Maneuvering deeper into the woods behind a row of houses, the wind soughing through branches overhead. Eventually, the trees gave way to an open field. He dropped behind some dense brush and scanned the main road.

A hundred feet away stood a lone house. In the yard, a man progressed through his martial arts forms, precise and unhurried—and then Reilly saw his face.

Travis Weston.

The name landed like a stone in his gut. *Finally.*

He eased behind another cluster of pines, thirty feet out. His pulse throbbed, questioning. Confront the man outright? Or aim and release—one clean shot, the way he'd ended the others? The bow felt warm in his grip, familiar as breathing.

Beyond the brief clash in the cave, Travis was a blank page to him—still, he was Black Arrow's enemy, and a possible reason Wren remained distance. The truck could wait. He was the prize, unexpected and overdue.

The door swung open, and another figure stepped out.

"Hello, Wren."

Reilly's blood surged hot. *I was right.* Fury flushed his cheeks as his fist clenched, knuckles whitening. "Not this time. You won't make a fool of me."

He nocked an arrow, leaned against a tree for support, the string kissing the corner of his mouth as Travis filled his aim.

A sharp pain suddenly shot through his own spine, obstructing his breathing. The bow fell, the arrow soaring wildly into the air. Turning with shaky legs, "You... can't..." he rasped. "Not... my time."

Sacha stepped closer, projecting a shadow in the morning light. "It's not? Not theirs either."

"I know... you," Reilly rasped. Vision blurring, knees buckling. He crumpled into the pine needles.

Sacha's eyes were flat. "I'm sure you don't." He reached down to wipe the bloodied knife on Reilly's shirt as Travis and Wren sprinted up the hill.

Wren gazed down and kneeled beside him. "Oh, no."

Sacha put a hand on her shoulder. "He had his bow drawn on you both. I first saw him at the forest's edge, watching. Only recognized him when he drew—but I couldn't let him loose that arrow."

Travis exhaled, a memory flooding back to him: their first encounter with Sacha, when he'd stumbled upon their camp. He'd spotted another archer aiming a projectile at him. "That's the second time you've pulled me from death's door. Thanks."

"You'd have done the same."

Travis dropped to one knee beside Wren. "I'm sorry. I know he mattered to you once."

"I never thought about how finding him like this might make me feel," she replied, reaching for Sacha's hand. "This was bound to happen. Reilly hurt people because that's what Brody shaped him into—someone no one cared for."

"If I'd known—"

"It wasn't your fault." She stood, brushing needles from her knees. The wind stirred again, carrying the faint, acrid scent of chimney smoke from town. "I need to get back to camp and tell Father. He'll have returned by now and will want to know."

Travis rose. "You don't know how the camp reacted when your father mentioned joining us. He might have pushed Brody too hard."

"Everything will be fine." Wren's voice steadied. "I'll slip in after dark. Father's house is small, tucked at the edge of camp—he'll be asleep. I know a back path. No one will see me."

"Then I'm coming." Travis's tone left no room for argument. "I'll wait in the woods while you talk to him."

Wren nodded. "Then let's go now, please."

Travis looked at Sacha. "Can you take care of Reilly?"

"Yes. Hurry, both of you."

"We'll just grab our gear."

Chapter 36

Brody listened to Cohen's report detailing the murder of a man in Clarksville. As the details came to light, he realized Reilly Brewin was likely responsible. His grip on the chipped enamel coffee cup tightened; the ceramic gave a sharp crack and shattered, hot liquid splashing on his knuckles. A thin line of blood welled along his palm. He reached for a frayed rag from the wall hook near the heater.

"Coco, could you please clean up this mess?" he called toward the doorway. He held his hand over the dented trash can, wiping blood onto the rag. "Cohen, has Reilly gone nuts?"

"Seems that way, sir," Cohen replied.

"That man makes me want to slap him."

"He may not return to us."

Brody drew a long breath; the air tasted of woodsmoke. "Might be for the best. If he does, lock him in our jail. In the meantime, do you have any updates on our trackers?"

"Yes, they arrived from the first trip—saw no sign of him. I sent them out again after they rested, to another section of the forest."

"He's in those woods somewhere, but Reilly's one of the best at not leaving a trail."

Cohen nodded, boots scraping faintly on the worn pine floor. "Yes, he is." He looked down at the cut on Brody's hand. "Better take good care of that."

"Yeah, I will. So, what happened to our men on the horses?" Brody asked.

"Sam heard the truck come through, headed north. We figured they might follow the same route back."

"Right."

"I instructed them to wait, monitor that road, and to stop it," Cohen said.

"Cohen, we *need* those weapons to further our objective," Brody said, eyes locked on him. "Our assassins yielded meager benefits—and the people could use some motivation."

"The fighters told me they blocked the road with a fallen tree, but when the truck came through and stopped, one of them got out and fired at them, killing one of our horses. The gunfire sent the rest into a frenzy. It was a close call, but thankfully, none of the men were hurt."

"You mean to tell me we got *nothing* out of it but a dead horse? We traded good meat for those horses. I need those darn guns. Cohen, it infuriates me every time I think about how that town used guns against our attack." He turned to face Cohen straight on. "You don't look so good, friend. Are you alright?"

"Yes... sir," Cohen stammered, eyes dropping to the scuffed floor as he sat down again. "Brody, there's something I need to tell you. I met with some Pattonville folks a few days ago."

"You did *what?*" Brody's voice sharpened. "That's the People of the Faith. You did this behind my back?"

"It wasn't my intention. I found out my daughter had befriended one of them. Wren caught me off guard. She asked me to go hunting with her, but it turned out to be a trap to get me away from camp. They cornered me and forced me to accompany them."

"You went to their camp? Our *enemy's* camp?"

"I'm sorry, Brody," Cohen said. "I learned some very important things regarding the northern region."

"And you're just now sharing it with me?"

"I tried several times, but I was worried about how you would react."

"Well, I'm all ears," Brody replied, his jaw tightening.

"Sure," Cohen said, hesitantly. "They said the North will likely never permit us to return home. Their intelligence also reveals that Militant rebels from the east are gaining access through Canada and have positioned themselves in the north—Minneapolis, for one—possibly they've infiltrated other cities."

"I'm sure those are rumors. There have always been accounts of other countries trying to start a war with us. You can't rely on any of it."

Cohen's fingers flexed against the threadbare couch arm. "Sir, the important thing I learned is that a covert army awaits word, ready with an arsenal at their disposal to defend the states. They asked me to pass along this message: they need our help—every Southern soldier, they said—to join forces with them in the fight. The northern military isn't as strong as it was when we were part of it.

Brody's expression shifted from surprise to anger. "Oh, *wow!* I'll overlook the fact that you allowed them to capture you. But why would we help if they have no intention of honoring their promise?"

"No! These aren't the same people we spoke with before. But they are prepared to defend against both the foreign militants and the northern military."

Brody gave a lopsided grin. "Cohen, you have allowed a rival faction, an adversary, to take you captive, and now you expect me to believe this… this *cockamamie* story they fed you?"

"Sir, an agent from the covert group is at their camp."

"And they used *you* to bring me the message. So, how *did* your daughter get involved with this bunch? You know this violates Black Arrow regulations. But the bigger question is why an experienced Colonel would fall for their lies."

Cohen shook his head. "I don't believe they are lies, sir. The details they provided appear valid and worth our consideration."

"So, Cohen, how many more of our people have ventured to this town? You admitted that your daughter has? Who else?"

Cohen drummed his fingers on the couch, the faint tap echoing in the small room. "Wren hasn't caused our people any harm, sir."

"That's for me to determine." Brody turned and crossed his arms. "Maybe it's easier than I realized to lure one of our soldiers away and fill them with false hope."

"The message isn't false." Cohen's palm slapped the couch cushion, and dust drifted upward.

"Oh my gosh, Cohen!" Brody exhaled deeply and set down his second cup; the enamel clinked against a dirty glass and the scratched table. "You should know this is one of the enemy's tactics. Even I thought you were hunting. Now, I learn that an adversary has manipulated you because you fell for the oldest trick in the book." He stared into Cohen's face. "Have you forgotten that a soldier is never to allow the enemy inside their head?"

"I would never permit such a thing." He fixed his eyes on Brody. "You should listen to me. This war is inevitable, and we should help them. It's our country, too."

Brody chuckled. "I've heard enough of this *nonsense!*"

Turning toward the door, he called, "Mark, come in here!"

Mark and another young guard entered the room. Cold air slipped in behind them, carrying the scent of pine and smoke. They stood before the two men, staring.

"Please escort Mr. Daniels from my presence," Brody ordered as he gestured toward the door. "Put him in the holding cell."

In disbelief, the guards locked eyes with each other.

"Now—please! The man is insubordinate and also a traitor. Take him to our jail."

"Yes, sir." Mark reached for Cohen's hands as he stood and secured them with coarse twine. The two guards walked him toward the dark, damp cell, boots thudding on the dead grass and sand,

Brody trailed behind, still angry. "I never thought you'd do this to me."

"Me? What happened to you?" Cohen asked over his shoulder. "The last few years, you've turned so cold inside."

"My loyalties are unquestionable," Brody countered, "but I *can't* say the same for you. Friends all these years, and now I have to *execute* you. Not to mention what we'll do to your daughter when we find her."

"You would stoop that low—*kill* my child?" Cohen asked.

"You told me Wren's a traitor. How can I dismiss it? What example would I be setting for the soldiers if I allowed them to conspire with other groups—they'd easily believe the same lies.

"You're mistaken about Wren." Cohen asserted. "Her connection is only a boy. Wren and I will never go against you. They only wanted me to bring a message asking if you'd join them in fighting the North and the rebels to save the country. That is the truth."

"Even if the intel they gave you is reliable," Brody added, "I cannot jeopardize the promise the North offered. We shook hands on it, and they expect us to fulfill our part of the bargain. We only need to step up the fight—and those guns would be a great help."

"We can't *trust* the North," Cohen replied. They'll never allow us back without a fight. We're doing their dirty work, you know. I thought you wanted to win back our country. Well, there's a chance if we join these folks."

Brody extended his hand through the cold metal bars, finger jabbing the air. "That bunch will realize exactly when I visit them. We'll confiscate those weapons and then *show* them how friendly we can be."

Brody sighed. "You betrayed me, Cohen." Brody's eyes bore into his old friend. Then he turned and walked away, his boots shuffling down the trail.

The guards, witnessing the scene, exchanged uneasy glances. They followed Brody back to his house, where Coco was already sweeping the broken glass into the trash basket, shards glinting briefly in the soft candlelight.

Brody invited Mark to stay as he dropped into an old chair. "Mark, Cohen was my best friend," he uttered.

"I'm sorry, sir. Is there anything you need me to do?"

"You know, there is. Fetch Solomon Warner. Tell him I have something for him to do."

"Yes, sir. I'll find him right away." Mark stood and left through the door.

Brody grabbed another cup of coffee—the metal pot still warm on the heater—and returned to his chair. "Why can't I have officers who *listen* to me? I always treated Cohen and his family with respect because he saved my life. *This* is my reward for kindness."

The door creaked open. Solomon Warner entered, bringing another draft of cold air. "You wanted to see me, sir?"

"Solomon, come in and take a seat. I've got a new assignment for you. Our chief officer has committed treason and will no longer lead the men. You'll receive orders from me now. Today I need someone trustworthy to carry out a special assignment."

"What do you have in mind?" Solomon asked.

Brody glanced across the room at Coco with a mop in her hands. "Are you not finished yet, Mendoza? Hurry and get out."

"I'm leaving." Coco gathered her things and hurried out, the door latch clicking shut behind her.

Brody turned to face the young archer. "All right, soldier, let's get down to business."

Chapter 37

Heavy rain pounded the forest canopy, and lightning tore across the night sky, forcing Travis and Wren to take shelter in the weathered shack along the trail to the Black Arrow camp. Finding dry kindling proved nearly impossible in the downpour. So, Travis peeled away strips of sappy pine bark with his knife from nearby pine trees. In a short while, a hearty blaze crackled to life, its golden warmth displacing the chill that had occupied the shack.

Wren set her backpack against the rough wooden wall and watched Travis tend the fire, as the flames danced across his features. "Travis, your mind seems far away tonight."

"Yeah," he admitted, poking at the logs with a stick. "I'm worried about Father. I wish he'd slow down. Every time he pushes himself, the pain comes roaring back to his joints."

"What about this woman he's staying with?"

"I met her once. She seems kind,"

"I'm sure she'll look after him."

"I think so too," Travis said, glancing up at her through the shifting firelight. "What do you make of Sacha's news?"

"I only heard the part he shared with my father at the church," Wren replied gazing into the flames. "Seems he held back some things."

"Maybe. It feels like a real chance for us—for everyone."

"You know this path will lead to fighting—and casualties. I've always hoped we could avoid bloodshed. And if Brody refuses... what happens to my father?"

"Reasonable concerns," he conceded. "There will be losses, no doubt. But picture it: freedom to travel to places beyond these woods. Sacha says the plan will move forward with or without Brody and Black Arrow, even if he balks."

"I know. I just hope Brody doesn't interfere with our preparation," she replied, turning onto her stomach, resting her palms against her chin, casting her gaze at the dirt floor, as flame danced around her.

Sensing the weight of the idea on her, Travis softened his voice. "It'll be worth it. My father told me stories of the old days—the real schools, cars, and lots of people. He had a job fixing automobiles, had money to buy things—even their own car. I've stared at the faded photographs for hours, trying to imagine that life. For him to lose it all... I want Father to taste it again. To live like they once did—"

"I've heard those tales," she said softly, "but don't you think Sacha's plan is too rushed? Without lots of planning, people will be hurt or killed. You and I could end up right in the thick of it, and one of us might not make it home. That's a heavy price for dreams pieced together from old photographs and the word of a man we barely know."

"Sacha asks a lot," Travis replied, resting a hand on his hip as sparks popped in the fire, "but he saved my life twice and yours once. I will never forget it. Father also told stories about the old wars—tens of thousands sacrificing so others could live free. Thousands of deaths bought freedom for millions. They remind me of Jesus on the cross, giving His life so souls could be free from sin."

Wren tilted her head, the firelight catching in her eyes. "Why would Jesus do that?"

"Because He loves us. There's a verse: *Greater love hath no man than this, that a man lay down his life for his friends.* That's the kind of love that shows God is truly our friend."

"Is this what you believe, Travis?"

"With all my heart. Jesus bore my sins on the cross. The story's right there in the Bible I gave you."

"Did He die for me?"

Travis looked at her with a faint smile. "Jesus died for whosoever will believe."

"How can I believe as you do?"

He told her that faith comes by hearing God's Word and turning from sin, and then quoted another passage: *If you confess with your mouth the Lord Jesus and believe in your heart that God has raised Him from the dead, you will be saved.* "How simple is that?" he asked.

"Travis, I'm not sure I can do—"

"You've been reading the scriptures I showed you, right?"

"You know that I don't read well."

"Then pray after me?" Mirroring how his father had led him years ago, Travis guided Wren through a simple prayer of surrender and faith. As the words faded into the crackle of the fire, they sat in quiet reverence.

"I felt a burning in my heart—does that mean I'm saved?" she whispered.

"Yes," he said. "Now live for Him and be a light to others."

She leaned back against her pack, the pine smoke curling around them like a comforting veil.

"More miles tomorrow. Let's rest," Travis said, settling on the opposite side of the campfire.

***

By morning, the storm had passed, leaving the air crisp and scented with wet pine and fresh earth. The two packed their gear and pressed on, pushing through swollen creeks and sodden under-growth that soaked their legs anew. As dusk approached, the Black Arrow stronghold emerged through the trees.

Wren paused at the edge of the woods. "Travis, stay hidden here. I'll slip through the fence and circle to the back. Getting inside could take a while, but I'll return before dawn. If I don't... know something's wrong. Leave this place. Don't wait. Men come and go all day—so stay alert."

"I can't sit idle if I sense trouble," he said. "If you're late, I'll come for you."

"No, Travis. They'd kill you on sight."

He drew a deep breath. "Then I'll be right here until you return."

She reached up, fingers brushing the nape of his neck, and pulled him close for a brief, passionate kiss before slipping away down the trail.

He grinned as he fixed his gaze on her. "You shouldn't have done that. Now waiting's going to be torture."

She pointed a finger back at him with a grin. "You stay."

The young huntress followed the familiar beaten path, jogging until she reached the rusted barbed-wire fence. She ducked beneath the sagging strands at the worn spot she'd made over time and scanned the camp's open ground. Circling near the soldiers' quarters, she spotted two dark figures approaching. *Guards?*

She crouched behind a rusted trash barrel, heart pounding, as they drew near.

"Wren, is that you?" a soft voice whispered.

Coco? she guessed.

Rising slowly, she peered out. "Coco?"

"Yes, and Mallory. We've been waiting for you. Where have you been?" Coco asked as they hurried closer.

"What's happening?"

"Honey," Mallory said, "they have Cohen."

"What do you mean?"

Coco gripped her arm. "Brody and his men locked your father in the prisoner's cell."

"I told them Brody wouldn't listen," Wren breathed.

"Rumors are flying that Cohen's a traitor—that he had information about outsiders seeking help against the North, that he met with a faction group without Brody's approval."

"I have to get him out," Wren said and turned to go.

"No," Mallory insisted. "Brody's men will arrest you. I've been terrified they'd throw me in with him."

Wren shook her head, staring into the shadowed camp. "I can't abandon him."

Coco placed both hands on her shoulders. "You have no choice. Your father asked me to get you and Mallory out. He made me promise."

"What? No, Coco, I can't leave my father in that cell!"

"Wren, trust me. Brody's unhinged. Reilly killed a man without their approval, another faction shot at his riders and killed a horse, then Cohen upset him more with his message. He's furious, unpredictable. If he catches you…" Coco hesitated. "He knows about your ties to that other group—and the boy."

"He knows about Travis?"

"Your father must have mentioned him, trying to sway Brody."

"Oh, no."

"Come with us now," Coco urged. "Once we're clear, we'll find a way to help him."

"You're leaving too?" Wren asked.

"Yes. I'm going with you and Mallory. I'll explain everything later. We have to move—now."

When they reached Travis in the woods, they broke the news of Cohen's imprisonment.

"This is terrible," he said. "Can't we get him out."

"Not tonight," Coco replied firmly. "You'll need help and a solid plan. We can work it out, but don't rush. Brody seems to relish watching your father suffer. But he plans to execute him in a few days."

"That's exactly why we can't wait!" Wren said.

"Wren," Coco responded, "Brody's men are posted all around that cell. You don't have the numbers for a rescue. It would be suicide. Get him out when you have a real chance."

"Then we hurry and find help."

"So... are you ready to run?" Travis asked.

"I suppose I'll have to be," Wren said, her voice strained. "Coco, you and Mallory—can you keep our pace?"

"Probably not," Coco admitted, "but we'll manage. I'll track you through the woods. Tell Sacha we're right behind you."

"*Sacha?*" Wren and Travis echoed together, brows furrowing as they broke into a sprint, the scent of wet leaves and damp earth trailing them into the night.

Chapter 38

Tears traced cold lines down Wren's cheeks as she sat closely beside Travis on the rough log bench. The image of her father, isolated in a cold and lonely cell, haunted her thoughts. With Coco and Mallory already departed from the camp, her fear about Brody's intentions for Cohen intensified—a tightening knot in her gut.

Travis wrapped his arm around her, his hand warm against her back. "We'll bring him here. He'll be safe with us."

She remembered the day Brody had dragged a prisoner into the open and ended him with a single shot, the crack of the rifle still echoing in her memory like a slammed door. The Black Arrow leader ruled through terror; he would choose the cruelest punishment for Cohen, turning the execution into a lesson carved deep for every fighter who might dare to leave.

"Wren?" Travis's voice pulled her back. "Did you hear me?"

"I'm not sure there's time," she replied. "I know Brody. If the trial's today, he'll celebrate the victory and have the sentence carried out at dawn tomorrow."

"Maybe not. Sacha and the others are gathering their gear right now. They'll be ready to move soon."

"You'll have to fight your way in."

"We understand that." He nodded firmly. "One way or another, we're getting him out. He's your father."

Wren took a deep breath. "I can't believe you'd risk your life for someone you barely know."

Travis's gaze softened. "Remember the verse I read you? Greater love hath no man than this, that a man lay down his life for his friends. We care about you and your father. We'll do whatever it takes."

She buried her face against his chest, her arms wrapped around him. "I love you," she managed, voice cracking. "No one's ever… been this good to me."

"I love you too." He pressed a kiss to her forehead, lingering a moment in the cold air. "But now we have to go."

They grabbed their gear and stepped outside into the darkness. Sacha waited with a rifle slung over his shoulder, flanked by two men from Pattonville and two of Roy Wayne's archers—each with bows, knives hung at their belts.

"Ready?" Sacha asked, his breath fogging.

"Let's move," Travis answered, shouldering his bow. "But fast."

★★★

Wren's knowledge of the trails guided them through the dark woods. Before first light, the unmistakable smell of woodsmoke drifted to them on the breeze—heavy and close.

Sacha motioned the others to hold their position outside the camp while he, Travis, and Wren headed inside. "Stay sharp," he told them. "When we bring the Colonel out, cover us."

The gate stood unmanned, and they wondered if the guards had fallen asleep. Wren led them through, slipping into the darkness beyond the bunkhouses until they reached the edge of the court-yard clearing.

"Soldiers sometimes watch from here," she breathed. "I don't see anyone, but that doesn't mean they're gone. I'll cross first and signal when it's clear."

"Go," Sacha urged quietly.

Wren proceeded through the area, pausing behind a building to survey it, then turned and waved them over. They made their way down the next building against the rough surface of the wall.

She darted across the open ground, heart hammering, then paused behind the next building, scanning the area. A quick wave brought them over. At the next building, they pressed along a plank wall.

Wren's hand shot up. "Wait."

Around the corner, a guard slouched in a chair, back against the building.

Sacha didn't hesitate. He strolled forward, casual as a man looking for conversation. "Hey—seen anything tonight?"

"Nothin'," the guard muttered.

"Yeah, me neither." Sacha punched the side of his head; he crumpled without a sound. "Over here," Sacha hissed.

They hurried on until Wren pointed to the isolated wooden structure. "That's it."

"Let's take it slow," Sacha warned, eyes sweeping the shadows. "Guards might be waiting inside. We don't need surprises."

He eased the door open. A faint candle flame flickered atop an old chest, poultry wire stretched across the building's sides, sheet metal covering it. Behind locked cell bars, Cohen lay on a narrow cot, breathing steadily as he slept. A rusted bucket sat on the dirt floor.

Wren rushed to the cell door. "Father—we've come for you."

Cohen stirred, eyes snapping open. "You shouldn't be here. Do you know how dangerous—"

"I brought friends."

"Let us get that door opened," Sacha said.

"Sacha Bourget?" Cohen pushed upright, recognizing the ponytail. A tired smile broke through. "Good to see you, my new friend."

"We're going to get you out, sir." Sacha stood at the cell door, pulling a slender tool from his pocket, inserting it into the mechanism. Travis and Wren watched as he worked the lock with careful turns until it clicked. "There."

"Cohen stepped free—just as a voice cut through the gloom. "What's going on here?"

Travis pivoted, his leg snapping up into the kick Sacha had drilled into him. The guard's head rocked back, and he slammed against the wall, slipping to the ground.

Wren threw her arms around her father. "I was so scared."

"Don't fuss about me," Cohen murmured, patting her back. "They fed me, at least."

"We think Brody was going to execute you any day."

"He wouldn't have gone through with it," Cohen replied. "He loves interrogating me too much."

Sacha peeked outside. "You folks can chat all you want after we hit the woods."

"We have to wake Mallory," Cohen expressed urgently. "We can't leave her. Brody will use her against me—or worse."

Wren reached out and took hold of Cohen's arm. "She's safe, Father. Mallory left with Coco and me and Travis."

"Are you certain?"

"Yes, they left a few nights ago."

"Coco, too?"

"We'll explain later," Sacha said. "We have to move out."

They slipped out of the building and retraced their steps. The guard Sacha had sent to the ground was staggering upright. Sacha dropped him again with a clean punch.

"Goodnight," Travis muttered with a smile as they ran past.

They hugged the perimeter toward the gate. Two guards stood talking from the high tower, voices low.

"The guards are back," Wren whispered. "I know another way."

She led them to a section of fence several buildings away, her old secret gap. Barbed wire sagged at the bottom.

"Lift it and crawl under," she said.

Travis and Sacha heaved the wire high. Cohen slid through first, Wren next. They traded places, holding it for the others.

Sacha was halfway under when a shout split the night: "Alert! Intruders in the courtyard!"

The tower guards spotted them. An arrow hissed past, thudding into the dirt inches from Sacha's head.

"Sacha—hurry!" Wren cried.

Two of Brody's men flanked them outside the camp and seized Cohen, catching Travis and Wren off guard. One pressed a knife to his throat. "You're going back inside," he growled.

Sacha rolled free and sprinted toward them.

"I'll cut him," the guard snarled, spotting Sacha charging his way.

Sacha never slowed. He barreled through the first, drawing the other's attention. Travis sprinted toward the other, landing punches to the man's head and stomach.

As they fought, two archers raced along the fence line. One nocked an arrow but then dropped to the ground, a shaft from the forest buried in his shoulder.

The group plunged into a thicket for cover, pausing to catch their breath,

"We cannot stop!" Cohen rasped. "Brody knows I'm gone. He'll have men out already."

"Where to?" Travis asked, voice rough with exhaustion. "We're spent."

Wren pointed into the dark. "The shack. It's out of the way—if we're quiet, they won't track us there tonight. We can rest."

"It's a haul," Travis responded, "but doable."

"Then let's find it," Sacha said.

Chapter 39

The group arrived in Pattonville, weary and worn, boots covered with creek mud. Only once in the woods had they truly believed they would have to fight—Brody's men lucking up on their trail. Sacha's quick thinking sent them trudging through a shallow creek until the pursuit faded into silence.

Jacoby Meyers stood on the Westons' porch, arms crossed against the cool breeze. "We were getting concerned, folks, but I'm glad you made it through."

"What are you doing here?" Travis asked.

"I cut some wood for Logan while you were gone. He promised me a handsaw for payment."

"That's good. I guess my dad's still at the farm?"

"Yes—he wanted the wood cut for when he came home."

"Jacoby, we're starving. Would you mind frying up some deer steak? We have plenty in the smoke shed."

"Sure—I can handle that. You all just sit and relax."

In a short while, Jacoby carried plates of venison to the kitchen table. They ate in quiet at first, until Brody Myles' name became the subject of conversation.

"I figure Brody's fuming about now," Cohen said, wiping his chin. "He'll chew out his guards for letting us escape. His trackers will know which way we went, but the fact that you've got those guns should give him pause."

Sacha finished his meal, set his fork down, and stood. "Brody's a hard man. His people will suffer for it."

Cohen nodded as he stood beside him. "He doesn't make life easy."

Sacha crossed to the corner and picked up his rifle from where it leaned against the wall. "I'll check around the edge of the woods. Just in case they show up."

Cohen turned to him. "Sacha, before you leave, I want to thank you. You and Travis kept Wren safe. I appreciate your dedication to restoring our country. You are true patriots."

"Thank you, sir." Sacha threw the rifle over his shoulder. "Plenty carry this burden. Our dream is to restore freedom for all Americans. We have so much to offer to allow foreigners who hate us to tear it down."

Cohen gave a quiet nod and watched Sacha as he stepped outside.

"Father, was the trip from camp difficult for you?" Wren asked as she sat down in front of him. "You never complained, and we moved really quickly."

Cohen grinned, the lines around his eyes deepening. "It did help me realize I'm not the same man I used to be—but I'm fine."

"That's good."

"Thank you, Wren and Travis, for getting Mallory out and bringing her here. Brody would have used her against me. As I suspected, he wouldn't listen to Sacha's message. I should have never supported his plan to move against the other factions. Until recently, Brody valued life. Our separation seems to have brought out a darker side of him."

"The separation hurt us all," Wren said softly. "Maybe one day, Travis and I can enjoy what some of you had all those years."

Cohen looked between them. "Listen closely, both of you. Sacha has the military know-how—be careful in these times. Brody's exactly the kind of man who'll hurt you if he decides to."

Travis nodded. "Mr. Daniels, I need to tell you that I have strong feelings for your daughter."

Cohen fought back a smile. "I can see that. The bond you share is rare, and one we all know might not sit well with everyone. We'll see how it plays out."

"He's joshing," Wren said. "It's Father's way of saying he approves."

Cohen chuckled. "Daughter, do you know where Mallory is?"

"She's at the Salisbury farm," Jacoby said, standing beside the doorframe. "Derrick took them there after they arrived."

"What about your father, Travis?" Cohen asked. "How's he doing?"

"When I saw Logan yesterday," Jacoby said, "he was walking gingerly. Still hurting plenty."

"What is wrong with him?" Cohen questioned.

"His joints, sir. He has arthritis and something he called rheumatism," Travis answered.

"So sad," Cohen said. "Jacoby, do you think Mr. Weston might feel up to talking?"

"He can talk fine. Maybe he's rested by now."

"Travis, I hate to ask after that long haul through the woods," Cohen said, "but could you show me to the Salisbury place? I'd like to see Mallory—and talk with your father."

"Sure. It's only a few miles. The farm might be safer for you anyway. Maybe Sacha will come along."

"Yes, that sounds good."

"Travis, I'm heading home." Jacoby said, sighing. "Cutting wood took what energy I had left."

"Thanks a lot for everything, buddy."

"I didn't do that much," Jacoby said.

They gathered their gear, found Sacha waiting near the trees, and headed for the Salisbury farm under a sky smelling faintly of coming rain.

After nearly an hour, they arrived at the farmhouse. Travis knocked on the door, but there was no answer.

Wren circled behind the house and saw no one. "Wonder where they've gone."

Moments later, Gaela Woods and Mallory Daniels stepped out of the hay barn.

"Are you looking for us?" Gaela called, spotting them.

Cohen jogged closer. "Mallory, are you all right?"

She hugged him. "I'm fine. I shouldn't have left you with Brody so angry, but Wren and Travis planned to come back—."

"Brody would have hurt you if you'd stayed. I only needed to know you and Wren were safe."

"We are," she said, squeezing his arm.

"Gaela, this is Cohen Daniels, Mallory's husband and Wren's father," Travis said. "I was hoping he could stay here with the others until we're sure Black Arrow isn't hunting them."

"Nice to meet you, Mr. Daniels. Yes, it's a large house. Hey, Sacha, Coco is inside, lying down. She asked for you when she and Mallory arrived, and Derrick brought them here to wait for you. You can use one of the rooms or sleep in the barn."

Sacha nodded. "What about Logan?"

"He's in my room. I set up one of the roll-away beds that was left here, thinking it'd be best to be close in case Logan needed help."

"How *is* Father?" Travis asked.

"Logan was asleep when we left for the barn. Derrick and Kincaid are there deciding how to arrange things for the weapons."

"Mrs. Woods," Travis said, "I meant his pain."

"He's better today. Come inside—he'll be up soon."

Gaela led them to the kitchen, where the smell of freshly brewed coffee filled the air.

"Yes, coffee," Sacha said. "Smells wonderful."

"I'll make a fresh pot. Aren't you glad we found those cases of coffee in that old house?"

The others looked at them, curious.

Sacha noticed them staring. "Gaela, Coco, and I spent a night in an abandoned house on our way from Little Rock. Some family left behind cases of coffee. We both love coffee. Packed all we could carry. I'm glad for it, but right now I'm eager to find out if there are any messages."

Gaela gestured toward the next room. "One message. The war is heating up in the north. Foreign militants are mobilized on the outskirts of Minneapolis."

"Guess they're still pouring across the border," Sacha said, with a bitter expression on his face.

"I think so."

"They'll let *anybody* in this fight," came a gravelly voice from the doorway behind them.

Travis turned and saw Logan leaning against the doorframe. "I hope we didn't wake you," he said.

"Slept long enough. Is that Mr. Daniels?"

"Hello, Mr. Weston. Call me Cohen."

"Then, call me Logan."

"It's a deal."

"Any trouble getting him out, Sacha?" Logan asked.

"Minor. Except one of ours had to shoot an archer behind their guard tower."

"Sorry to hear that. So, what's next on our list?"

"Honestly, Logan, I'm not sure. Maybe we should try again to convince Brody to move forward with us. I'm just afraid his connections to other groups could cause us some trouble. We'll need a lot of good fighters to pull this off. After last night, talking to him will be more difficult."

"Difficult, yes, but worth the trouble," Logan said. "Right off, they'd strengthen our forces. If they don't join us, we'll have to keep an eye out for Black Arrow interfering in our training."

"As Sacha said, Brody will have called for help from the outside groups he's close to," Cohen declared. "It won't be easy with his mind set on the North's promises, though that distraction might benefit your plans. Another thing about him: if Brody thinks you're deceiving him, he'll fight with everything he has."

Cohen's comment brought silence to the room, and everyone shifted their attention to him.

Logan scowled. "We've got to give this a few days—put our heads together and come up with a workable plan." He looked across the room and saw the tired look in Cohen's face. "Cohen, you should rest."

Gaela rose. "Yes, come with me, sir. I'll show you your room. Wren and Mallory will be with you as well. You can figure out the sleeping arrangements—there's another fold-away bed."

"Thank you, we'll need it." Cohen rose and followed her down the hallway.

Wren watched him leave, then turned to Travis. "I suppose I'm on the fold-away bed beside Father and Mallory. Where will you be?"

"I'd head home, but it's late. Think I'll find a place in the hay barn with Derrick and Kincaid."

"Okay, then goodnight, everyone," Wren said softly.

Travis left through the door, and Logan turned to Sacha. "If only Brody would listen the way Cohen does. Did you hear what I said?"

Sacha walked in from the kitchen holding a fresh cup of coffee. "Yes, I did hear you. In my view, there are two paths. Brody joins us—or he does everything he can to wreck our plans."

"Yeah, the second one is what I'm afraid of because it could jeopardize our plans going forward and cost lives," Logan replied.

"Oh, how I know—and there will be plenty of that when we journey north."

Logan sighed. "Right you are."

Prophecy

Finally, brothers, rejoice. Aim for restoration, comfort one another, agree with one another, live in peace; and the God of love and peace will be with you. 2 Corinthians 13:11 ESV

What shall we then say to these things? If God be for us, who can be against us? Romans 8:31 KJV

Chapter 40

Pastor Greyson Parker stirred awake, heart still pounding from the vivid, unsettling dream. The room carried the faint, comforting scent of old wood and linens worn soft by years. He reached for the tattered Bible on the bedside table and read by the pale morning light filtering through the curtains. After a time, he eased to his knees on the rough pinewood floor, bowed his head, and poured out his soul in quiet, fervent prayer, seeking clarity as the echoes of the vision still lingered.

Soon, he rose, joints protesting, splashed cold water on his face from the basin, and packed a few essentials—a small leather-bound Bible, a tin cup, a few pieces of jerked meat—into his weathered satchel. Then he stepped out into the crisp dawn air, the familiar scent of smoke from nearby homes lingering on the breeze, as he began the long walk north.

Years had passed since he last traveled this dusty road. He remembered the last time clearly: jolting along in the town's communal wagon to visit Dan Salisbury at his large farm.

When the old Salisbury place came into view, the rusted iron gate—once proud—caught his eye first. It now lay toppled, leaning drunkenly against a splintered post like a fallen sentinel. Parker moved slowly through the encroaching tangle of weeds and briars, stepping carefully around the deep ruts and potholes that time and neglect had carved into the path.

The house stood much as he remembered it, though its paint had peeled further, and the porch sagged under the weight of forgotten seasons. *A few solid repairs would bring it back to life*, he thought. He knocked on the door; the sound echoed across the quiet yard. Nearby, a mule lifted its heavy head from the sparse grass, ears flicking forward, dark eyes fixing on him with mild curiosity.

The door groaned open, and Travis stood inside, stunned surprise on his face. "Pastor Parker? What brings you all this way?"

"Is your father here, Travis? I thought he, and some of the others, might have gathered at this place."

"Come on in. They're in the kitchen, drinking coffee and talking low."

"Are they all there?"

"No, not all."

Parker's brows drew together sharply. "Where are the rest?"

"Derrick and Kincaid walked here earlier. They're bunking down in the big hay barn now."

"Alright. Take me to the kitchen first, then fetch those two. They need to hear this."

Travis led him through the dim living room, past faded photographs and a cold stone fireplace, then down the hallway to the dining room where the others sat. "Guess who showed up at the door," he said.

Logan stood quickly from his chair at the long oak table. "Pastor. Well, this is a surprise."

"Oh, sit down," Parker said with a small, weary wave. "The Lord leads us to unexpected places on our journey. Seems He had marked this one on His map for today."

He spotted an empty chair and eased into it, a faint grunt in his voice. "These old legs aren't what they used to be."

A soft footstep caught his attention. Gaela stepped out from the kitchen, wiping her hands on a faded apron. "Would you care for some coffee, sir?"

Parker's face brightened with genuine surprise. "I'd be most grateful for a cup, ma'am. It's been years since I tasted real coffee."

"Pastor, have you met Gaela Woods?" Logan asked.

"Not yet. A pleasure, Ms. Woods."

"The pleasure's mine. I've only heard good things about you."

"At least I've got that much in my favor," he replied with a modest smile.

Logan gestured across the table. "The others are Cohen and Mallory, Wren's father and stepmom, Coco, and of course, you've met Sacha."

"Yes, I have," he said. "So glad to meet you all."

"Pastor," Logan continued, "this is Gaela's home now. She's kindly let us use the big hay barn to store... certain supplies."

"I see."

The back door swung open with a creak. Travis entered, trailed by Derrick and Kincaid.

Parker glanced over his shoulder. "Good. Everyone's here now. Did I hear right that you're preparing to possibly clash with Black Arrow, then push north to fight for what's left of the country?"

"Yes, Pastor," Logan answered. "We'd rather not fight Black Arrow at all—if they'd join us instead, all the better. But if not..."

"And the North?" Parker pressed.

"Sacha's got a group waiting for us to join them soon," Logan said. "They need us to help take back the country."

"Then that must be why the Lord sent this dream."

Cohen leaned back in his chair, arms crossed, a wry edge to his tone. "Maybe you just ate too late last night, Pastor. Could've been nothing but indigestion talking."

"Father!" Wren snapped, cheeks flushing. "Why would you even say that?"

Cohen shrugged, unrepentant. "I've heard plenty of preachers spin 'prophecies' that belonged in a fantasy novel. They called it divine revelation, stood on them—and every last one of them turned out dead wrong."

Parker met Cohen's gaze without flinching, his voice calm but carrying assured certainty. "It's true—there were false prophets thick as flies in those days, and some may still linger. But I assure you, Cohen, I wouldn't have walked these miles and dragged my old bones through the briars to stand here if I thought this was some fevered fancy of my own making. This came heavy on me, and I've tested it against the Word and prayer. It's no indigestion. It's a warning—and, I believe, a promise."

"We'll see."

He drew a slow breath, the warm steam from his coffee curling upward like a quiet prayer. "Last night I had a dream—one I can't dismiss. Scripture tells us that in the last days, old men will dream dreams and young men will see visions. I believe what came to me carries spiritual significance for things ahead."

He felt their attention settle over him, heavy and expectant, while the kitchen grew suddenly quiet except for the soft tick of a wall clock. "Even after I woke, those images clung to me like campfire smoke. I turned to the Word for answers, found some comfort, but the unease remained. So I kneeled and prayed—long and hard—asking the Lord to make it plain."

He met their eyes one by one. "Brace yourselves, for what I am compelled to recount may shake the very foundations of your spirit. Yet in the mercy of the Almighty, may it ignite a flame of hope. The vision is laden with profound symbols—some yet linger beyond my grasp, awaiting the Lord's unveiling in His perfect hour. Hear now, exactly as it was shown to me.

"A group akin to our own assembled in a deep, emerald forest, feasting together. But the meat was strange—from beasts long fallen, rotting flesh—and ravenous beasts prowled the fringes, snarling and snapping at the selfsame scraps. The folk were wasted, eyes sunken like pits of despair, their frames bowed beneath a heaviness thicker than the cloying mist that enveloped them.

"In the distance rose a colossal wall, stone massive and seamless, stretching toward the sky. Figures struggled upward, hands raw on thick ropes, hauling themselves inch by agonizing inch. Scarce had one reached the summit."

"Oh, my," Gaela murmured, her arms prickling with goosebumps. "The sound of it gives me chills."

"I'm sorry, but there's more," Parker pressed on, his gaze distant as if beholding the vision anew. "From high above the wall, I saw sentinels—lizard-like fiends wreathed in thorny diadems, their scales sheathed in black mail. Eyes like embers in the pit glared forth. With gauntleted claws, they brandished swords aflame, hewing down all who ventured near. A scant few stole past in the darkness—many plunged into the void below."

Wren shook her head slowly, lips sealed in grim silence.

"Beyond the wall emerged a towering figure, its shadow swallowing the land. Atop its brow rested a golden crown—unadorned with gems, yet carved deeply with countless scenes of torment and despair.

"How can I bear to hear this?" Gaela whispered, her voice a-tremble.

"You must. The survivors fought fiercely against the lesser creatures. Only the strong prevailed. Together, they drove the giant back, forcing its retreat.

"Then, a moment of divine triumph unfolded. Swords clanged to the ground on the other side. The warriors sat, exhausted—and in that instant, all was transfigured. The warriors became like a gentle flock of sheep, and I wondered, were these the faithful departed?

The Lord turned my eyes afar. An expanse stretched before me—hills and valleys covered in gentle grass, and sheep peacefully grazing. Then a remote roar rent the stillness—a guttural cry from the abyss that the beast would rise again.

Parker paused, lifted his cup, and took a slow sip, letting the bitter warmth steady him. "I woke, shaken and searching. Only through Scripture and prayer did the meaning begin to unfold."

Logan cleared his throat. "You wouldn't have walked all this way unless you thought that the dream involved us."

Parker carefully set the cup down. "Yes. The opening scene—the weary souls gnawing carrion—mirrors our own lean years, scavenging the scraps of survival amid our misery.

"The wall," he pressed on, rising to pace slowly, "symbolizes the parallel line dividing us—the boundary between here and the northern realm. To breach it, courts doom. Those thorn-crowned guardians? The demon spirits that now hold sway over the land. But war is coming—it will be both flesh and spirit. Hone your blades, the battle already rages in the spiritual realm. The adversary may roar, but behold—the Lord Jehovah marches afore you, to demolish every fortress and high thing exalting itself!"

"Wonderful," Sacha said.

Parker halted abruptly, pivoting to confront them. "Hear me, people: these hellish legions fight without mercy the Almighty and His people. Victory dawns not from flesh, but from spiritual warfare—supplications that rend the heavens. Some of you will stand on the very edge of the battle. Without leaning fast to the Lord, your courage will crumble. But prayer is the weapon the devil cannot break. Forsake it, and you lose before you begin.

"Cling to this promise from Proverbs: *The name of the Lord is a strong tower; the righteous run into it and are safe.* Run to the Lord in every trial. He will shelter you. Walk closely with Him, and He will walk with you—faithfully, every step."

Parker eased back into his chair. They were paying attention—he could feel it in the stillness, the way no one shifted or looked away.

A broad smile spread across his lined face. "Now here's what made my feet move before dawn. Amid the coming storm, God showed me a glimpse of what awaits on the other side: peace.

An endless pasture, sheep resting without fear. Such undisturbed rest is described in Scripture about the end of days or a profound restoration. Only God knows the hour. But this vision speaks to our time. Our land will once again resound with jubilation, people free to worship without looking over their shoulders. This is the heart of the vision the Lord revealed."

Silence settled in the room, thick and thoughtful, broken only by the faint rustle of wind through the open window.

After a moment of quiet, Travis spoke softly. "I've never heard anything like that."

"Your vision stirs dread in me for the days ahead," Wren admitted, voice low.

Parker nodded. "There's darkness in it, yes. But knowing is better than blindness. More than that, it's proof God still speaks—still walks with His people and promises to go before them."

"Wow," Logan breathed. "So you're actually hopeful we can win this thing?"

"With God on our side? Yes. Unequivocally," Parker replied.

"This excites me, Pastor," Sacha said, eyes bright, "that God hasn't forgotten us."

Parker's smile returned, softer now. "It certainly does."

Chapter 41

Throughout the day, Greyson Parker's dream remained the pulse of every conversation inside the house. People pressed him for more details, but all he would offer was a cryptic response, hinting at the mysteries God had yet to unveil.

While the others deciphered Greyson's dream inside the house, Travis and Wren slipped out into the backyard. A cool breeze greeted them, carrying the faint sweetness of sun-warmed pine. They walked to their favorite spot, the old covered shed out back. There, beneath the slanted roof, they hoped to steal a quiet hour for Wren's reading and writing practice.

Wren studied the word Travis had scratched onto the paper. "So that's how you spell your name?"

"Yes. Can you write it?" Travis said with a soft, patient voice.

She took the pencil, tongue caught lightly between her teeth, and formed each letter with deliberate care—T–R–A–V–I–S—watching the graphite leave its faint gray trail.

"Perfect," he said. "Now, how about your father's name? And mine?" He slid the paper toward her after adding COHEN and LOGAN in his neat hand.

Wren tilted her head. "What are *you* going to do while I'm busy learning all this?"

Travis reached out, fingertips brushing her cheek in a slow, feather-light stroke. "Oh, I don't know… enjoy watching you."

His touch sent a warm shiver racing down her spine. "You'll enjoy watching me? Why?" She had pushed men away—Reilly most of all, with his cutting remarks—Travis's felt different, dangerously different.

He traced the curve of her jaw, eyes lingering on the soft glow of her skin and the shifting hazel of her irises, flecked with gold in the dappled light. "Because you're beautiful."

Wren arched a brow, teasing. "And how exactly would *you* know what beauty looks like, Travis Weston?"

He leaned closer, voice dropping to a murmur. "Because I'm a man, Wren Daniels, and men have special powers when it comes to recognizing a woman's beauty."

Her gaze locked with his. She leaned closer, drawn by the warmth radiating from him, the faint scent of the open air clinging to his shirt. "Do you remember when we first met? Out in the woods, by the creek?"

"How could I forget?" His thumb traced the shell of her ear.

With a gentle tug, she drew his hand away. "I saw you charging toward me, and I nocked an arrow—not sure if you were friend or foe. I nearly loosed it… until I noticed how unfairly handsome you were." She laughed softly. "I almost lost my grip on the string."

His eyes narrowed. "So you were closer to murdering me than I realized."

"Unintentionally," she said, grin widening. "Very unintentionally."

"You're telling me I'm only alive because *you* almost shot me?"

"Travis, stop twisting my words." She shoved him hard enough that he toppled off the low concrete ledge onto the sun-warmed grass. Before he could recover, she pounced, straddling him, pinning his wrists lightly beside his head.

He gently took her wrists, pinning them at his sides. "So… where's that bow of yours now?"

She leaned in and kissed him—quick, bold, tasting faintly of mint and sunlight—then pulled back, locking eyes. "*Kissing* is my superpower, not my bow."

"Are you taking prisoners?" he murmured.

"Only one." Her fingers skimmed his jaw. "I'll blindfold you, tie your hands, toss you in my jail, and turn jailkeeper so I can keep both eyes on you."

"Oh, well," he said with exaggerated resignation. "At least I'll get to see you every day—even if it's just when you slide bread and water through the bars."

She faked an exaggerated gasp. "You will? Then maybe I'll starve you a little… make you desire me more."

"I already desire you all the time."

Heat flooded her cheeks. "You do?"

He slipped from under her and sat on his side, propping himself on one elbow beside her. The grass was cool against her back, the breeze stirring her hair. "Why don't we get married?" he asked.

She scrambled upright, eyes wide. "You're *proposing*? After everything that's happened?"

"Why not?"

"Your timing is terrible."

"Don't worry about the timing." He sat up, facing her. "Just tell me what you say. I *want* an answer."

She grinned. "And what if I don't give you one?"

He stood, pulling her up with him, then arranged his face into theatrical sorrow—lips down turned, brows knit in mock despair. "I'll mope until you say yes."

A bubbly laugh escaped her mouth as she studied him—the charming tilt of his mouth, the earnest light in his eyes. In the short time they'd had, a quiet bond had taken root, yet marriage had never crossed her mind as something he'd want. She lifted one finger. "I will… under one condition."

He shook his head, amused. "You already have conditions?"

"Hush, silly. Only one." Her voice softened and grew serious. "Promise me you'll never leave me behind, not for hunting, not for some dangerous run north, not for anything. There's no one else I want beside me, and the thought of losing you—" She swallowed. "It's unbearable. We stay together."

His smile softened. "You don't need to worry. I want you right beside me. What could matter more?"

"You just better not forget."

The back door banged against its frame. Sacha stepped out, scanning the yard, and found them standing close, faces inches apart. He fought a smile. "Your fathers were wondering where you two disappeared to."

Travis eased back a half-step. "We were—"

"Working on my reading and writing," Wren finished quickly, cheeks reddening.

"Reading and writing. Right." Sacha echoed, his eyebrow lifted. "Well, I need a quick word with Travis. Logan's asking if you'd go hunting. Meat supplies are getting low with so many mouths to feed. But I can go instead if you'd rather stay here... studying."

"No," Travis said at once. "Wren and I will hunt."

Wren gave an awkward laugh. "Yeah. Hunting sounds a lot more fun than reading anyway."

Sacha raised an eyebrow. "You sure?"

Wren, averting her gaze from him, nodded. "We'll bring back meat for everyone."

"Be careful out there." Sacha turned and disappeared inside.

Travis exhaled, then leaned in to steal a kiss on Wren's cheek.

She sidestepped with a smirk. "*Nuh-uh*. Hunting first. Kissing later—lots later." She spun toward the back door, the breeze tugging at her hair as she opened the door with Travis following behind.

They gathered their gear and ventured outside for an afternoon hunting expedition, the pleasant scent of pine filling the air as they left.

Chapter 42

Deep in the forest, Solomon Warner stumbled upon a secluded camping spot. The night had been restful beside the fire. At first light, he gathered his gear and set out in search of breakfast. Before long, he picked up a promising deer trail, their fresh prints pressed into the damp earth. As he scanned the ground for more signs, a flurry of gray squirrels raced along the path ahead. *I wish you were closer*, he thought.

Solomon pressed on until the trees thinned to an open field, and he noticed a cluster of pine trees beside a medium-sized pond. Fresh deer tracks covered the ground. *This place might work*, he decided. He slipped behind a dense patch of sagebrush and settled in to wait.

Thoughts of Cohen Daniels soon crept into his thoughts. Given the man's reputation, Solomon knew his plan had to be flawless. He could sneak up close with his knife—quick, silent—or use his bow. He wasn't as skilled as Reilly had been, but if the wind stayed calm, a shot from short range would do the job cleanly. *Either would work*, he told himself, flexing his fingers around the smooth wood of his bow.

Brody Myles had promised him his former first officer's possessions if he succeeded. The proposition was Solomon's best offer since joining Black Arrow. With that reward in mind, he set out to find Pattonville and complete the assignment.

First, he must win their trust and then convince Cohen Daniels that his departure from Black Arrow was real. The only way to achieve this was to exploit Daniels' confinement, disapprove of his imprisonment, and criticize their treatment of him. He could then obtain the intelligence he came for and ultimately bring down Daniels. It was a perfect plan, provided it worked.

Now, where are those deer?

★★★

Travis had hunted these woods south of the Salisbury farm many times before, but after two long hours of nothing but birds singing and the rustle of leaves, he decided today would not yield a kill. He walked a few hundred feet when a familiar voice carried through the trees. Wren had found a promising spot near a pond next to an open field, several hundred feet away. He spotted her waving him over.

A small deer lay at her feet as he approached. "Nice," Travis said, relief softening his voice. "I haven't seen a thing."

Wren bent down and began tying a rope around the deer's legs. "It's small, but at least it's meat."

They had the animal dressed and quartered when Travis caught a flicker of movement about a hundred yards away. Squinting against the glare of the sun, a lone figure in dark clothing strode toward them, with a bow held loosely at his side. "Wren, we've got company. Not sure if he's friendly, but he might be one of yours."

She slipped a strip of meat into her pack and glanced up, her expression hardening. "I know him. That's Solomon Warner. He's one of Brody's assassins." Dropping her knife, she grabbed her bow and nocked an arrow.

They watched as the stranger drew closer.

"Don't trust him, Travis."

The visitor slowed to a stop twenty paces away. "I thought that was you, Wren."

Wren kept her bowstring taut, the arrow aimed. "Solomon, what are you doing here?"

"Could you lower that thing, please?" he asked, one palm half-raised. "I'm not here to hurt anyone."

"You're one of Brody's assassins. How do I know I can trust you?"

"You know me—I would never hurt you. Things are different for me now," Solomon said.

"How so?"

"Oh, it's a long story."

Wren relaxed the tension on the string and slipped the arrow back into her quiver, though her eyes stayed sharp. "Tell it anyway."

Solomon dropped to one knee, set his bow carefully on the ground, and pulled a rag from his pocket to wipe the sweat from his forehead. "Did you know Reilly left us? The trackers searched the woods but never found him. Brody assumes he's gone AWOL."

"Reilly's dead," Travis said flatly.

Solomon's eyes widened in disbelief. Reilly was one of the best soldiers in his camp. "What happened?"

"He tried to assassinate someone and was taken out for his trouble."

"I'm sorry to hear that. Brody gave me some of Reilly's duties, but now—" Solomon met Wren's gaze. "Wren, when I heard what they did to your father, I couldn't keep taking orders from Brody. I decided the best thing was to *leave* Black Arrow and have nothing more to do with them."

Wren tilted her head, studying him like a hunter reading tracks. "You're part of Brody's assassination crew, Solomon."

"Oh, he sent me out, but I *never* killed anyone. That's not who I am—though Brody would put me in jail or kill me if he knew. Doesn't matter now. I'm *not* going back. He only wants to keep the factions at each other's throats and kill wherever he can. He sent me a few days ago to cover one of Reilly's assignments, so I made my break. Figured it might be my only real chance to get free. Brody mentioned he thought you were running with these folks now."

Travis dropped another piece of meat into his pack. "Why did he think that?"

Solomon gave a casual shrug. "We went to your town, remember? Your people came out against us with guns. That was something—guns against our bows."

Travis straightened, wiping his hands on his trousers. "What *other* reason did you think she was now running with us? Wren wasn't even there that day."

"Um... I don't know any other reason. Brody must've heard it from Reilly before he... well."

Wren zipped her backpack and fixed Solomon with a hard look. "Are you lying, Solomon? *Why* are you really here? Maybe Brody sent you to take out someone else from the People of the Faith."

"No!" Solomon said quickly. "As I already told you, I *left* that camp—I'm not going back. I hoped to join your group. A fresh start—that's what I need."

He rose to his feet. "Wren, I need somewhere I can fit in. I want to stand with you and your father—he was my commander. I'll pull my weight." He pointed to the deer carcass hanging from the limb. "I can hunt, too."

Wren looked over at Travis as he finished packing the meat. "What do you think?"

They had caught Solomon in at least one lie. Yet what if the young man's intentions were sincere? They should at least let him tell his story to the others.

Travis shook his head sharply. "I *don't* want to glance over my shoulder every second, wondering if he's got an *arrow* pointed at me or a knife ready to stab me."

"But I think I believe him," Wren said softly. "He wouldn't risk coming here unless he'd truly broken ranks with Black Arrow."

Travis maintained his gaze on the man. "I hope you're right. Solomon, you can follow along and repeat your story to the group. *They'll* decide your fate—not us."

"That's all I ask."

"What makes you think we won't just arrest and throw you in jail like Brody did Colonel Daniels?"

"I don't," Solomon replied. "I took a huge risk coming here. I needed to do something and was hoping Wren would speak for me, us being friends."

Travis cautiously reflected on the man's last words as a gust of wind swept across the pines. "Alright. We'll feed you, then you can return with us. But I can't guarantee how they'll react."

"I understand."

"Then, let's cook some meat."

"Sounds great."

As they built a small fire, Solomon's request did little to ease the darkness that began to settle over Wren. Like snakes rising from the water, his sudden appearance brought old memories of Black Arrow and Brody Myles to the surface. She wondered, even as the first strips of venison began to sizzle and pop over the flames, if bringing him back with them was a mistake she would come to regret.

Chapter 43

For days, Logan had urged his friends to include Black Arrow in their northern plans, only to draw shrugs and dismissals. He assembled them once more around the wood heater as wisps of woodsmoke and coffee lingered in the room. But after an hour of debates, every ploy crumbled against the raw threat of a Black Arrow insurgency.

Gaela spoke up, her voice cutting through the murmur. "Everyone, please listen to Coco. She's got something worth hearing."

Coco Mendoza leaned against the door frame behind Gaela.

"Please, come in and sit," Logan said, gesturing to an empty chair. "Tell us what you know."

Coco slipped into the seat near Logan and Sacha. "Brody was furious when he learned about the guns," she said. "The whole camp heard him shouting."

Derrick wiped honey from his beard with a towel. "I can believe it. He knows our weapons are better than his."

"Brody's convinced the North is the one arming you," Coco continued. "I overheard him say they've abandoned us—that their promises mean nothing now."

Logan leaned forward in his chair, the wood creaking under him. "You're sure that's what he said?"

"Yes. I was cleaning the room that day." Coco nodded as her fingers traced a small scar on the table's edge. "He kept repeating it, over and over."

"So Brody believes we're in bed with the North?" Sacha asked.

"And that their promises are nothing but lies."

Was this the way forward, Sacha wondered? Brody had remained fixated on the assurances of the North. "This could be exactly what we need," Sacha said, eyes sharpening. "If Brody thinks the North has turned on him, he might be open to reason. He has no real cause to fight the other factions... unless he's playing us."

"I can see them setting us up," Derrick muttered, licking the last trace of honey from his fingers. "Remember, Black Arrow doesn't need much excuse to start a fight."

Logan turned back to Coco. "I don't doubt what you said, but is it possible Brody knew you were listening?"

"Very, because he doesn't trust anyone, though he never said a word to me about it."

Logan exhaled slowly and addressed the group. "Folks, we can't verify this information, but we can't sit on our hands either. I say we surround the camp, hold our position, and wait until Brody realizes he has no choice but to hear us out. He'll have to come to the table."

"Maybe," Sacha replied, rubbing his jaw. "If he feels trapped, he might come out fighting. I think we should ease toward the camp like neighbors—knock on the door, make it clear we've come in peace. Our people should already understand that we're trying to avoid bloodshed."

Kincaid sat with his arms crossed. "I still think we're better off heading north with the other factions—leave Black Arrow behind. There'll be no one left for them to fight or antagonize."

No one replied. Most felt they needed Black Arrow because of their experience.

Cohen Daniels cleared his throat. "There's an element you're forgetting. Whoever talks to Brody must be someone he already knows. Otherwise, he'll smell a trap and shut down completely."

Logan nodded. "Agreed. But Cohen, who? Brody never believed what you said. By now, he knows Sacha, Coco, and Mallory have left his camp. He's probably furious with all of them."

Cohen stared at the floorboards, a deep crease forming between his brows as he wrestled with the words. The air grew thick with anticipation. "There's one other person we could send, that he might still trust... even if I hate the idea. My daughter. Brody always said he loved Wren like his own."

"You can't send Wren," Gaela said. "Trust or not, he might kill her."

"Send me where?" Wren's voice echoed from the other room.

She and Travis had stepped into the kitchen with Solomon close behind, catching the tail end of the conversation.

"Where am I supposed to go, Father?" Wren asked, her tone steady despite the tension.

"To the Black Arrow camp. To speak with Brody," Cohen said.

Travis moved in front of Wren, facing Cohen directly. "No. Absolutely not. Brody could lock her up the way he did you—or worse, kill her out of pure spite."

Sacha cut in, "It's not the same situation. We'll be right there, ready to protect her."

"Please don't ask her to do this," Travis pleaded, shaking his head, his hand reaching for Wren's.

She shook loose his hand. "Listen to their plan."

"Travis," Logan explained calmly, "we're planning to surround the camp anyway. Brody already knows about the guns, and that gives us the advantage. Once we're in position, we'll call for him to hear our proposal. If Cohen believes he might actually listen to Wren, it could be our only real chance to bring him over to our side against the North."

Travis remembered Black Arrow's brutal attack on the town—the screams, the chaos. Without his father and the others arriving with guns, more lives might have been lost. But Wren—she was the one he cared for above all, the one he meant to marry and build a life with. A fierce ache twisted in his chest at the thought; if anything happened to her, he wasn't sure what his life would become—empty, adrift, a hollow shell of the man. Surely someone else, anyone else, could face this danger—not Wren.

"Father's right," Wren said quietly. "Brody and our family go back years. He once told me he loved me like the daughter he never had."

Travis threw his hands up, frustration in his voice. "This is crazy. We broke in and took your father. Do you really think Brody will accept this peacefully?" He turned to Logan, pleading. "It's a mistake to send her out there."

"Travis, calm down," Wren urged, her hand resting lightly on his arm. "I have to do this—for all of us. Remember when we first met? We dreamed of a world where people could live without constant fear. I hate fighting because people die, but this is the chance we've been waiting for. Everyone will be watching, ready to step in. They'll surround the camp. Brody will have no choice but to listen."

Logan appreciated Wren's hope for a future world where they were free. But recalling Pastor Parker's dream, he knew that even if they added Black Arrow to their ranks, the path ahead was far more formidable than they could imagine.

Cohen leaned sideways, peering through the doorway into the kitchen, where others stood listening. "Daughter," he said, "you've brought the enemy into our camp."

A sudden hush fell over the room. All eyes shifted toward the kitchen entrance.

Wren followed her father's gaze and realized he meant Solomon Warner. "Father, we found Solomon wandering in the woods, half-starved and looking for food. He's left Black Arrow for good."

Cohen shot up from his chair, gaze locked on the young man. Before he could cross the room, Sacha stepped into his path. "Colonel, we're not like Brody or his men. We give people a second chance."

Cohen gritted his teeth. "I know you're right, but I still don't trust him." He exhaled and sank back into his seat.

Solomon shifted nervously on the other foot as they stared at him. "I disagreed with Brody locking you up," he said. "He sent me out again, so I took the chance to slip away. What they did to you was wrong, sir."

Cohen fixed a stern gaze on the young assassin. "If you disagreed with Brody, why did you not rescue me that first night?"

"Well, I was out hunting until right after these folks broke you out."

Cohen knew Solomon was lying, but he let it pass. "Maybe you should answer for the people you've killed under his orders."

"I've killed no one," Solomon insisted. "That's why I left." *Surely, that will satisfy him,* he thought.

As the tense exchange continued, Coco slipped quietly past the group from the kitchen, her heart tight in her chest. She prayed Solomon hadn't recognized her from that night they took Cohen. She remembered that Brody had called her in to clean up the shattered cup he'd smashed, and he called for Solomon moments after they locked Cohen away.

A sharp knock rattled the front door. Sacha opened it to find Jacoby standing there, chest heaving, sweat beading on his forehead. "Jacoby, what's happening?"

"Black Arrow is attacking the town," he gasped, words spilling out. "Roy Wayne and his people are fighting back, but it doesn't look good."

"Is anyone hurt?" Sacha pressed.

"Yes, several. Pat Simmons is dead."

"I'm sorry, Jacoby."

Logan moved quickly to the door. "Jacoby, catch your breath and then go around to the back." He turned to the others. "We have to move now. Travis, Derrick, Kincaid—load some weapons into the truck and bring it around. Black Arrow isn't waiting for us to make the first move."

"So much for thinking Brody might be open to persuasion," Sacha said, glancing at Logan.

"Would've been so much easier if they had listened to Cohen," Logan said, shaking his head.

Chapter 44

As they hurried toward town, Derrick's grip tightened on the steering wheel. Logan stared out the passenger window as the trees blurred past in a rush of green and shadows. In the back, Sacha and the rest of the group sat tense, shoulders pressed together.

"This is all my fault," Cohen said quietly. "I should have stayed at Brody's camp. He's only attacking because of me."

Wren reached across and took her father's calloused hand. "This isn't your fault, Father. It's Brody's. He's the one sending assassins to towns, and he'll pay for it."

Cohen exhaled sharply, the sound lost beneath the rumble of tires on rough road. "Brody seems determined to cause pain. I should have expected something like this when you broke me out. His behavior has worsened over the past few years. You saw it. I thought nothing of it."

"Father, what more could you have done? Brody would never listen if you tried."

"He'd better start listening now."

Derrick eased off the gas as the first buildings came into view, his eyes scanning the tree line for any flicker of movement. A man from Roy Wayne's group stepped into the road with one hand raised, signaling them to stop, the other gripping a rifle.

"They're on both sides of town, hidden in the trees," he said, breath fogging slightly in the cool air. "You should separate your team."

Travis and Jacoby bailed out of the truck first. Wren followed close behind Travis, then turned back to Cohen. "Be careful, Father. If Brody sees you, he won't hesitate to kill you."

"Brody better look out for me," Cohen replied, jaw set. With Sacha and Solomon beside him, he headed toward the north side of town.

Jacoby and Travis sprinted in the opposite direction while Wren hurried to catch up.

Sacha's crew reached the edge of the woods. "I see some of Brody's fighters ahead," Sacha said, eyes fixed on the woods. "We should spread out among these trees. I'll take the upper side." He peeled off toward a thick patch of oaks thirty yards away, rifle slung across his shoulder.

Cohen glanced over at Solomon, who had dropped back about twenty yards. "Son, this is your chance to prove you've moved on from Brody. Make it count."

Solomon met his gaze and gave a single, solemn nod. "I will."

A flash of black fabric caught Cohen's eye—a Black Arrow hoodie. He flicked the safety off and squeezed the trigger. The rifle kicked against his shoulder with a sharp crack. The man collapsed to the ground. "I'm sorry, Mark," Cohen whispered, the words tasting bitter on his tongue.

Travis and Wren took up positions on a low hill near Travis's home while Jacoby pressed on into town alone.

Frustrated, Wren tossed the peculiar rifle. "Travis, I can't use that gun."

"That's why we brought our bows."

"I thought Logan would be upset if I didn't try to use it."

"Our priority is stopping those who are attacking. Use what you're comfortable with."

"Then I gotta get closer. I'll follow the trail around your house."

"Be careful. The woods are crawling with them. You might not see 'em coming."

Just as Wren started down the narrow trail, a Black Arrow fighter spotted her from behind the underbrush.

Just as Wren started down the narrow trail, a Black Arrow fighter spotted her from the underbrush. Travis caught the shadow moving among the pines, then saw the man draw an arrow from his quiver and nock it. He shouted a warning, but the words drowned in a burst of gunfire. *It's as good a time as any to test the weapon*, Travis thought. Remembering Sacha's training, he raised the .30-30 Marlin, squeezed the trigger, and felt the recoil jolt through him. The attacker's bow slipped from his fingers; his arrow flew harmlessly into the treetops. A pang twisted in Travis's gut at the sight of the fallen man. *Lord, don't ever let me get used to killing*, he prayed silently.

Wren froze, then locked eyes with Travis across the distance. Realization dawned on her face. He gave her a quick, reassuring smile and signaled her onward as he chambered another round.

Cohen dropped another attacker, then gazed over at Sacha as he took down two more. Turning toward Solomon, he realized the young man hadn't fired a single shot. "I'm watching you," Cohen said.

Solomon nodded once and scanned the tree line, spotting a Black Arrow attacker aiming at Cohen. *Maybe Bruce will take him out first*, he hoped. Cohen twisted aside at the last second, and the arrow sank harmlessly into a tree behind them.

Adrenaline surged through Solomon's veins as he stepped forward to satisfy the old man. When he accepted the assignment, he never expected he'd have to fight Black Arrow. They were all friends. Brody might penalize him, but he couldn't reveal to the People of the Faith that he was Black Arrow. He lifted the rifle and fired. The deafening sound echoed through the air as the attacker collapsed to the ground. "Sorry, Jesse." Solomon turned, meeting Cohen's stoic gaze. *Maybe that will satisfy him*, he thought. Cohen looked at him for just a moment before turning back to the fight.

Solomon fired a round harmlessly into the air, the report echoing through the trees. If he could convince Cohen that he was engaged in the fight, he could slip away from his position. The young assassin moved quickly behind a large oak and waited out of Cohen's sight.

Moments later, Cohen looked back, frowning when he noticed Solomon was gone. He shook his head and returned to the fight.

As good a time as any, Solomon decided. Standing twenty feet away, he still couldn't land a clean hit. His heart pounded, and he crept forward as more gunfire rang out.

Ten steps away. He drew the hunting knife slowly from his belt. Eight steps. His grip tightened on the handle. Two steps away, he raised the weapon high. One more step—

Uunhh!

Solomon stood frozen, the knife slipping from his fingers, bouncing on the pine needles. Cohen's own knife had landed in the young man's side, hammering against his ribs.

"Are you alright?" Sacha called, smashing through the underbrush upon seeing the assassin's attempt.

"I am now," Cohen answered, breathing heavily. "I know why Solomon came here now."

"I'm sorry, Colonel. Was meaning to keep an eye on him, but I got caught up in the attack."

"So did I—just never expected Solomon to come at me like a coward. I never trusted his presence here."

"We do things in war we'd never do otherwise. I'm sure Brody promised him a lot—goods, favors, whatever it took."

Cohen nodded grimly. "You are right."

"I'm glad you turned around when you did," Sacha said. "Well, I need to check on the others. I believe we turned the Black Arrow archers with our guns."

Cohen turned the body face up and looked at Sacha. "I remember when Solomon came into the Black Arrow camp. He was young, eager, and learned fast. His life didn't have to end like this."

Sacha shook his head. "It's not on you, Colonel."

"I know, this is on Brody, and he will get his due. I guess I need to bury him."

"That's Logan's place over there." Sacha pointed toward a house. "There should be a shovel in his shed—maybe a wheelbarrow." He tapped Cohen lightly on the shoulder and then left the Colonel staring down at the young assassin's still form.

Sacha quickly spotted Travis and Wren on the road and turned toward them. "Is everyone alright, Travis?"

"I think so, but I don't know where my father is."

"I'll look for him."

"Sacha, five or six of the Black Arrow archers slipped away into the woods," Wren said. "They'll take the animal trails toward home. Travis and I can track them and cut them off."

"That's way too dangerous."

"They attacked us, and they need to understand there are consequences for hurting innocent people."

"I won't stop you, but heading into the woods after well-trained men is risky. If you go, take every precaution. And don't trust Brody for a second—he's shrewd."

"Got it," Travis said.

Sacha pushed in front of Wren as she turned to leave. "You'll find your father at Travis's house. Solomon tried to take him out—he's hunting for a shovel to bury him."

"Solomon is dead?"

"Yes."

Travis tugged on Wren's coat. "We don't have time for anything else if we're going to catch them."

"I have to check on my father," Wren said. "I just need a minute."

Travis shook his head reluctantly. "Fine. One minute. Sacha, tell my father where we'll be."

"Sure thing, Travis," he replied. "We'll pray for your safety. You have three days—then I'm coming for you."

Travis nodded, and they turned toward his house. Cohen stood motionless, staring at the place he'd dug, a shovel in his hand.

Wren ran up to him and hugged him. "I'm so sorry."

"Brody will pay for this," Cohen growled.

"Let it go, Father," Wren urged softly. 'Vengeance is mine, saith the Lord.'"

Cohen searched her face, his anger fracturing. "I suppose you're right."

She glanced back—Travis shifted impatiently, eyes on the woods. "We have to track those archers, or we'd stay and help dig."

"No," Cohen said firmly. "I need to do this alone."

Wren squeezed his arm. "Then we'll see you soon."

He nodded silently, and Travis and Wren slipped into the woods.

Chapter 45

Travis studied the footprints pressed into the damp earth. "These aren't our folks."

"Then it has to be Brody's bunch," Wren replied.

"Their pace tells me they don't think anyone would follow."

"That works in our favor. Let's keep moving."

They continued along the same trail Wren used to reach Pattonville. The ground grew softer underfoot, releasing the rich, loamy scent of turned soil. Soon, they came across fresh raccoon and coyote tracks overlapping the heavier boot prints left by Brody's men. Hours passed in quiet tension until the trail narrowed into a shadowed gorge between two wooded hills, revealing only a partial view of the land beyond.

"Wren, hold up." Travis raised a hand and scanned the tight passage. "I don't trust Brody."

"Do you think they will ambush us?"

"Let's not risk it. We'll circle this hill and pick up the trail again." He veered off the path, and Wren fell in behind him, the crunch of dry needles under their boots the only sound between them. After a few miles, they paused to catch their breath.

"Do you think they will stop to camp tonight?" Wren questioned.

"If I were them, I'd push hard to get home after what they pulled. But that depends on Brody's level of confidence."

"Brody Myles doesn't lack confidence."

Travis sighed, jaw tightening. "Wren, I still don't understand why we need them. Brody and Black Arrow are a major problem. They murdered my friend and others in town. I *don't* trust them. When our people head north, everything has to go smoothly, and I'm worried Brody might do something to damage our relationship with the Patriot Endeavor."

"Maybe you should talk to your father about this. Logan appears determined to have them join us. But I agree with you, Travis. How many more people have to suffer at Black Arrow's hands?"

"I'm worried about the others back in town. During the conflict, I couldn't even see where Father and his friends were."

"Yeah, I hope Solomon is the only casualty."

"Right," Travis said. "We'd better keep our voices down from here on."

They kept going past the gorge and rejoined the trail. A few miles later, the ground softened near a shallow creek, the water gurgling over smooth rocks.

Travis paused and crouched, examining the ground. "They stopped here. Some tracks head west, the rest continue straight. I wonder if they realize we're behind them."

Wren glanced over his shoulder. "I bet Brody sent some of them out to hunt. Maybe he's thinking about food. It was always scarce at camp—too many mouths. So... should we split up?"

"No. We gotta pick one direction."

"I hope it's not the group Brody's in. He's deadly with a bow and as dangerous with a knife."

Travis met her eyes. "What do you say?"

Wren exhaled, tasting a cool breath of creek air. "I say we follow those we think are hunters. A high percentage that Brody's not with them."

"Maybe."

"We'll face him if we have to," she said.

Travis kneeled, cupped cool creek water to his lips, then stepped back as Wren drank.

Then he turned west, following the fresh prints. The trail led them into a narrow clearing where old wooden poles and sagging electrical wiring still stood like skeletal remains. Travis remembered his father calling them highline sections. He paused, studying the disturbed dirt.

"What is it?" Wren asked.

"They've slowed down. But why?"

"Maybe someone's hurt."

"Could be," he said, "but I don't see blood. My guess is it's something else."

"A trap?"

"Possibly. And we're exposed out here."

"Let's get deeper into the woods and find another trail," Wren suggested.

They slipped onto an animal-trampled path, the dense undergrowth brushing against their legs. The woods smelled of damp earth and distant woodsmoke. A sudden rustle made them turn and stop. Three deer leaped through the thick trees, their white tails flashing.

"Brody's hunters must have missed those," Wren whispered.

"Hunting wasn't the reason Brody came."

Wren was about to respond when she picked up the scent, stronger now. "Travis, I smell smoke, close."

They ducked behind a large tree, peering ahead. The faint scent of woodsmoke drifted on the breeze, sharp and unmistakable.

"They must be camping for the night?" Travis said.

Wren nodded. "Looks like it. What's our plan?"

I don't plan to kill anyone, but I will if I have to. Overnight, we'll try to restrain them and bring them back to town in the morning.

"Travis, I'm glad you decided against killing them. I was worried that with them hitting the town, you might want to. But extracting them won't be easy if Brody is with them."

"Oh, I'm angry about what they did, but I also know that Brody is the one we need to reach with our message."

"Good." Wren nodded and edged forward for a better look. "Hey, I see the campfire."

"Let's split up. You take the right, and I'll come in from the backside. Speak up if you get there first, so I'll know where you are."

"I'll whistle." She made a sound like a whippoorwill.

Travis offered a faint smile before they separated, moving low and silent. Wren reached the edge of the camp first and gave her signal. Three men sat near the fire, and Brody was among them. Her pulse hammered as she waited in the shadows, listening to Brody rant about the men they'd lost in Pattonville.

Travis had heard Wren's signal and emerged from the trees on the far side. "Hold it right there," he called loudly. "We know you're the ones who attacked us today. We've come to take you back to town."

Brody and his men froze.

"So how's this going to work, mister?" Brody smirked, eyes glinting against the firelight. "You can't hold that bow and tie us up at the same time."

"He's not alone," Wren said from twenty yards behind him, arrow nocked.

"Wren the traitor. Just like your father."

"My father is not a traitor," she said firmly. "You should have listened. All we ever wanted was to bring you important information."

"What are you doing?" Travis asked. "Wait until we get him back."

"He needs to listen now," Wren explained.

Brody chuckled, amusement in his voice as he turned toward her. "So they sent you two with the same sad spiel as your father tried."

"You know, Brody," Wren said, "I didn't get the chance you and my father had before everything fell apart. I'd love to live in a free world, go where I want, and have the things that were available then. That chance is right in front of us now. What my father told you was true, but you were too wrapped up believing he conspired with the enemy."

"He did! Cohen deserved punishment for the wrongs he committed. Those are the rules."

"*Your* rules," Wren said sharply. "All he did was suggest you talk to another group? He only wanted something better for all the factions." She saw Brody's face harden and realized she was getting nowhere. Then his eyes shifted from her to Travis, and back.

"Travis!" she shouted. "*Look out!*"

Brody dove sideways, reached for his knife as the other two men scrambled for their bows. Travis loosed an arrow that whistled past one man. The second attacker fired back, forcing Travis to dodge the projectile. Wren released hers at Brody, but he rolled clear and hurled his knife. It whizzed past her ear and thudded deep into a tree trunk.

Realizing they'd both missed, Wren yelled out, "*Run*, Travis!"

They bolted from the camp, crashing through the underbrush until they met again on the main trail, chests heaving.

Brody shrugged as his men stood staring into the woods. "Well, go after them. This is what you trained for. Mess this up, and you're dead."

"Yes, sir. We'll find them." The two men hurried away from camp.

Travis and Wren turned away fast, sprinting through the woods as the cool evening air brushed against their skin. Near the gorge, they slowed to catch their breath.

"I don't see them," Wren panted, glancing back. "Hopefully, Brody kept his men at the camp."

"Nah, they are coming. I'm not sure if Brody is with them, but we're not running."

"You want to set up an Ambush?" Wren asked.

"Yes, at the gorge."

They pushed on until the narrow cut between the hills rose around them.

"Let's scan for cover," Travis said.

"I see two good spots. You take those bushes. I'll use the fallen tree limbs for a blind."

"We can catch them in a crossfire."

Wren cut two limbs with her hunting knife, more from the ground, and laid them against a tree to build a quick blind.

Moments later, the snap of breaking branches carried through the forest.

"They're coming," Travis said.

"Do we shoot to kill?"

"I don't know. Wounds will slow them enough."

Wren stepped back into position. The footsteps grew louder, twigs cracking under boots. As the men drew near, one held up a hand to signal to the other that something wasn't right. They slowed, scanning the ground and the hidden places.

One man noticed the disturbed leaves and needles, pointing to various spots in the soil.

Wren stepped from behind the blind. Her projectile flew true, punching into the first man's thigh. At the same moment, Travis rose from the bushes and sent his arrow into the second man's backside. Both attackers cried out and dropped to the ground, writhing in pain.

Travis moved in quickly. The man he shot was still dangerous. He snatched up a fallen limb and cracked it across the man's head, sending him unconscious. The second assailant lunged toward Wren as she turned her focus on Travis. Travis closed the distance in a hurry and smashed the man's arm with his bow, snapping the bone.

The young man bellowed.

"That will keep them for a while," he said.

"Travis—I hear someone coming."

"Must be Brody. Let's go. He'll have his hands full with these two."

Chapter 46

Logan and Sacha decided the time was right to make their move on the Black Arrow camp, the sting of the recent attack still sharp in the air. Extra soldiers would tilt the odds in their favor, so they sent Jacoby and Chevy to Deport with a message requesting Marius's help to execute their plan.

"I'm worried about Travis and Wren," Logan said. "I wish you hadn't sent them."

"I *didn't* send them," Sacha clarified, sitting in a chair. "Chasing those men was their own idea. They'll be fine."

"What were they thinking?" Logan continued. "And *why* didn't you stop them?"

"I figured it would give them useful experience."

"Experience?" Logan's brow tightened. "What exactly are you up to, Sacha?"

Sacha reclined in his seat, fingers laced behind his head, wearing a smile. "I want Travis to come north with me when the time comes."

The words struck Logan like a cold blade slicing between his ribs. He had already lost his wife amid the chaos at the crossing. The thought of losing his son as they slipped back through carved a hollow ache behind his sternum. "So you thought sending him after a battle-hardened veteran from the old war would challenge him?"

Sacha offered a slight shrug. "When you say it like that, it sounds a little heavy. I just sensed Travis was ready and had great instincts, but instincts need sharpening. You could help."

Logan stared through the open doorway into the next room, the distant murmur of voices and the faint scent of woodsmoke drifting in. "I'm still waiting to hear why you need *my* son up north with you."

"Because he'd make a fine partner for reconnaissance, gathering of vital intelligence... maybe even slipping into the enemy camp. The Patriotic Endeavor desperately needs men like Travis if we are ever to retake our country. His work with the POF men will forge him into the warrior required for the perilous days ahead."

"On-the-job training?"

"More like meaningful enterprise," Sacha replied. "The experience will serve him well as an undercover asset."

"A *spy*?" Logan's voice dropped. "I never pictured my son as a spy. And how do you think I can help?"

"Encourage him to lead the POF men in training. You're their natural leader, Logan. Travis just needs a nudge, and who better to give it than—"

"*Fine*," Logan cut in. "But he may not want the responsibility."

"Just speak with him before I head north again."

Logan rose from his chair, and the floor groaned beneath his boots as he took a few steps. He paused at the hallway entrance and glanced back. "After my nap, I'll talk to him."

"Thank you."

★★★

Travis and Wren arrived at the Salisbury farm under the midday sun's glare. The air carried the sweet, dusty scent of dry winter grass. With Derrick and Kincaid gone home to catch up on things, Sacha had left the two of them in charge of guarding the weapons.

"I think I'll lie down for a while," Wren said as they stepped into the shadowed building. "Since these men are gone, I'll take Derrick's bed."

"Might as well both rest," Travis agreed. "I'll use Kincaid's."

Several hours later, they stirred, ready to work on Wren's writing skills. She had just spread a few sheets of paper across the small table when the door creaked open and then clicked shut.

Gaela walked toward them, brushing a strand of hair from her face. "Travis, your father wants to speak with you."

He stood quickly. "Is he all right?"

"Logan's been napping in the bedroom," she said, stepping closer. "He has something important to discuss with you. I'll stay and keep Wren company while you go."

"Thanks."

Travis made his way to the house and found his father in the second bedroom at the end of the hallway. Logan lay on his side, eyes half-closed.

"You're still in bed?" Travis asked quietly from the doorway.

Logan rolled onto his back with a quiet grunt. "Rest seems to do more good than anything these days."

"Maybe you should keep resting instead of talking to me," Travis said, pulling a chair up beside the dresser.

"I'm good for now," Logan replied, adjusting himself higher on his pillow.

"Are you enjoying your time with Ms. Woods?" Travis asked, taking in the room.

"Gaela's been gracious. She doesn't seem to mind looking after me. Truth is, she might have taken a shine to me. Does that bother you?"

"Not at all," Travis responded. "I'm just not sure you know her well enough yet."

"That's exactly why I want to be here," Logan said, a faint smile touching his lips. "The best way to know people is to spend time with them. You and Wren have been spending plenty of time together, I notice. Must be helping you learn about each other."

"If you enjoy Gaela's company, don't worry about how I feel."

"Thank you, son." Logan's tone grew serious. "Now… what I need to tell you is important."

Travis leaned forward, wondering what could matter more than their upcoming meeting with Black Arrow. "I'm listening."

"Son, you know the men in our town have always regarded me as a leader, even though I never asked for it. Things seem to have naturally progressed that way." Logan paused, choosing his words carefully. "Travis, I need your help with something. Right now, I can't fill the role they expect of me."

Travis shifted to the edge of his chair. "Help with what?"

"I'd like you to lead our people while I'm laid up—train them and guide them to the Black Arrow camp. They need a steady hand, someone they trust."

"*Me?*" Travis asked. "Why can't Sacha do it? He's trained for this."

"They *might* follow him for a time, but they don't know him. I'm not sure they'd obey his orders when the fighting starts."

"They might not obey mine either."

"Our people know you. You're a capable young man, a good hunter who doesn't shy away from hard work. You're like me in the ways that matter. They'll stand behind you the same way they've stood behind me." Logan caught his son's gaze. "I need someone with confidence in charge. If you're not ready, Sacha will have to step in, but it could get messy."

Travis rose and paced beside the bed, his boots scuffing softly on the floorboards. Logan had sometimes spoken of men who led others well, but he never saw himself as some sort of commander. "Father, this is a hard thing you ask of me. And I might fail."

Logan looked into his eyes and saw the uncertainty that comes with youth. He reached for Travis's hand, his grip still strong despite his health. "Failure's *always* possible—even for me. I only ask that you do your best. Train our men. Lead them to the camp and get them into position. Stay sharp and be ready to adapt as the situation evolves. Be prepared for any deception from an enemy like this one. Brody Myles is known for his sneaky tactics. We all hope to come away with them joining us, avoiding an all-out war."

Travis gave his father a curious glance at the name. Logan had made odd remarks about the Black Arrow leader before, yet except for those two clashes with the rogue group, their paths had never crossed, as far as he could recall.

He released Logan's hand, crossed the room, then returned and pulled the chair closer to the bed. "All right. I'll try." His voice was soft yet firm. "Can we expect Marius and his men soon?"

"Hopefully. We still need to prepare for them. Work with Gaela and the others. Set up sleeping quarters in the grain storage sheds. If there isn't enough room, prioritize it for Marius's officers. See if the townsfolk can spare extra blankets. If space runs out, use the hay barn, but keep only trusted people near the weapons."

Travis nodded. "We'll make sure the weapons stay safe until they're needed."

"Good."

"I think we should send men out to hunt for fresh meat every day," Travis added.

"That's a great idea. Sacha and Cohen are probably out there now. We'll need plenty once this group arrives." Logan's expression softened. "Remember this, Travis: it's easier to keep a warrior happy when their belly is full."

"Or hers."

Logan smiled. "Yes, or hers. Thank you for agreeing to this."

"Sure. I'd better find Wren and get her help."

Chapter 47

Wren found Cohen sitting on the edge of the old well, shoulders slumped in quiet thought. The cool stone held the damp chill of the earth. "Father, what happened to Solomon was terrible."

Cohen lifted his eyes to hers, the lines around them deeper than she remembered. "Yes, it was, dear. I remember Solomon joining Black Arrow after his parents died. He was quite a spirited young man, full of fire."

She stepped close and wrapped her arms around his shoulders, breathing in the familiar scent of worn flannel and pine that clung to him. "You should try to let it go. You're *not* to blame for his death."

"You're right," he murmured, his voice held a heaviness. "Solomon's blood is on Brody. Still... I hate that it happened."

The back door of the house creaked shut. Travis crossed the yard and dropped onto the well's edge beside them. "Sorry to interrupt. Wren, I could use your help if you're free."

"Sure," she said, straightening. "What are we doing?"

"Father wants us to convert the old storage buildings into sleeping quarters for Marius's men before they get here."

Wren gave Cohen's hand a gentle squeeze as she stood. "Father, I'll see you later."

Cohen managed a small nod. "I'm all right, dear. Go on and help Travis."

The storage buildings were basic wooden structures, single rooms once used to store grain after the harvest. Their timbers held the musty, dry scent of forgotten seasons. One building had decayed into a sagging ruin, but three had endured. The simple frames would shelter Marius's fighters from the cold and wind.

Travis and Wren spent the first hours clearing out the interiors, hauling away dusty furniture and forgotten odds and ends someone had tucked away long ago. The air carried the faint scent of old hay and mildew. They kept the old mattresses in case any guests wanted to use them.

Inside the main house, Coco, Mallory, and Gaela were busy preparing food for everyone, filling the air with the savory aroma of roasting deer. Meanwhile, Sacha and Cohen had gone off to hunt, while Derrick and Kincaid, just returning from their own homes, took care of smoking and preserving the meat outside.

Later that afternoon, Travis and Wren rigged a sturdy barrier inside the barn using plywood they found to conceal the weapons until the time came to use them.

***

By lunchtime, the group had gathered in the kitchen. Gaela and the other women set out a simple meal of bread and roasted deer. "I wish we had more wheat flour for making bread," Gaela said, wiping her hands on her apron. "I'm down to the last bag of ground wheat."

"You're fortunate to have that," Logan replied. "I was told Mr. Salisbury raised wheat on his place. Must have kept a good stash for himself. We should check the other outbuildings and the cellar. Never know what he might have hidden."

"Please do, though I don't think you'll find any."

Travis looked at his father across the table. "I'm glad you're up and about, Father."

"Seems like a good morning. I am tired of being stuck in that bed, though," Logan replied, then blessed the food.

"Derrick and Kincaid said they didn't want to get grease on anything, so they took food with them," Gaela said.

"Are they working on the truck again?" Logan asked.

Travis swallowed a mouthful of meat. "Tires. Derrick said they took some to the barn. They'd found several at the junkyard, under a collapsed building, and put them away for when we need them."

"It sure has been nice to have that truck around… when it's running."

"I'm thankful we have it for you," Wren declared.

"I am too," Logan replied, setting down his fork as he swallowed. "Sorry, everyone, but I need to change the subject." He turned to Travis and Wren. "I thought you two might run an errand for us."

Travis looked up from his food. "What kind of errand?"

"Reconnaissance of the Black Arrow camp."

A flicker of unease tightened in Wren's chest. "Do you realize how dangerous that is after what happened? Brody will have men watching more closely now."

"I trust that both of you can avoid trouble," Logan said. "We need an updated look at that camp. I'd like to know whether anything has changed since Cohen left."

She stared at him. "*Brody* doesn't change much."

"He might, daughter," Cohen said. "Brody has a long list of plans unknown to anyone."

"Let's get eyes on that place before we send our people into this blind," Logan added. "Better safe than sorry."

"He's right," Travis acknowledged. "We should scout it. Father, when do you expect Marius?"

"Any day now. That's why this can't wait. Listen—*everyone* will need to hunt hard once those men arrive. We'll have extra mouths to feed. Be sure to assign hunting before you go."

"Jacoby and his friends are helping. I wanted to, but we've had our hands full."

Logan set his glass down. "I know. Once Marius's men arrive, they'll lend a hand. If Derrick can keep the truck running, I want to take the hunters to the old game reserve north of here. Game's getting thin."

"Good idea," Sacha said. "We hunted for hours but didn't see anything worth killing."

Travis wiped his mouth with a cloth and set it beside his plate. "Wren and I will head out first thing tomorrow."

"Actually," Logan said, "I'd rather you leave right after lunch. It's a late start, and you may need to camp overnight, but the sooner we know what Black Arrow is up to, the better."

"Then we'll get ready." Travis rose from his chair.

Wren pushed back her chair with a quiet scrape, her eyes narrowing at the thought of Brody's men lurking in wait for them. If he caught them now, she and Travis would endure unimaginable suffering until they returned her father to face his execution. She sighed. "Guess we'd better grab some dried meat, too." She offered a small, wry smile. "Looks like we're on the move again."

Chapter 48

A few hours into Travis and Wren's journey toward the Black Arrow camp, a steady, cool drizzle began to fall. They slipped into their worn-out raincoats and pushed on through the damp ferns, brushing against their legs, until they reached the lean-to.

"I'm thankful to be out of the rain," Travis said, setting down his backpack. "My pants are soaked through." He spotted the pile of dried branches they'd left behind on their last visit. "I'd forgotten about the wood we stashed. I'll get a fire going."

"Will help dry us," Wren replied, "but we can't stay long. We should leave before daylight."

"I'm good with that."

"At least we're together for a little while." She gave a small, rueful smile. "Though I got a bit angry when Logan asked us to do this."

"I think I heard it in your voice," Travis said, smiling as he stooped by the kindling.

"You did?" She brushed a wet strand of hair from her cheek. "I wanted time with you, and we'd just gotten back."

"I know, but we can spend time together when we return."

"Travis... have you thought about a wedding day?"

He shook his head as the firelight flickered across his face. "Uh, not exactly. Guess with everything that's happened... Sorry."

"Maybe we should set a date after we confront Brody," she offered, kneeling to unpack her gear. "What do you think? Or is it too soon?"

"No, that's fine," he said. "But remember, we still haven't told the others we're getting married."

Wren looked up, eyes steady in the firelight. "I want you to tell them, and ask Pastor Parker to marry us."

Travis gazed into the flames, letting her words settle amid the soft crackle of burning wood and the steady drip of rain on the roof. "Yes," he said at last. "I'll do that when we return."

"Fantastic." She unrolled her blanket on the floor beside the fire. "We'd better get some sleep."

As Travis reclined, the raindrops tapping on the roof stirred old memories. So much in their lives had changed. He turned his thoughts to Wren and ached for the day they might finally step back into something normal, away from the constant hustle through the woods.

***

The next morning, a light mist still clung to the air, turning the forest paths into silent gray corridors. Travis and Wren gathered their gear and left the run-down shanty, their boots whispering over the springy carpet of pine needles. By midday, they reached the Black Arrow camp.

Wren led them to a familiar spot behind a tall stand of pines, with rattan vines and poison ivy tangled around the trees, providing cover. Inside the compound, the air thrummed with the sounds of soldiers training—grunts of effort, the slap of boots on the wet ground, and sharp commands. They watched through the mist as Brody instructed one group in hand-to-hand combat, their bodies colliding with solid thuds. Another group tackled an intense obstacle course, while the next group crawled through mud that clung to them like wet clay. Some scaled slippery ropes hand over hand, while others strained under weight-lifting bars.

Wren shook her head in disbelief. "There are far more men here than before," she whispered. "Brody must have sent for some of the outlying posts."

"So this kind of training isn't normal?" Travis asked.

"Not at all. His men usually throw knives and shoot arrows at targets for their training. Judging by this… Brody's preparing for something bigger."

"Yeah," Travis said. "A war against us."

"I think you're right. Let's circle to the other side."

They slipped down a trail she knew well, pushing through Virginia creeper vines that draped the path and keeping clear of the guards in the watchtower. From the new vantage, the mist carried sharper scents of the camp—wood and meat smoke—mingling with the loamy damp leaves underfoot. A flickering campfire blazed between the buildings. Fighters, men and women, sat on crates and logs, enjoying a meal, while three women and a man in faded military fatigues ladled out portions.

One man spoke loudly, saying, "We believe they will arrive today," in response to a question.

"How many?" another voice asked.

"I'm guessing a hundred or more."

Wren tugged at Travis's coat sleeve and whispered, "That is Daryl Morrison. Brody must have put him in charge after my father left. Did you hear what he said?"

Travis nodded, rainwater dripping from his coat's hood. "Sounds like more men are coming to join them."

A sudden disturbance—shouts and the crunch of boots—echoed from the front of the compound.

"I wonder what that is?" Wren murmured.

Travis shrugged. "Let's get around there."

They hurried through the woods to the opposite side and found cover near a deteriorating section of wooden fence, half-swallowed by peppervine and dewberry briars. Travis noticed a large tree that had fallen across a shallow gully, its trunk laced with rattan vines. "Wren, climb upon that tree so you can see."

She scaled it quickly and peered through the mist. "Travis, these are the men Daryl mentioned. There could be a hundred or more. Brody is making our meeting with him even more difficult."

Difficult, yes, Travis mused, his mind racing. He could envision the raw power they'd wield if this faction stood with them—strength forged in unity, unbreakable against the northern tide. "We have to think bigger," he said aloud, gazing toward the camp. "Gotta look to the future. Brody's strategy has its flaws, no doubt, but summoning these men here is clever. Now I understand why convincing them to join us is crucial. Our mission of confronting the north would stand a far better chance with these forces on our side."

"Your father was right to send us," Wren said, hopping down. "We see how much work and planning this will take. I hope

Marius Nevins comes soon with enough men to show a force against Brody's men. He must take us seriously and realize we mean business."

"He'd better."

"We should hurry back," Wren added. "Logan and Sacha will want to hear every detail."

"Yes, for sure."

They turned to leave, and the wet brush stirred close by.

"Behind the tree, Wren," Travis whispered. "Someone's coming."

A swift sound sliced through the light rain, followed quickly by a solid thud against the tree they took shelter behind—an arrow quivered in the bark, its fletching humming with the force of the shot.

"We've got to go," Travis said, wheeling to lead them back down the trail at a run.

Wren caught up, her boots slapping through the wet leaves. "I thought we were quiet."

"I guess not," Travis replied, glancing back with a crooked, cross-eyed glance that almost made her laugh despite the fear. "We have to get away from them."

"You think?" she blurted.

They stuck to the well-used hunting trail for several miles, the path hemmed by tangles of blackberry briars that snagged at their raincoats and pants. The air hung heavy with the musky scent of pine and Virginia creeper, wet with the winter's light rain.

Soon, Travis slowed to a stop and turned to look at her. "We don't want to give away the location of your shack."

Wren nodded, breathing heavily. "How far to the old house you came to after we parted? You know, right after I removed the arrow from Reilly's hip."

"It's a good four or five miles from here," Travis said, searching his memory for a semblance of the path he would have taken. "That seems the best choice. Let's shed these raincoats—too easy to spot against the undergrowth."

"We'll get wetter," she said, "but you're right. Maybe the light rain will hold and wash away our tracks."

A few moments later, they were moving again, Travis in the lead, hoping the former route still lived in his bones. He planned to swing wide of the shack before hooking onto the road to the place in the woods.

They slipped down the animal trails at a steady jog for the next hour, the wet undergrowth slapping against their legs—the faint essence of rattan and oak leaves cutting through the air. Travis halted at a road, chest heaving, and turned to check on Wren.

"I'm good," she said, meeting his eyes with a quick, warm smile that seemed to melt the chill. "Is this the road?"

"I think so, though I came in from another direction last time."

"You came from the cave."

He gestured with a nod and pushed on. A half mile down, he spotted a lane and slowed again. "I think this is it."

"If it's not," Wren said, still catching her breath, "maybe we can find someplace else to rest and dry out."

"Yeah, maybe." He scanned the quiet woods. "At least I haven't heard Brody's men again. Wherever we stop, I think we're safe now."

"Then let's walk from here," she replied.

He grinned, easing into a walk, and she fell in beside him until an old house came into view, its porch sagging under the weight of heavy vines. Travis noted the front door still hung crooked on one hinge, unrepaired and lonely. "This is it."

Wren shook her head as she studied the place. "It's in bad shape."

He stepped onto the porch, and she followed. "Yeah, it is. We'll stay in the kitchen. Go ahead while I look for dry wood. We'll build our fire in the sink."

"Okay. Hope we don't burn it down."

Travis tore an interior door from its hinges and broke it apart. He carried the pieces to the kitchen and stacked them on the floor before the sink. When he straightened, he saw Wren wrapped in a small blanket, her wet clothes—pants, top, socks, and under-things—scattered across the bar top like shed skins.

She caught the surprised look on his face. "I hope I didn't shock you. I couldn't stand to have those wet clothes on any longer."

Noticing the bare curve of her shoulders and wet brownish blonde hair, the hoodie's edge didn't cover, Travis turned away. "It's fine."

"You can look, Travis. I won't expose myself if that's what's worrying you. It won't be long until we're married and you'll have nothing to worry about."

Travis turned back, meeting her eyes, his face warming to a light shade of red. "You're beautiful with clothes on, so I'm already tempted."

Wren offered a huge smile that brightened the dim room. "You'll make it, but I'm glad to know you think I am."

He focused on the sink. "I built a fire here before, and it worked well. The broken glass should pull the smoke out."

Once the flames caught, Travis moved through the other rooms gathering more fuel. He brought it back and stacked it on the floor. "This should hold us through the night."

"We'd better eat some dried meat," Wren added. "We both need rest."

"I know. It's a long way home tomorrow."

Chapter 49

The rain had ended, prompting Gaela and the other women to serve the noon meal outside on a makeshift picnic table.

Sacha sat at the end seat. "Your meals are always amazing, ladies."

"If we had more supplies, we could do more," Coco said.

"If we find something usable, we'll bring it to you."

Logan sat down next to Gaela. "I'm curious about what Travis and Wren have learned," he said.

"Shouldn't they be back soon?" Derrick questioned.

Gaela reached for Logan's arm. "Bless the meal first, please."

They bowed their heads as Logan prayed. Gazing at Derrick after he said amen, "To answer your question, I hoped so, or by morning."

Sacha laid a towel on his lap to wipe his hands. "I hope nothing has changed, though I suspect Brody has a surprise up his sleeve. He has friends in Oklahoma and other places in Texas."

"How many men?" Kincaid asked.

"I never heard a specific number, but I felt it was significant. I'm guessing around a thousand unless Brody's men were exaggerating."

Logan noticed Cohen had not spoken a word. "Would you know, Cohen?"

Cohen looked up and turned to Logan. "Um...I don't and I'm surprised Sacha heard what he did. There were certain things Brody trusted no one with. We met with groups for bow and knife competitions over the years, and they competed well. Those outside groups had more men at the events than we had in our camp. Brody liked to use the contests to enhance our training. He thought it added competition and fun for the men."

"Brody seems a capable leader. We could use more like him," uttered Derrick.

"Yes, but Brody needs a purpose," Cohen shared. "That is what motivates a man like him. If we can persuade him to join us, we should offer him something. He will perform well."

"I know you're right," Sacha said, placing his water glass on the table. Brody's talents are wasted here. His leadership skills will be invaluable in the times ahead."

Logan saw Cohen peering down the lane. "Cohen, everything okay? You seem distracted."

"Just concerned about Wren. I am always anxious when she's away. The thought of her being where Brody is...makes me uneasy."

"They are bright kids. They'll come through fine."

Sacha finished his last bite. "Without a doubt, they are highly intelligent and exhibit leadership qualities. While Travis may be young, his impressive reasoning abilities may soon prove valuable. He and Wren make a great team."

Hearing Sacha reminded Logan of his recent conversation with Travis. "Speaking of which, since I've been feeling under the weather, I've requested Travis to help lead our people when we head toward Black Arrow's camp. I believe Travis will do well in this role. When I approached him, you'd think I set him up as mayor of New York City. He took a moment to process, but he agreed."

Derrick nodded. "That's great. It takes Kincaid and me both to keep that rattletrap of a truck running."

"You know how I feel, Logan," Sacha said, half-grinning. "They aren't too young to get started."

Gaela turned her ear to a strange sound. "Gentlemen, your conversation is vital, but I think I hear horses."

A deep rumbling and horses' nickering echoed from the lane.

"That must be Marius," Logan responded as he rose from his chair. "I'm glad they've arrived."

"Logan, finish your meal," Gaela uttered. "They will be a while coming through."

"Dear, I *have* finished," he said, smiling.

A procession of horseback riders and supply wagons appeared at the opening. Two well-organized columns of men marched behind them, armed and carrying backpacks, followed by more wagons and horses. Marius Nevins waved as he passed by on his horse.

The entourage advanced steadily until halting near the hay barn. After giving instructions, Marius Nevins rode away from his men, dismounting near the house. "Hello, folks," he said.

"Glad to see you, Marius," Logan said. "Would you like to have lunch with us?"

"No, we stopped and ate from our supply wagons. We should be fine for a few days. Our men can help with any hunting needed while we're here."

"I was going to speak with you about that."

Sacha reached to shake hands with Marius. "That's quite an army you have there, sir," he said.

"Our group is exceptional, and this is just the first unit. Um, Logan, is there a designated area to set up camp?"

"Past the hay barn, a trail leads to a mostly open field, maybe forty acres. Please feel free to set up there. If that doesn't work, we will find a different place."

"No, it sounds good. Thank you. I will lead our men around and get them ready. If you'll excuse me."

"Oh, Marius. We've readied those storage buildings beside the barn for you," Logan explained, pointing toward them. "I suggest using those spaces for yourself and your officers."

"I appreciate the offer and will discuss this with the men."

By early afternoon, Marius and his men had raised over fifty tents in the open field. Some officers chose the storage buildings. Within hours, the hayfield took on the appearance of a fully operational outpost.

As the group from Deport set up, Cohen focused his attention on tending to the smoker. He looked up and saw two figures strolling up the lane. "Logan, take a look."

Logan smiled, seeing Travis and Wren walking towards them. "Hey, you're back."

"You two made better time than I expected," Cohen said.

Wren hugged her father. "It wasn't the easiest trekking through the woods in the rain."

"Have a seat and tell us what you know," Logan said.

Travis set down his gear and explained, "When we first arrived, Brody's men were busy with training exercises. Then, as we watched, a large group of soldiers from outside the camp showed up. Looks like Brody is preparing for a war."

"I thought something like this might happen. This changes things," Logan remarked. "We can't allow Brody to get a step ahead of us."

"You're right," Cohen said, recalling his daughter's upcoming task. "Brody having those extra men might add to his unwillingness to hear us out."

"I hoped that since he knew the North had given up on their deal, Brody would pause the fighting. I suppose he's forgotten that he's fighting his own people."

"Derrick expressed it most effectively," Cohen remarked. "He said, 'Black Arrow loves a good fight,' and he's right."

Logan shook his head. "I believe it, and that means we must prepare well before we reach that camp, or someone will get hurt."

Chapter 50

The next morning, a column of soldiers rolled into the Salisbury farm, dust trailing behind them. The man in charge, Nathan Cameron, led them down the lane on a white horse. More riders halted near the hay barn, while the rest of the division stretched along the driveway from the main gate toward Pattonville.

"Hello, Nathan," Marius Nevins said as he dismounted. "You brought a fine-looking group."

"Yes, sir. We're ready to stay as long as needed—and maybe push north with you when the time comes," Nathan replied, his voice carrying with confidence.

Marius glanced over and saw Logan's people drifting closer. "Hey, Nathan, come meet someone. This is Logan Weston, a good friend of mine. Logan, meet Nathan Cameron—he leads the Southern Friends, as they call themselves. They've come from Louisiana, Mississippi, Alabama—"

"And Georgia," Nathan finished with a thick Southern drawl, extending a calloused hand. "I'm a Georgia boy, born and raised. Logan, pleasure to meet you."

"Welcome," Logan said, gripping the hand firmly. "Mr. Cameron, thank you for coming to help."

"Just Nathan, please. Now, is there room on this farm for all my men?"

"I figured we'd talk to Mitchel Meyers," Logan replied. "His place sits closer to town and still has plenty of unused farmland. Should hold your people comfortable. If you and Marius would like to join me, we'll take the old truck."

"*Truck!*" Nathan's eyes lit up. "You have a running vehicle! We've had no fuel in ages."

"Fuel is an issue for us, too. Sometimes we have a running truck; sometimes we don't. Our guys work on it almost every day. Hop in, and we'll take a spin. And pray we don't break down."

★★★

Travis perched atop the old well house, watching the column of soldiers still coming in. So many of them—boots stirring the dry dust, their expressions purposeful. The sight twisted his gut, taking his thoughts back to his father's recent request: Oversee our people. Lead them to the Black Arrow camp when the time comes.

I've got to get away from here, he decided.

He dropped to the ground and walked into the house. Laughter and the clatter of pots drifted from the kitchen, where the women worked. "Hey, Wren," he called, grabbing his gear from the side room. "I'm going hunting. Want to go with me?"

Wren wiped her hands on a cloth, then shrugged, half-smiling at the others seated nearby. "Travis, your timing's not the best with all these new folks rolling in." She nodded toward the door. "But I'll grab my things."

By the time she stepped outside, Travis was nearly down the lane. The new arrivals paused to watch her pass. She quickened her pace and caught up as he turned onto the main road.

They walked in silence until they reached the stretch of land between the Salisbury farm and Meyers' road. Travis veered into a field of dry sagegrass and broomsedge. For half an hour, they scanned the area for deer sign—tracks, droppings, and scrapes—before he crossed an old barbed-wire fence and slipped onto a narrow trail that wound into the piney woods.

The deeper they went, the more the terrain shifted—rocky patches breaking through thin soil, lifeless tufts of grass giving way to scattered yaupon and the occasional fallen pine limb, its needles dry and crackling. It wasn't the hunting ground he remembered.

Wren eyed the rocky, lifeless terrain, her brow furrowing. "Travis, you sure about this spot? What could the animals even find to eat out here?" She took a few more steps, her boots stirring the dry earth. "Have you hunted here before?"

Travis kept walking, the weight of unspoken words pressing heavier on her.

After a moment, Wren stopped. "All right, enough of this, Travis. What's up with you?"

"What do you mean?" he asked, slowing to a few deliberate steps.

"You know *exactly* what I mean. The way you're acting doesn't feel like you at all. Did you even plan to hunt today?" Her expression tightened with frustration as the dry, cold wind tugged at loose strands of her hair. "Please—just *stop* walking."

At last, he halted abruptly and turned to face her. His silence hung thicker than any reply.

She closed the distance and laid a hand on his arm, her voice softening. "What's wrong, Travis? Talk to me."

His eyes had gone glassy, reflecting the filtered light through the pines. "All these fighters showing up... it just reminds me of what my father recently asked me to do. I'm not sure I can do it."

"*Huh?* What exactly did Logan ask you to do?"

"He's been sick, and the men from Pattonville still look to him. He always knows the right words. Even Derrick and Kincaid turn to him for answers. He told me leading just... happened for him. Nothing he ever planned."

"I'm not following, Travis. Are you worried he can't lead because he's ill?"

"*No*—don't you see? Because he can't right now, he wants *me* to lead the men from town. He says they'll follow me. But what if they don't? What if I make the wrong call and someone gets hurt? I don't want to embarrass him. I can't even imagine what they'd think of me if something went wrong."

"Travis, you can't worry about what others think. Your father asked this because he believes in you."

"Do *you* believe I can do it, Wren?"

"Yes. I do." She held his gaze. "I've seen how Derrick and Kincaid look at you, though younger than them, but they respect you deeply. I think the rest of the town does too."

"I've never seen myself as a leader. We already lost good people when Black Arrow hit us—twice. Now I'm supposed to lead our people against them."

"How many fighting men are there from Pattonville?"

"Maybe a hundred. Nothing like Marius's men or this new Southern Friends group."

"Still, that's a lot of lives and a heavy responsibility. But this could be the time you learn who you really are, Travis. What if God is shaping you for something bigger?" She softened her tone. "I heard what Marius said about that day in the woods—how God protected you. Remember when that man tried to kill you? And when Reilly drew an arrow at both of us? Sacha showed up out of nowhere and stopped him. Do you really think that was by chance? I don't."

Travis lowered himself onto a nearby fallen log. "Where'd you hear about the woods incident?"

"Your father told me. I believe God sent Sacha to protect you—and so does he. The Bible talks about being faithful with a few things, so you can be trusted with more. Maybe I'm not quoting it perfectly—"

"Close enough."

"Travis, just be faithful. If nothing else, do this for your father. But I hope you'll do it for God, too. He's watching over you and has a plan. Do it for yourself as well—so you can shake off this fear that's got its hooks in you. Win or lose, giving it everything you've got will strengthen you."

"Well... it *must* be right, since Father asked."

Wren stood with her hands on her hips, looking down at him with quiet fire in her eyes. "Yet here *you* are, getting all twisted up over what you know you must do. Can't you see how God is preparing you? He wants *you* for this. Not Sacha, not your father, not any of the others. They each have their place. But this one is fitted just for you—if you'll open your heart to serve Him. Maybe he'll make you capable of leading."

"Travis gazed up at her. "I never looked at it that way."

"Maybe you should also pray before you let it eat you alive."

Wren's insight left him quiet, almost awed. Since the day he'd first handed her that small Bible, she had grown in her faith with a quiet steadiness that humbled him.

"So," she asked, a small smile returning, "are we actually going to hunt here?"

Travis picked up his gear with a slight, reluctant grin. "Like you said—there's no game here. Let's head home."

Chapter 51

Brody Myles completed the first exercise drills with his men and wiped the sweat from his forehead. Aware of the demanding workload that awaited him, he eagerly awaited the arrival of the Oklahoma group, which meant his men would have the opportunity to train alongside them. The majority of them had served in the military and worked as mercenaries and would share some of their training techniques.

The use of firearms against his troops increased the sense of urgency. Bows and arrows wouldn't stand a chance against these weapons. Yet victory might still be attained by applying covert black ops strategies, and the Oklahoma group's expertise in this field would benefit them.

He would train his soldiers to move through the forest like ghosts and infiltrate the enemy. His latest plan had three phases: locate Pattonville's food supply and take it out, eliminate the leadership and sow confusion, and uncover the weapon stash, therefore shifting the power in their favor.

His men also had to undergo several weeks of rigorous training exercises to make them ready. And one other major task he must attend to—a small yet crucial detail. Cohen Daniels' escape from his cell made Brody seem incompetent. His old friend, the traitor, must at last be judged before his men and meet his demise. This was one of Black Arrow's laws.

A knock sounded on the door.

"Come in."

Daryl Morrison stepped inside, his face revealing concern.

"What is it, Daryl? Looking at your face, I'd say you're in a bad mood."

"No, sir, but we're running low on fresh meat. Should I arrange for a hunting team to go out?"

"I thought we already sent Ricky and Jim?"

"Sir, that was four days back. They brought in two deer and four rabbits. We need a lot more for our men."

"I suppose we do. Send out four teams today and four tomorrow. Instruct them to hunt hard and help us catch up. We have a group of men scheduled to arrive soon, so we'll need all the meat we can gather. Make sure they hunt the grounds those Pattonville folks hunt. Might be another way to get back at them."

"Yes, sir. I'm on it."

Brody flung a map down on his desk and rose from the chair. "Hey, Daryl, hold up a minute. Is there anyone in camp who might know the training location for those Pattonville folks? They stood their ground, which suggests they'd prepare for another attack."

"I don't know, sir. I'd be happy to send someone to spy for you."

"Nah, let's wait on that. They might get in their heads some reckless idea like Reilly and meet their demise. I have some plans in the works, so we'll wait. Just arrange the next group's training session, and I'll be out soon."

"Yes, sir."

After Daryl left the room, Brody stared out the window, pleased with how his men performed in the earlier combat drills. Those with military expertise excelled, while others displayed remarkable talent in knife-throwing and archery. He had adjusted each drill to maximize the men's strengths and address their deficiencies. With each passing day, Brody grew more and more confident in their ability to handle whatever obstacles came their way. But the day wasn't over. He reached for a set of dry clothes from a drawer, put them on, and headed for the exercise area.

Daryl waited outside with seven others to start their training. "We are ready, sir," he said.

"Thank you, Daryl. After I start them, would you go to the tower and instruct those men to notify me when our guests from Oklahoma are in sight?"

"Sir?"

Brody rolled his eyes and added, "I may need to put on more dry clothes before they get settled inside."

"Oh, yes, sir."

"Now go!"

Brody introduced the men to a hand-to-hand blocking exercise he had acquired during his time in the military. To emphasize the importance of self-defense, he picked two of them to go head-to-head.

A whistle blew, and Brody turned to see them waving from the tower. *That was sooner than I expected,* he thought. "Tim, lead the drills until Daryl returns," Brody said. "Tell him, after this, move on to knife throwing."

"Yes, sir."

As Brody looked on, the Oklahoma group drew nearer. A group of around forty men entered through the gate, including three on horseback and two on the supply wagon. The rest of the soldiers marched in, carrying their weapons and dressed in fatigues and caps. The scene reminded Brody of a similar moment in the military. *That's how discipline should look,* he mused.

A clean-shaven man riding a black horse reined away from the rest when he spotted Brody standing nearby. He pulled the horse to a halt and dismounted with a salute. "Sir, it is great to be here," Colonel Krieger said.

Brody returned a salute. "At ease, Frank. We're glad to have you and your men with us. A bunkhouse awaits you at the end of the lane, though it might not have enough space for all."

"We'll figure something out, Major General Myles," Colonel Krieger remarked. "We have tents."

No one had called Brody Major General in over twenty years, and the term seemed out of context in their environment. "Frank, let's skip the formalities while we're at camp. I'm grateful for the acknowledgment, but we maintain a low profile here. Please refer to me as Brody?"

"Of course. My men and I will start setting up right away. Is there anything you require from us today?"

"Not that I can think of. Our drills will begin right after breakfast tomorrow. Inform your men that supper will be served right before sunset."

"Yes, sir. We'll catch you later," Frank said with a nod, turning toward his horse.

A smile spread across Brody's face. "This is what we've been looking for. The POF will be astonished," he remarked, watching as Frank and his crew moved toward the sleeping quarters.

Chapter 52

Hoping to catch Travis's attention during the late-morning drills, one hundred eager volunteers stood together. Travis selected a group of thirty men from them and guided them towards the farm. They stood watching as Sacha put Nathan's group through a vigorous workout. After a while, Sacha handed over the responsibility to one of Nathan's men, who led them in jogging.

While he waited, Travis walked over to Sacha as Marius started the next group. "That was quite a workout with the first group. What do you want us to do?"

Sacha turned and looked him in the eyes. "Follow me. There's something I want to show you."

"Show me?"

"Yeah, how to make a firebomb?"

"I must be a lucky man today," Travis smiled.

"You may thank me someday for this knowledge."

Sacha had set up a table just outside the main barn door. He reached and picked up a soda bottle. "What we're making is called Molotov Cocktails. That name, 'Molotov Cocktail,' became famous after a Soviet foreign minister named Vyacheslav Molotov dropped large bombs on Finland during the early 1900s. The rebels fighting against them had little to work with, but they came up with the idea of building firebombs against the Soviets. These cocktails were named after him since he was responsible for bombing their country. History tells us that the Finns are estimated to have destroyed around 400 Soviet tanks using Molotov cocktails. And that's your history lesson for the day."

"I don't even know what a tank is," remarked Travis. "But I suppose I'm blessed to learn this."

As the lesson commenced, Sacha explained to Travis the step-by-step process of making the cocktails, using glass soda bottles and a kerosene and methanol mixture as the explosive. Once a bottle was ready, Sacha tore an old shirt into strips for wicks, inserting them into the liquid, with a portion hanging outside for lighting.

He sealed the bottle with a wooden stick sharpened to a point. "When we're ready to use one of these, just light the wick and throw it. Since we're low on kerosene and methanol, let's use these sparingly."

"We can't use gasoline?" Travis asked.

"Gasoline is too volatile, but we can mix it with other agents like wax and tar—I just can't put my hands on any. There have been cases where gasoline explosions have caused people to lose an arm."

"I'd rather keep my arm."

"Okay, now that you learned to make them, you can show Wren. More people should know in case one of us doesn't survive."

The thought of one of them dying had never crossed Travis' mind. "Maybe we're rushing too much to get to that camp."

"We just have to be careful how we place them, which will be your job. This is a huge responsibility, but I believe you can do it."

"I understand my role, but I don't want anyone to die. We have guns, and now we're making firebombs—I'm not sure I'm ready for this."

Sacha shrugged. "There are moments in our lives when we must rise to the occasion, even in times of uncertainty. So often others perceive our potential even when we cannot."

Travis gave a nod. "Maybe so."

"Perhaps you should consider a different perspective. We are not in conflict with the people of the North. We are battling principalities in high places."

"I remember that scripture," Travis said.

"Yes, from Ephesians. Evil spirits are looking to control whatever they can. Your pastor emphasized the importance of prayer in the ongoing battle between good and evil. Your father and I, and many others, experienced it when evil forced Christians below the thirty-sixth parallel, so I understand your pastor's dream. The creatures he saw symbolize malevolent spirits seeking whom they can devour. Amid all of that, one of our tasks is to show love to those ensnared by the spirits and assist them in breaking free from his grip. Not a straightforward task, but we must try."

Travis stared at him through narrow lids for several seconds, then gave a nod. "I know there will be moments when we'll have to face evil head-on."

"Yes, and I suspect you're ready. Lean on your instinct and what you've learned."

"I'm not a soldier like you, Sacha, and I've noticed how you can move forward after ending someone's life."

"Oh, it's not easy, but when you or a person close to you is facing a life-threatening situation, you find a source of inner strength."

Sacha could see from Travis's expression that he had absorbed every word. Still, he felt it was important to emphasize the need for faith in God amid uncertain times. "To win in battle, we need more than a powerful army and impressive weapons. With prayer as our ultimate weapon and God as our source of strength, we can face any challenge with confidence."

"I've never heard you speak like this before."

"As an undercover asset, I'm required to withhold personal things, but I should have been more honest with you. I hope you can look beyond my facade and understand who I am."

"I do, and thanks for the encouragement."

After Travis placed his second firebomb cocktail on a shelf, Sacha picked it up and soaked the wick with the kerosene mixture.

"What are you doing?" Travis asked.

Sacha turned and walked outside with the bottle as Travis followed behind. "Check this out." He lit the wick and tossed it about twenty feet toward an old stump. The bottle burst on impact, igniting the stump in a fiery blaze and sending shards of glass into the air as it broke.

"Wow! That is amazing!" Travis remarked.

"Firebombs aren't the most efficient weapon, but they can offer a distraction."

After returning to the work area, Sacha watched as Travis assembled four more firebombs until they summoned Travis and his men to the field for the workouts, where he put them through a rigorous routine and then led them on a jog.

Nearing the road to the farm on their return, Travis noticed someone in dark clothes sprinting across the road. With his hand raised, he signaled for the men to stop while he observed the intruder take to a field.

"Should I go after Sacha?" Jacoby questioned.

Travis wiped the sweat from his brow, and he turned to address the men. "He'd never catch him. I will let Sacha know as soon as we return."

"Black Arrow must be spying on us like you and Wren did them."

"I think you may be right, Jacoby. Another time, though. Let's finish our run, men."

Chapter 53

Gaela paused at the sound of movement from the bedroom and stepped into the doorway. "Logan, what are you doing out of bed?"

"I feel pretty good this morning," he said, his voice still carrying the gravel of sleep.

"Not good enough to ride out with the others, though, right?"

"No, but I might want to discuss things with Travis and Sacha. When are they leaving?"

"Tomorrow," she answered, moving toward the counter. "You want some bread and coffee? Jacoby brought us a bag of wheat meal. He said a friend gave him several, so he gave one to us."

Logan's face brightened. "That sounds great. We'll miss that grain once it's gone. Maybe things will be different up north."

Gaela kneaded the dough with steady hands. The savory-sweet scent wafted up, warm and comforting—a small luxury in these uncertain times—mingling with the woodsy aroma from the cast-iron cookstove. She didn't hear Logan approach until his arms slipped around her waist from behind, drawing her gently against him.

"I'm grateful for everything you've done," he murmured, his breath warm against her hair. "I can't tell you how much your kindness has meant to me."

"You wouldn't have done any less for me," Gaela said, leaning back into the solid comfort of his chest.

He pressed a soft kiss to the side of her neck. "You know I adore you, right? Still don't know what you see in a broken-down man like me."

She turned in his arms, meeting his eyes. "Actually... I've been wanting to talk to you about that."

"Oh?"

"The truth is," she said, her heart beating a little faster, "I'm crazy about you, too. In fact, Logan, I'm in love with you. But I have a problem. The Endeavor will call me north soon."

His arms tightened around her. "Do you *have* to go?"

"Someone's been handling my responsibilities, and they can manage for a while longer. But they'll expect my return once Sacha starts back... unless—"

Logan chimed in, "There's an escalation in the war? Or the fighting in the North turning southward?"

"Or another reason."

Logan smiled, reflecting on the hidden meaning. "If we were to marry, would that be enough to justify your staying?"

"I'm sure it would. Are you asking?" she said.

"I am, if you will. I don't think I could stand watching you walk into a war zone without me. Just the thought of it sends my joints aching again."

She stared into his eyes, seeing the depth of his feelings. "Well, let's get married." Then she leaned in, and their lips met in a tender, unhurried kiss.

He pulled back just enough to whisper against her mouth, "Let's do it."

Footsteps approached from behind them. "Oops," Gaela whispered, glancing over Logan's shoulder.

Travis and Wren stood at the kitchen entrance, hand in hand.

"*What's* going on?" Travis asked.

A smile danced across Gaela's and Logan's faces as they turned toward each other. "We're getting *married!*" they said in unison.

"*What?*" Wren replied, her eyes widening. "That's wonderful! Well, since you are, maybe we should share our news." She turned to Travis and gave him an encouraging nod.

Travis cleared his throat, a touch of reddening in his cheeks. "Father, Wren, and I have also decided to get married."

"Well, I guess I'm not surprised," Logan said.

"That's *fantastic!*" Gaela exclaimed.

Wren's face lit up like the morning sun breaking through the clouds. "Yes, it is. Gaela, when can we expect the wedding? Do you have a time frame in mind?"

Gaela and Logan exchanged a quick glance. "He asked me a few minutes before you walked in," she admitted. "How about you two?"

"In a couple of weeks, if nothing else happens," Travis answered.

"What if we held our weddings at the same time?" Gaela suggested.

Wren leaped into Travis's arms with a delighted laugh. "*That* would be amazing. We can plan the wedding together."

"Pastor Parker should do the honors," Travis added.

Logan sensed the women were on the verge of diving headfirst into wedding plans. He pictured the soft scatter of fabric and flowers, and vows humming in the air like a distant melody. He caught Travis's eye. "Travis, don't we need to find Sacha? We have something important to discuss with him."

"Yes, we do."

The two men slipped outside, the screen door creaking softly behind them, and made their way to the stone wall at the old well, where they sat. "I'm no use with all that wedding talk," Logan said with a rueful chuckle. "Women can get carried away when it comes to these things."

"Sorry for the distraction," Travis replied. "I know we should keep our minds on preparing for the trek to the Black Arrow camp."

"But sometimes it's good to step away from things," Logan said.

The back door swung open with a sudden burst, and Wren darted out. "Travis! Gaela said to find Sacha—there's a message coming in on the radio."

Logan followed Wren back inside while Travis sprinted toward the barn. Gaela was already at the radio, a pencil in hand, poised to scratch down the message.

"What was that?" she asked into the microphone. "Say it again."

A voice cut through the crackle on the radio: "Please provide a response code. We'll hold."

"Affirmative. Snowplow is the response code. Hold," Gaela replied.

The speaker hissed again. "That's correct." After a short pause, the voice said, "A weather warning for you: Avalanche is delayed. Hold."

Gaela leaned closer. "What time is the weather expected to change, Snowstorm? Hold."

The voice echoed clearly through the speaker. "Delay the avalanche for approximately two months. Await the summons. Hold."

"What other changes in weather patterns?" Gaela asked. "Hold."

They waited amid the speaker's hiss for a long, tense moment. Then a distorted voice broke through: "Rocky Mountain rains occur in two weeks. Hold."

"Which regions? Hold." Frustration crept into Gaela's voice with each delayed response.

"The lion's rain will meet in the Mojave region—refer to the map. The grizzly's will assemble in the Talon region, and the bear's will gather in the Razor region. Hold."

"Affirmative and hold," Gaela said.

Static hissed over the radio as they waited. "Snowstorm out," was the voice's final words.

Distortion burst from the speaker until Gaela reached and switched it off.

"Did you understand all that?" Wren asked.

"Yes, it's coded," Gaela replied.

Sacha and Travis stepped in from the hallway. "We missed most of it," Sacha said. "Did you confirm the date?"

"Delayed for at least two months."

Sacha shook his head.

Travis frowned. "What's an avalanche?"

Sacha's expression grew more serious. "That's the signal for the fighters here to head toward the thirty-sixth parallel."

"So, the fight is still on?" Travis asked.

"Yes, only delayed a bit longer. Endeavor would only push back the timeline when they have a good reason, but I wish they'd hurry."

"Sacha, there's more," Gaela said quietly.

He waited, a flicker of unease crossing his face. "You mean—"

"I'm afraid so."

Wren leaned forward. "There was much *more* in that message. What else do those codes say? I heard you ask about other storms."

"That's right," Gaela replied. "Some were codes for us to head home. They're calling us back to the Missouri camp in two weeks. Bear is the code for Sacha, Coco, and me. Razor is the code for the Missouri camp. The rest were for others doing undercover work."

"But *you're* getting married," Wren protested. "You *can't* leave."

"What's that? Since when?" Sacha asked, a curious expression etching his features.

"Just now, minutes ago," Wren said. "Logan asked her to marry him."

Sacha gazed at Gaela, his jaw tightening. "I was afraid of this, but you should have warned me."

"I only learned less than thirty minutes ago."

"That's right. I just asked her," Logan confirmed, stepping closer. "Which raises the question. *Will* you let Gaela stay behind?"

Gaela reached out and touched Logan's arm. "I told you Endeavor would expect my return."

Sacha tapped his finger rhythmically on the top of an old wooden chest. "Not necessarily," he said.

"What do you mean?" Gaela replied.

"I have the authority to decide whether you stay or leave," Sacha told her. "But I wasn't looking forward to crossing that border alone, and Coco has already asked to stay. It's better to have someone watching your back when you reach the periphery. I honestly never expected you to stay."

"I'm sorry, but life changes," she said softly.

Sacha gazed at her with a shrug. "I know."

Travis shook his head as he glanced at Sacha. "You're leaving when we need you here? Our training has just begun."

Sacha let out a deep breath as the weight of the decisions settled heavily on his shoulders. Training wasn't a major issue, but the Endeavor wouldn't appreciate Gaela's choice to stay behind—it could even get her kicked off the team. He might face retribution himself for allowing it.

"There are several who can help with the training here," he said. "Besides, *I* was the one who pushed hard to use the southern men to aid the North. I came here hoping to convince some of you to join us. You did, and now they're expecting you."

A trace of confusion crossed Travis's face. "You're admitting that you *used* us?"

Sacha shook his head firmly. "I only told them that the southern men have some top-notch fighters. The first time I came through was two years ago. I learned about the various factions—how you've survived and your resilience. When I mentioned you, most of our people believed you folks had already suffered enough. But you've endured because of your faith in God, and that strength is invaluable."

He gazed at them, noticing little reaction. "Each faction has gifts we need. Travis, I would never take advantage of you. I only recently shared the truth about myself. It was the Endeavor who asked me to keep it hidden. Now, you've all become my dearest friends."

The room fell quiet for a moment. Logan nodded slowly. "Thanks for explaining things. We understand better now… and we feel the same way about you."

Travis rested his hands on Sacha's shoulders and squeezed gently. "I'm sorry for what I said. I should have known better."

"Not a problem, Travis."

"If I were healthier, I'd go with you," Logan said.

Gaela looked at Logan. "I'm *not* staying unless you're with me."

Sacha raised a hand. "Gaela, let me think about it. I'll get back to you." He stepped outside.

Wren crossed the room to the older woman. "So, does that mean your marriage is still on?"

"I suppose so," Gaela replied with a smile. "Sacha will figure something out."

Chapter 54

Travis chose a group of trusted men from Pattonville, several from Marius, and a solid contingent from Roy Wayne's ranks to join the rendezvous as they headed for the Black Arrow camp. Pastor Parker gathered the company beside the wagons for prayer as the sun rose behind the trees. When the final amen faded into the cool morning air, those who had received weapons training were handed rifles. The rest relied on their bows.

With their knowledge of the best routes for the wagons, Travis and Wren guided the procession. By nightfall, they arrived at the campsite where Travis and Wren had their unexpected encounter by the creek.

The company made camp without haste. Soon, the rich scent of woodsmoke curled through the cool night air, drifting low over the water. The creek murmured steadily in the background, a constant, soothing voice beneath the occasional hoot of an owl and the gentle rustle of wind through the branches overhead.

Wren laid out her bedroll on a patch of soft ground, then sank onto it with a tired sigh. "Travis," she said, a small smile touching her lips, "we should come back to this spot again someday—just to hunt."

"Only if you give me a head start," Travis answered, grinning as he settled nearby. "I still remember you stealing my deer."

"That was *my* deer," she answered, a thread of laughter in her voice. "Are you really still claiming her after all this time?"

"Wait a minute. How long had you been coming to this place to hunt?" he asked.

"I spotted her the day before," she explained, propping herself up on one elbow. "I walked down from the old lean-to and found fresh tracks leading to the creek. There she stood, half-hidden in the trees. I returned before dawn the next morning."

"That was my *fifth* day of hunting that week," Travis added. "I reckon you're the reason the deer stayed hidden those first few mornings."

"Don't blame me," she replied with a playful huff. "You can't claim a deer just by following her tracks."

Sacha passed by and slowed his steps, catching the tail end of their conversation. "You two, set your arguing aside. Tomorrow demands clear heads. We can't afford any mistakes. Save your energy for then."

Wren sat up, her smile fading to seriousness. "You're right, Sacha. No time for play. Would you walk us through it again?"

Sacha crouched near their bedrolls, speaking calmly. "We'll handle any Black Arrow scouts we encounter outside the camp as the situation requires. Once we're in position and everything is ready, I'll give the signal to call Brody out."

"Sounds straightforward," Travis said, though doubt edged his words. "The real question is whether we can pull it off."

"We have the numbers and the weapons," Sacha answered. "Our success depends on everyone holding to their role—including you, Wren. Convincing Brody won't be easy, especially if he senses armed men waiting in the trees. Stay extra careful. Don't step into the clearing until it feels right. We're all praying your words will draw him out so he can hear what we have to say."

"I hope you're not planning anything dangerous," Wren said.

"I'd love nothing more than to take him clean," Sacha admitted. "But Brody's too sharp for simple traps—especially after we took Cohen. All we truly need is a conversation to get things started."

Travis sat up on his blanket. "I still don't like that Wren is the one facing him. Brody threw her father in jail. The man is dangerous."

"Travis," Sacha said, dropping to one knee beside him. "Remember, we have those guns now. A few arrows *won't* match our bullets. He knows that. But if things turn for the worse, we have a surprise waiting." He placed a steadying hand on Travis's shoulder. "Keep your focus."

"I'll just be glad when this is over," Travis murmured.

"It will go smoothly if we hold to the plan. Wren, speak to Brody as you always have—steady and clear. Keep your composure."

Wren nodded slowly, her brow creased in quiet thought. "I can't see him stepping outside the camp."

"We'll keep trying until he does. For now, both of you should get some rest."

As Sacha rose, Pastor Parker approached. "Could we take a moment to pray together?"

Sacha nodded. "*That's* a fine idea, Pastor."

Others nearby drifted closer as Parker bowed his head. The creek's soft murmur seemed to weave into the moment. "Father, we ask for Your protection over every soul here. Wrap these men and women in Your arms of defense as they step into tomorrow. Let mercy and grace prevail in all that lies ahead. May the outcome align with Your perfect will. Amen."

"Amen," Sacha echoed. "Thank you for coming with us, Pastor. The trail couldn't have been easy."

"A little wearisome," Parker admitted with a faint smile, "but I came because I believe the time has come for darkness to loosen its grip on this land and for light to prevail." He blinked back sudden tears. "When God gave me that dream, I felt I would soon witness the answer to my prayers." He gave a faint grin and looked at him. "Sacha, if things don't unfold exactly as planned, don't lose heart. God is with you. Simply trust Him."

"Thank you. I will."

"Now, I'd better get my rest."

"Yes, me too."

As the pastor moved away to his bedroll, Travis reached over and gently touched Wren's arm. "Pray with me that nothing goes wrong tomorrow when you step forward."

"Travis, don't worry about me," she whispered. "Brody won't hurt me. My bigger fear is that he won't even listen."

"If he gets angry, as your father expects, then all this work could be for nothing."

Wren shrugged. "Then we'll head north without them."

Travis lay back, staring up at the stars. "Right. Short by a hundred and fifty to two hundred good fighters."

"If they aren't on our side, we're better off without them."

He fell quiet for a long while, turning over the risks of the long journey north without the Black Arrow men. Whispers of dangerous drones still hovering at the edges of known territory lingered in his mind. Would they make it through without loss? How many unseen threats waited ahead, even ones Sacha didn't know about? *Lord, grant us victory*, he prayed silently. *This is new ground for all of us. Guide our steps and keep us safe.*

Most of the camp had already slipped into sleep, their breathing soft and even beneath the drifting woodsmoke and the creek's endless lullaby. Travis turned on his bedroll to face Wren. She met his gaze in the dim firelight, and a quiet, reassuring smile passed between them. He let out a slow breath, feeling some of the tension ease from his shoulders, and soon fell into a deep, hard-earned rest.

Chapter 55

Sacha and Travis rousted the camp before dawn. Once everyone had taken water and chewed down their dried meat, the group set out to finish the long journey. By midmorning, the scouts reported they were nearly there.

Marius urged his horse alongside Travis. "One of my men found a trail leading to the back of the camp. I'd like to send a few to watch for anyone trying to slip away."

Travis replied, "Great idea. Spread the rest out on this side, but keep them hidden unless fighting starts. Remember, our people are at the main gate."

"No problem. I prefer you folks handle the talking."

Wren recalled a detail and approached the big man. "Marius, tell your men to watch for hunters moving in and out. They come and go from the camp all day."

"Will do. See you later." Marius wheeled his horse and rode off.

As they drew closer, the guards in the tower came into view. Inside the walls, Brody's men went about their tasks, unaware of the visitors just beyond the tree line.

Travis quietly warned those close by to stay alert for returning hunters, then motioned to Jacoby. "The firebombs are in the back of the wagon. Soak two wicks in the kerosene mix and keep them ready."

"Sure will." Jacoby turned and headed toward the wagon.

One of Roy Wayne's young men, waited a short distance behind them. "Chevy, watch for my signal," Travis said. "You know what to do."

Chevy nodded and slipped back toward the wagon and out of sight behind the dense brush.

Wren studied the gate and tower from about two hundred feet away as Sacha stepped out from cover. "Ready?"

"As ready as I can be," she said.

"You in the camp, listen up!" Sacha shouted, then darted back behind the oak. "We need to speak with Brody."

When there was no reply, Sacha cupped his hands and called again. "You in the camp—did you hear me?"

"Who's out there?" a young voice called back.

At the response, a commotion stirred in the woods behind them.

Travis glanced over his shoulder. "What's that noise?" He motioned to Derrick and Randall. "Find out, but be quick. We can't afford anything to go wrong now."

The two men melted into the trees as Sacha called toward the tower once more. "We're here to speak with Brody Myles!"

The man on watch remarked, "Brody's not taking visitors today." His companions nearby chuckled.

"Is that so?" Sacha raised his .30-30 Winchester and fired three rounds into the air. "Is he now?"

A brief silence followed, broken only by the soft sounds of men shifting into position behind the camp wall.

"Do you think that was wise?" Wren asked.

Sacha shrugged. "They already know we have guns. Had to get Brody's attention somehow."

Travis spotted Derrick and Randall returning, dragging a captive between them. "Tie him to the wagon and gag him."

"Two of Roy Wayne's men are watching for hunters," Derrick reported.

"Surely, they heard the gunshots," Travis said. "Have Marius's men keep an eye out for them too."

Travis gestured to Jacoby. "Ready?"

"I am," Jacoby replied.

A deep voice boomed across the clearing. "You have my attention!"

Sacha looked toward the camp. "Are you Myles?"

"I'm Myles. Who do I have the pleasure of addressing?"

"The People of the Faith and others."

"Figured that. So what do you want?" Brody's tone carried clear disdain.

"We're just here to talk." Sacha replied.

"I can hear you, but I'm not much for talking."

"We hoped to begin peace talks. Hated to do it this way, but your refusal to listen to Colonel Daniels left us little choice."

Brody's tone sharpened. "Colonel? He's no colonel." Brody shot back. "And all these men surrounding my camp don't exactly set you up for peace."

"We're not looking for a fight unless you force it," Sacha replied.

"I'm not sure I believe that." Brody paused, weighing the moment. "So what are your terms for these *so-called* peace talks?"

"To start, we have someone here you know. We'd appreciate it if you'd open the gate and meet them just outside."

Brody weighed the request. "You already have us at a disadvantage. Opening the gate leaves us exposed."

"You have my word," Sacha replied. "We came to talk, not fight."

"Let me think about it."

"Sacha, I've got a bad feeling about this," Travis said.

"Yeah, me too," Sacha replied, "but we don't have a choice. Don't worry about Wren. I won't take unnecessary risks with her."

Moments later, the gate creaked open. Six guards flanked Brody as he stepped out, stopping just beyond the threshold. "I'm here."

"Wren, it's time," Sacha called. "Don't go past the gate. If anything feels wrong, run."

"Don't worry about that," Wren replied, her voice wavering.

She sighed and forced herself forward a few steps. *No matter what I say, Brody won't listen*, she thought.

Her legs felt heavy as lead. "I can't do this." Then, louder: "Travis!"

Travis started toward her, but Sacha's arm shot out to stop him. "No. One person only—that's what we promised. We can't mess this up now."

"Something's wrong," Travis insisted.

"It's just nerves," Sacha replied, then raised his voice more. "Wren, you have to do this."

She glanced back at him. "I don't trust him."

"I'm right here, Wren," Travis called, his voice bearing a quiet strength. "We won't let anything happen to you."

Brody watched the exchange with a satisfied smirk.

"Are you sure about this?" Wren asked.

"We've got men covering you," Sacha assured her. "Just get close enough to deliver the message. We're watching like hawks."

She nodded slowly, steeling herself. *Dig in, Wren. Don't let him win.* The first step was agony, but each one after grew steadier. Their men moved with her, slipping from tree to brush, boosting her courage.

She paused fifty feet from the gate. Brody stood waiting, his expression one of open scorn. The fracture between them had never felt wider. Behind him, a group of men in green fatigues stood staring at her. *Travis,* she thought, *I wish you were here.*

Another wave of tremors rippled through her legs, but she held her ground. She had never seen these men before, but their military dress told her everything. Bows with arrows nocked, blades at their hips. She counted fifteen and suspected more waited beyond view. *Brody's clearly planning something,* she decided.

Meeting her old friend's gaze, she said, "Hello, Brody."

"Wren. I still can't believe you turned on us. And you were one of those who helped drag the traitor from my camp."

"Father is no traitor! He's your friend. His message should have encouraged you. The north is falling into enemy hands, yet you refuse to act."

Brody laughed coldly. "Why should I listen to a man who abandoned his allegiance?"

"Well, maybe you'll hear his daughter. And I remember you once saying I was like a daughter to you."

"That was before Cohen betrayed me. And you?" His voice turned mocking. "How long have you been sleeping in the enemy's camp, young lady?"

Wren felt the sting but pressed on. "My friend has nothing to do with this. I came with a message you should welcome. Please hear me."

"I hope it's not the same lies Cohen tried to feed me," Brody said, glancing to his flanks.

She sensed the shift but pushed forward. "Father told the truth. An army waits in the north—larger than you can imagine. A war is coming, and we thought you'd want to join us."

"A story fed by some government agent? Hardly. They lied to you, same as they lied to all of us."

"We have a contact with the Patriot Endeavor, an underground group set to fight the northern regime. I've heard the radio messages Don't you see how importance this is?"

Brody's face hardened. He was no longer listening.

"Seize her!" he roared.

Three soldiers burst from behind the gate and sprinted toward her. Wren spun to run.

Brody's archers raised their bows. A storm of arrows hissed toward the tree line.

Sacha fired a round from cover, kicking up dirt near a pursuer's feet. One soldier grabbed Wren's arm, dragging her back toward the gate. Sacha couldn't risk a shot with her in the mix. He dropped his rifle and charged. In seconds, he reached them, delivering a kick that sent the man sprawling.

He pulled Wren toward the trees when an arrow struck her foot. She stumbled, screaming. Sacha scooped her up just as another projectile sliced into his shoulder as it glided past.

Brody saw her escaping and broke into a run toward them.

Travis shouted for Chevy. The young man lit the first firebomb and hurled it. It shattered against the gate in a bloom of flame, igniting the wood and sending glass and fire into the air. The second bomb struck the far side, sending Brody's men scrambling back inside.

Amid the chaos of gunfire and crackling flames, a deep, thunderous rumble erupted from the bushes behind them.

The horses whinnied in terror. One reared. A sudden hush fell over the fighters as every eye and ear turned toward the ominous sound.

Chapter 56

The red truck rumbled to a stop at the clearing's edge, wheels kicking up a cloud of dust that hung in the air like a veil of disappointments. Logan Weston stepped out, hands raised high, palms open. "Hold up, fellows," he called, spotting Sacha and Travis.

He moved clear of the vehicle. "Brody Myles! Come out from behind your soldiers."

"Father, what are you doing?" Travis shouted.

"Stay back, everyone," Logan urged, gaze fixed ahead.

Brody emerged into the open, shoulders squared, sunlight glinting off his brow. "Logan Weston. I should have known you were behind all this."

"I'm here to expose the truth," Logan said, his voice ringing loudly across the dusty clearing. "Everything that's happened today—and for the last twenty years with these factions—rests squarely on your shoulders. You started this war between our people, and it's time you ended it." He held Brody's gaze without flinching. "Can you even remember the day Lara passed?"

"Sure, I can," Brody answered, his jaw tight. "How could I forget?"

"This entire conflict was born from your shame and regret."

"It's *my* shame, Logan. I'll settle it in my own way!"

"By letting innocent people die? How does that even work?"

Brody gestured with his hand. "Look at what we've built here. We took in the starving. Taught them to hunt, to fight—"

As the words drifted across the clearing, pieces clicked into place for Travis. His father's earlier slips of the tongue, now this. Was the long friction between their groups nothing more than a personal feud between two old men?

Logan pressed on, unyielding. "It's time we brought it all into the open."

"You don't need to do that," Brody cried, a note of pleading creeping in. "Logan. Please."

"Lara would never have trusted the North," Logan continued, the memory of her death thickening his throat. "They pushed us from our home and would have killed us if we hadn't crossed over the line. So, how could you make a deal with them?"

He stepped closer, the dry grass crunching softly beneath his boots. "You kept pushing that captain at the periphery, badgering him, calling his men commies. I hold you responsible for her death, Brody—and for every soul who fell that day."

The words struck Brody like a hammer. His face paled. He clamped his hands over his ears. As clearly as he'd ever remembered, he could see the people running through the forest, the military firing shots all around them before they reached the safe zone. "Leave it alone, Logan. Leave it! She was my sister, you know."

But Logan's voice pushed on, steady as the wind through the trees. "I want everyone to know you were the one who triggered the guns that killed her and so many others, and set this bitter rivalry in motion. I sat on the ground heartbroken, holding her lifeless body with little Travis in one arm. How many deaths does it take for you to understand that the North will never let us return?"

"They *promised* us, Logan!" Brody screamed, voice cracking. "You wouldn't understand.

"I know they've manipulated you to kill for them. You took out your grief on your own people."

"Stop, Logan!" Brody raised his hands as he fell to his knees and buried his face in them, tears flowing down.

Logan approached slowly and kneeled beside him. "Now is the time for a true alliance. Your country needs you again, soldier. A greater war is coming in the north. You and your soldiers could play a crucial role in reclaiming our nation. Opposing the small factions groups is pointless. The real battle lies ahead." His tone softened. "Join us, Brody. End this madness. We are your people."

Brody lifted his tear-streaked face. "Logan, can you ever forgive me?"

Logan rested a hand on the man's shoulder. "I can't say I liked what you did, and may struggle to fully forgive. But I know that God has already forgiven you." He bowed his head and prayed aloud, his words drifting on the breeze.

"Thank you, Lord?" Brody whispered.

"God's mercies never end," Logan prayed. "Give your burdens and pain to Him, and He'll set you free."

The Black Arrow leader remained on his knees, weeping and praying with Logan until peace settled over him.

A sudden movement at the tree line caught the corner of Logan's eye. A man drew a bow, his arrow glinting in the sunlight and aimed his way. "Hold up there." Logan pointed to him before lunging forward to shield Brody.

Travis pulled his rifle around. His shot cracked loudly, the recoil jolting through his shoulder. The arrow flew wild, slicing harmlessly through the air as the man crumpled to the ground, clutching his chest.

Logan turned back to Brody. "Only God and time will help people forget."

Brody wiped his face. "Hopefully, they will—someday."

Men from both the POF and Marius's group gathered as Charlie, one of Marius's, lay bleeding in the dirt. The big man stared down at him, shaking his head slowly. "Oh no, Charlie. Why?" He lifted his gaze to his men, voice heavy. "Whatever this is, it stops now. That man asked God for forgiveness," he said, pointing toward Brody. "If God has forgiven him, then so will we."

His men nodded, a murmur of reluctant agreement rippling through them.

Marius turned to Travis, regret in his eyes. "You shouldn't have had to do that, son."

Travis gazed at him with a nod. "He aimed it toward my father—I had no choice."

"I'm sorry, for this."

As Logan and Brody approached the scene, all eyes shifted toward them.

Brody met the guarded stares, feeling the weight of their distrust. "Please listen. I've made tons of mistakes and led my camp down an unfortunate path. From this day forward, I pledge we will not fight against our own people. I ask your forgiveness as we begin this mission."

The group dispersed quietly, boots scuffing against the earth.

Brody shook his head. "They may never see me as one of them."

Logan lightly slapped his shoulder. "Give them time,"

As they walked, Brody glanced over to him. "Maybe this is not the best moment to ask, but tell me where did you find the weapons and ammunition?"

"Simple good fortune," Logan responded. "In two days, we're having a wedding celebration. The sooner you reach the farm with your men, the sooner I can tell you."

"A wedding?"

Logan allowed a small smile to break through. "Yeah. Travis and Wren, and Gaela—a fine woman you'll meet—and I are getting married during the celebration."

Brody's eyebrows rose. "Oh, wow. I wouldn't miss that for the world."

Chapter 57

The budding camaraderie between the factions marked a genuine step forward, yet Sacha couldn't shake the uncertainty that it might fray once he departed for the Endeavor. Before heading north, he needed to settle two pressing matters: whether Logan needed extra hands here and whether Gaela would remain behind. Even if he found a relatively safe route, crossing the parallel remained perilous. Soldiers watched every viable path and crossing. Jeeps prowled the roads, hunting those fleeing north or slipping back from the south. Worse, the drones' thermal imaging could detect a human heat signature from hundreds of feet above. Traveling alone was not an option.

Sacha had already begun preparing Travis for the southern troops' departure. Travis's archery had sharpened, his fighting skills had grown formidable, and his physical endurance now rivaled Sacha's own. The trip would also grant him invaluable experience in the intelligence work that kept the Endeavor alive. But would he accept—especially with the wedding only days away?

He spotted Travis walking alongside Randall and Kincaid and angled toward them. "Travis, may I have a word?"

"Sure. How's the shoulder?" Travis asked.

"A flesh wound," Sacha said, tilting his head to glance at his injured shoulder. "Listen, I have an unfortunate issue I need to lay on you. Don't agree until you've heard me out."

Travis nodded curiously, brows furrowed.

"Gaela wants to stay with Logan after they are married. She'll still handle the incoming radio messages, but I need someone to take her place at my side on the journey north. Crossing the secured zone is no small feat. Drones, patrols, thermal scans… I'd like you at my side—extra eyes and ears. Once we reach the other side, you'd work from one of our safe houses."

Travis's eyes widened. "You're asking me to cross the periphery with you?"

"Yeah, I can think of no one better to evade drones than you," Sacha replied, his smile widening. "It won't be easy, but we could accomplish great things for the Endeavor. You can bring Wren along if she's willing. She's a fine archer, and the two of you work well together. I'll speak with Logan and Cohen, and I expect their blessing."

"So, we will prepare the way, sort of like John the Baptist?"

"Something like that," Sacha replied. "Travis, this is an opportunity for both of you to learn about intelligence gathering. You'll work on valuable and sensitive operations."

"You'll have to explain that."

"Unfortunately, I'm not privy to the latest needs since I'm here, but we'll find suitable positions for you both."

"Will we ever return home to Pattonville?"

"That will be up to you, but not for a while. Once we call for the southern troops to infiltrate the north, we'll meet up with the entourage. The work is dangerous, but I can guarantee some funding for you and Wren."

"Do I have to answer at this moment?"

"Oh, no, but you should discuss it with Wren, and you will want to pray about it. If you decide against it, I need some time to find another. Let me know as soon as you can."

"I'll talk with her tonight. When do you plan to leave?"

"In about a week, maybe longer," Sacha replied. "There's time for your wedding and honeymoon."

As they talked, Wren had been watching from the wagon. She shifted against the seat, wincing as she tried to swing her injured foot down. "Ouch. If only this blasted foot—"

"Wren, you can't get down," Jacoby said. "I don't want Travis upset with me if you hurt that leg more."

"Yeah, yeah," she sighed, leaning back against the wagon seat. The canvas above creaked softly in the breeze, and the familiar sway of the wheels over uneven ground reminded her of how far they had yet to go.

"You won't be sidelined forever."

"I know," she said. "If I can't go to him, he can come to me," she shouted, "Travis! "

Travis heard her, spun around, and saw Wren gesturing for him to come over, her words lost in the rattle of the harness and hoofbeats.

"She doesn't miss much. Already suspects something's up," Travis said, a faint smile tugging at his mouth.

Sacha nodded. "Perhaps you should trade places with Jacoby. Might be a good time to gauge her thoughts."

Travis exhaled. "I'd rather face a drone than do this, but waiting won't make it easier."

When the wagon drew alongside, he swapped places with Jacoby and climbed aboard. "What were you saying? I couldn't hear you."

With a determined gaze, Wren studied him. "I saw you and Sacha in conversation for a while, and was just curious what it was about."

"You won't believe what Sacha said." He explained the mission details, including the risks, but told her they would have time for their wedding.

Wren was quiet for a long moment, processing. "We'd have to leave our parents," she said softly. "I never expected Sacha to ask that of us."

"Gaela's staying, and he needs someone he trusts at his back. This mission is a great opportunity for us. We'd only be away from our fathers until the South moves north. We'd rejoin everyone then." He studied her. "What do you think?"

She slipped her arm around his waist and leaned into him. "I've been apart from Father before. It won't be forever. And Sacha's right about one thing—we should marry before we leave everyone behind. We may not get another chance for a long while."

Travis searched her face. "You're truly willing? The journey will be dangerous. Your leg is still healing, and there are reports of fighting farther north."

"Nothing is too hard if I'm with you." Her voice was soft but firm. "If you leave me behind, I'll only worry myself sick. Remember the promise you made? Wherever you go, I want to be there. I mean it, Travis."

He let out a slow breath, a faint smile tugging at his mouth. "It's clear as a raindrop." After a moment, he added, "We'll pray about it while we finish wedding plans. I need to give Sacha an answer soon."

"Give me the reins," Wren said. "Jump down and tell him now."

Travis nodded, kissed her temple, and dropped to the ground as the wagon continued its steady roll toward Pattonville.

Chapter 58

Sacha set his empty coffee cup on the wooden table, the faint aroma still lingering in the air. "Logan, when I look at these men, it brings to mind that they will soon head north to face the most challenging battle of their lives. Many will be lost—we'll mourn our dead and give them a dignified farewell. Then we'll take up our weapons and advance to the next conflict. The notion sits heavy, almost beyond imagining, yet I know this is what we must do."

"Yes," Logan replied, his voice low. "I just hope Travis is not one of those casualties. You know, it was the sacrifices of men like these that built our country."

"But those sacrifices came on foreign soil, not our own. I never thought I would see the day when conflicts like these would happen in America."

"It's sad," Logan replied, "but that time has come. Whoever we lose, we will honor and remember them as heroes for generations to come."

"In a few days, we will leave to assist the Patriot Endeavor wherever we can," Sacha said. "And you, Brody, Cohen, and Marius, will keep our men sharp with their exercises until we call for you."

"Yeah, I can't believe we're that close." Logan's gaze drifted for a moment. "Soon, you'll lead Travis, Wren, and Chevy to gather intelligence. Wish I were going with you."

Sacha met his friend's gaze, the weight of the last months between them. "I will pray that you can join the others. Don't let rheumatism hold you back, Logan. There'll be medicine waiting once you cross over."

"You mean fight our way over," Logan corrected with a grim smile. "They're not going to let us just slip through."

"No, too many of you for that. But you'll take them out clean if you remember what we taught in training."

Logan could imagine some of their men sneaking across the invisible, guarded line using guerrilla tactics—slipping like shadows through the underbrush. "Yes, we will," he said quietly.

Sacha turned and looked out the window. "I think I'll head outside now."

"We won't be far behind you."

Travis strolled down the hallway from Logan's room just as Wren and Gaela emerged from another doorway, their footsteps soft on the worn floorboards.

"Are we all ready?" Gaela asked.

"I think so," Wren replied, smoothing her simple dress.

Logan glanced at his son, standing tall and confident beside his future daughter-in-law. Travis wore his best clothes—sturdy, plain, and far from elegant, yet they suited him perfectly. "Son, the moment has come. Are you ready for it?"

"Have to be now," he said with a quick grin. "A bit anxious, but not about the wedding. I don't doubt for a second that Wren is the best choice I could ever make."

"You're worried about the journey north with Sacha?"

"Yeah, it's been on my mind."

"Mine too," Logan admitted. "If I didn't trust Sacha to look after you, I'd tell him to find someone else."

"Wren and I prayed, Father. We're confident this is the right decision."

"Then everything will be okay," Logan said with a reassuring smile.

"Yes, sir," Wren added softly, stepping closer.

The door creaked open, and Cohen Daniels stepped inside. "Daughter, I had to see you again before you walk down the aisle. I wish I could adorn you in the most exquisite gown money could buy. Still, you're a gorgeous bride—though I might be biased as a father." He turned toward Travis. "And what a fine-looking man you are. I'm proud to soon call you my son-in-law. You two will build a long life together and then one day, give me grandchildren. Oh, won't that be a blessing?"

"Right, Father," Wren said, reaching to embrace him.

"It's not my place to pry," Cohen added with a warm chuckle, "but where do you plan to spend your honeymoon?"

Wren glanced at Travis, her smile soft and knowing. "We have a special place—a lean-to about half a day's walk through the woods."

"Ah, yes, the lean-to." Cohen's eyes twinkled with memory. "I remember staying there the night you broke me out of Brody's jail. At least you'll have some privacy amid the trees."

The door swung open again, and Sacha stood there with an easy grin. "Hey, folks. They're ready for you out there."

"Then we should go," Logan said.

Travis and Wren led the way through the crowd. Logan and Gaela followed close behind as a fiddle and guitar began playing the familiar wedding march. The melody drifted on the breeze, mingling with the murmur of voices and the rustle of leaves overhead.

Pastor Parker waited on the simple wooden platform set a hundred yards from the buildings. As they climbed the weathered steps and took their places, he drew a slow breath, surveyed the crowd with quiet gravity, then turned back to the two couples. "We gather here today—"

Chapter 59

The wedding festivities stretched late into the night, laughter and fiddle music drifting through the cool autumn air like a final blessing. Bathed in the silver hush of the harvest moon, Travis and Wren slipped away to the old lean-to shack. Its weathered timbers and moss-softened roof carried the scent of pine resin and earth, a quiet reminder of the fragile first days when their hearts had begun to entwine. Here, in this place of beginnings, they would spend their first night as husband and wife.

For two golden days, they let the world fall away. They lingered in each other's arms, rekindling the quiet fire between them, speaking in low voices of hopes and fears, of the uncertain road ahead. Mornings carried the scent of woodsmoke; evenings wrapped them in the rustle of leaves and the distant call of owls.

On the third morning, long before the sun crested the ridges, they rose in the chill predawn hush. The forest beckoned. They made their way through mist-laden trees to the creek, their boots sinking softly into damp soil still holding the night's frost. Wren chose her stand at the farther deer scrape. Travis settled beneath a low-hanging sycamore a hundred yards south, thirty feet from an old scrape.

Dawn arrived in slow veils of pearl and rose. Wren watched two mockingbirds tumble through the branches in a playful chase, their wings flashing white against the fog. As they darted away, a gray fox emerged, paused at the water's edge to drink, then vanished into the undergrowth. The woods felt hushed, almost holding its breath.

A short distance away, Travis smiled as two squirrels chattered and dipped their forage into the rippling stream. Then a turkey gobbled close enough to jolt his pulse. Before he could steady himself, a small doe burst from the brush and bounded past in a flicker of gray-brown. He let her go. Time stretched, thick with anticipation.

At last, an impressive eight-point buck stepped into view. The animal moved with wary grace, nostrils flared as it tested the air. Travis's breath caught. How in the world did Wren miss this one?

The buck turned its head, ears twitching at an unseen threat. Satisfied, it lowered its heavy rack against a young sapling and began to thrash, antlers rasping against the bark with a sound like dry thunder. Travis rose smoothly, drew his bow, and released. The arrow flew true, striking deep into the heart—the great deer crumpled with a final, shuddering breath, its warm blood scenting the morning mist.

Travis set down his bow and drew his skinning knife. He sliced through hide and membrane, the scent of blood mixing with the forest's damp aroma. He had nearly finished quartering the meat when a voice cut through the stillness.

"Excuse me. That's my deer, mister," came a soft voice.

Wren stood thirty feet away beside the creek, hands on her hips, one eyebrow arched in mock indignation. The morning light caught the faint flush on her cheeks and the determined spark in her eyes.

Travis stepped out from under the sagging limb, wiping his hands. "Today," he said with a slow grin, "it's not." He walked toward her, his boots crunching softly on fallen leaves.

Laughter rose between them, warm and easy, carrying them back to the very first day they had met in these same woods. Wren dropped her bow and hobbled toward him. Travis swept her up into his arms without hesitation. She kissed his face, then his lips, over and over, until he gently set her down.

"This is as much your deer as mine," he murmured, his forehead resting against hers. "We're married now."

"We are," she agreed softly. Then, more seriously: "Which means I'm still going north with you and Sacha, right? You haven't changed your mind just because of my foot, have you?"

Travis chuckled. "No, I hunt better when you're close by, and I'd rather not starve." He brushed a strand of hair from her face.

"Now I know what I'm good for," she said and kissed him again.

But as Travis turned back to the deer, his smile faded—the weight he had carried since waking pressed down on him.

"There's something I need to tell you," he said quietly.

Wren's expression sharpened. "What is it?"

"I didn't want to ruin our morning hunt," he said quietly, wiping his knife on a handful of leaves. "I had a disturbing dream last night. You remember Pastor Parker's dream about the beasts?"

Her face tightened as the playfulness drained from her eyes. "I do. It was awful."

"The image is still burning in my mind," Travis continued. "Two smaller beasts with teeth bared, raised swords against us. A larger, darker one watched from the shadows, waiting to see who would win. Their eyes glowed with the same unnatural fire Pastor spoke of. I saw Sacha chained, surrounded by the smaller ones... and a voice said to me, 'Beware the deceivers.' It felt like a warning, Wren."

She stood very still, searching his face as a light breeze stirred her hair.

Travis drew a slow breath. "Sacha reminded me that lives will be lost in the days ahead. We'll see things we've never seen before—opposition from the north and from the foreign fighters slipping into the land. Nothing will be the same after this."

Wren studied him for a long moment, her fingers tightening around the strap of her quiver. "Does this mean we're not going?"

"I haven't heard the Lord say to stay. Maybe the dream is part of our preparation for what's ahead, and God's warning to us." Travis reached for her hand. "We can't stop praying once we reach the north. Our victory is assured because God is with us; we just need to stay faithful to Him."

Behind them, leaves and branches crunched under approaching footsteps. They turned to see Sacha emerge from the trees, his face etched with urgency.

"What's he doing here?" Travis muttered.

Sacha raised a hand in apology as he stepped into the clearing. "Forgive the intrusion. A message from the Patriot Endeavor reached Gaela this morning. Rebel forces are moving troops down from the Canadian border. Foreign units have been spotted just a few hundred miles from the periphery. They'll call for Southern support sooner than we expected." He met their eyes. "We need to leave today."

"So soon?" Wren whispered. A cold fist seemed to clench around her stomach.

"I apologize for interrupting your time together," Sacha said as he stepped into the clearing. "The Endeavor needs people it can trust to move quietly, watch the enemy, and secure supplies. What we do there could also determine how quickly the southern troops head north."

Travis nodded slowly, though his jaw tightened. "We'll move as fast as Wren's foot will allow."

"That's why we should leave today," Sacha replied. "Gather your things and meet us back at the farm. We head out in two hours."

"We'll start that way," Travis said.

As Sacha turned and headed back through the woods, Travis looked at the deer, then at Wren. "The rest can finish dressing the meat. We'll gather our things, take the deer carcass, and head back." He saw the stunned sorrow on Wren's face and pulled her close. "I know it feels sudden, but we prayed, and God gave us assurance. Now let's spend the time we have left with our family. We don't know when we'll see them again."

Wren reached for her bow. "I'm going to miss Father. My leaving will hurt him deeply."

Travis wound a strip of leather around his bow, securing the quiver to it for the journey. "It has to happen at some point."

"I know," she said, nodding. "But it doesn't make me feel better."

"We will miss them both." Travis lifted the carcass onto his shoulders with a grunt and grabbed his bow. "Let's get this deer back to the farm."

Wren managed a faint smile. "You mean *my* deer?"

"Don't start," he chuckled softly. The lightheartedness lacked its usual spark, weighed down by the unseen burden they carried.

As they made their way through the sun-dappled woods, the familiar pressure of the days ahead settled more heavily on Travis's chest than any he had known before. The skirmishes with Black Arrow felt like children's games compared with the darkness they were about to face. *God, keep us safe in Your arms*, he prayed silently. *May evil learn that when it comes against us, it comes against You. If we are separated, Lord, shield my wife. Place a hedge of faith around her.*

They had barely broken camp when a distant, unnatural howl echoed from the ridges—a guttural cry that could belong only to a wolf. It lingered in the air, fading slowly, as if the darkness itself had drawn a warning breath.

Travis and Wren exchanged a single uneasy glance. Whatever waited for them in the north had already begun to stir within their spirits.

***

Thank you for reading **Assassin's Arrow**. We would appreciate an honest review at Amazon to help other readers determine if the book suits their reading preferences.

For more books by Michael J Spanhanks, go to https://book.spanhanks.com/or at Michael J Spanhanks's author page on Amazon.

About the author

Michael is a passionate writing enthusiast who crafts thrilling action-adventure stories. With ten years of experience as an author, he has written compelling tales across multiple genres, including Christian westerns, mystery and suspense, and post-apocalyptic fiction. He also looks forward to expanding his repertoire with science fiction.

After retiring from a twenty-seven-year career in the tire industry, Michael and his wife now enjoy the peaceful times of their 10-acre farm, shared with their two Siberian Huskies and the lively wildlife—including squirrels, rabbits, and birds. They cherish time with their two children, six grandchildren and two great-grandchildren.

More Books

Secret at Nimrod Lake

Book 1—Mystery of the Lake Series

A fourteen-year-old cold case. A dangerous secret. Can a journalist protect an innocent from a relentless killer stalking their every move?

Seizing a chance to scout for deer with his best friend on vacation, young journalist Andy Story is shocked to stumble upon a mysterious woman in the woods. Could she be the missing girl from a case long gone cold? Driven by curiosity, he and his friend follow her through the forest—until he's shot with an arrow.

When Andy awakens in an unfamiliar cabin, he ignores his friend's misgivings and is determined to assist the enigmatic blonde in her transition back to society. However, as the local police and FBI tie a tragic accident to her presence, he knows he must act fast to safeguard her. With danger lurking and lacking trust for authorities, Andy's only option is to vanish into the shadows with her by his side.

Can Andy untangle the web of deceit before it lands him and his companions in a shallow grave?

Secret at Nimrod Lake is the captivating first installment of Michael J. Spanhanks's Mystery Of The Lakes series. If you like steadfast heroes, unexpected twists, a hint of romance, and gripping natural settings, then you'll love Michael J Spanhanks's thrilling tale.

Get your copy of Secret at Nimrod Lake at Amazon and immerse yourself in the chase today!

Patriot Endeavor

Book 2—Journey From The Wilderness Series

First, the team must cross into unknown territory—unfamiliar to everyone except Sacha. Overhead drones scan the ground for heat signatures as they fly steadily along the periphery line. Upon arriving at the safe house, Travis and Wren encounter fierce opposition where its distrustful leader and tech professional immediately question their motives and loyalty.

Their marriage and faith soon come under relentless attack as spiritual warfare invades thee mission and even their most private moments. The overwhelming desperation of the hunt for their missing teammate, puts their lives in precarious danger. The tension reaches a breaking point when Travis is thrown in jail for carrying a weapon, leaving Wren to confront her deepest doubts alone. As obstacles multiply and darkness closes in, who can they trust? Can they hold fast to their faith before evil forces threatening to tear them apart succeed?

Watch for *Patriot Endeavor's* release, early 2027.

BOGGY CREEK PRESS®